EARTH

Also by Emile Zola
and available in the NEL Signet Classics series

L'ASSOMMOIR
THE BEAST IN MAN

Earth

Emile Zola

Translated from the French by
Margaret Crosland

NEL SIGNET CLASSICS

*NEL Signet Classics are published by The New English Library Limited from Barnard's
Inn, Holborn, London E.C.1. Made and printed in Great Britain by Richard Clay (The
Chaucer Press), Ltd., Bungay, Suffolk*

PART ONE

1

JEAN was sowing that morning, with his blue seed-bag tied round his waist; at every third step he took out a handful of corn and scattered it broadcast all at once. His rough shoes sank into the heavy, clinging soil as he swung along at a steady pace, and whenever he raised his arm the two red stripes on his old army jacket gleamed through the unending cloud of yellow grain. He walked on, tall in his solitude.

This strip of land, measuring barely an acre and a quarter, lay at the place known as Les Cornailles, and was so unimportant that Monsieur Hourdequin, the owner of La Borderie farm, had not wanted to send the mechanical drill, which was being used somewhere else. As Jean went up the field from south to north he faced the farm buildings, which were just over a mile away. When he reached the end of the furrow he raised his eyes, gazing blankly ahead, resting for a moment.

The low farm walls looked like a patch of old brown slates, isolated at the edge of the Beauce, the plain which stretched towards Chartres. Beneath the vast leaden late-October sky lay ten leagues of arable land, the bare yellow squares of rich ploughland alternating with green patches of lucerne and clover; not a single hill or tree broke up the plain as it faded into the distance, dipping over the horizon which was as firm and rounded as at sea. On the west only a little wood fringed the sky with a strip of russet brown. In the middle the chalk-white road that led from Châteaudun to Orleans followed a dead-straight line for four leagues, bordered by a row of telegraph poles in geometric formation. There was nothing more to be seen, only three or four wooden windmills built on log bases, their sails motionless. Villages looked like little islands of stone and in the distance a steeple rose from some church that lay hidden among the gentle folds of this corn-rich land.

Jean turned round and swung off again southwards, his left hand holding the seed-bag open, his right hand cleaving the air as he threw out an unending cloud of seed. Now he was facing the narrow valley of the Aigre river which lay close by and cut across the plain like a ditch; beyond it the vastness of the Beauce began again and continued as far as Orleans. The little village of Rognes was built on the slope, but only a few roof-tops could be seen by the church, below the tall grey stone steeple that was inhabited by ancient families of rooks. The chief town of the Canton, Cloyes, lay hidden two leagues away towards the east, beyond the Loir valley, and further away still the distant hills of Le Perche stood out against the sky, purple in the grey light.

Jean was going down for the last time when he caught sight of a young girl, almost a child, coming from Rognes and leading a cow by a rope, taking the path along the valley at the edge of the plain. Jean had turned his back and finished the last furrow when stifled cries and the sound of running footsteps made him look up again. The cow was rushing through a field of lucerne, followed by the girl who was desperately trying to stop her. Jean was afraid there would be an accident.

'Let her go!' he shouted.

The girl took no notice.

'Coliche!' she panted, cursing the cow in fear and fury. 'Stop it, damn you, Coliche!'

She had managed to follow the cow so far, running and jumping as fast as her short legs would allow her. Then she stumbled, fell, got up, and fell again further on. The cow became frenzied and dragged her along behind. Her body cut a passage through the lucerne and she was screaming.

'Let go, for God's sake!' shouted Jean again. 'Let her go!'

He shouted without thinking, in fear, for he had seen what was happening and now he was running too—the rope must have got knotted round the girl's wrist and every tug pulled it even tighter. Fortunately he cut across a ploughed field and headed off the cow, arriving at such speed that the stupid animal was frightened and stopped dead. Jean unfastened the rope at once and sat the girl up in the grass.

'No bones broken?'

But she had not even fainted. She stood up, felt herself and calmly lifted her skirts up to her thighs to look at her smarting knees. She was still too breathless to speak.

'Look, that's where it hurts. But it's not serious, I can

move. Oh, I was terrified: I was being cut to pieces on the road.'

She looked at the crimson ring round her strained wrist, put her lips against it and moistened it with spit.

'Coliche isn't really bad, but she's been driving us mad all morning, she's on heat . . . I'm taking her to the bull at La Borderie.'

'La Borderie?' said Jean, 'that's easy, I'm on my way back there, I'll go with you.'

He went on talking to her as though she were a child, for she was still very slim in spite of her fourteen years. She looked up and gazed seriously at this tall, brown-skinned boy, with his close-cropped chestnut hair and his full face with its regular features. He was twenty-nine, and to her he seemed an old man.

'Oh, I know who you are, you're Corporal, the carpenter who stayed on at Monsieur Hourdequin's as a farmhand.'

The young man smiled when he heard the name the country people had given him. He looked down at her, surprised to find she was almost a woman already, with her small firm breasts, oval face, deep black eyes and full lips, as fresh and rosy as ripening fruit. She wore a grey skirt, a black woollen jacket and a round cap on her head, while her skin was sunburnt to a golden brown.

'You must be Old Mouche's younger daughter,' he cried. 'I didn't recognize you. Your sister was Buteau's girl last spring when he was working with me at La Borderie.'

'Yes,' she replied simply, 'I'm Françoise. It was my sister Lise who went with our cousin Buteau, and now she's six months' gone . . . He's run away, he's near Orgères now, at La Chamade farm.'

'That's it,' agreed Jean. 'I saw them together.'

They remained silent for a moment, facing each other, he smiling at the memory of how he had surprised the two lovers behind a haystack one evening, and she still licking her injured wrist as though the moist touch of her lips could heal the smart.

The three strokes of the Angelus rang out through the lifeless air.

'Goodness, is it twelve o'clock already?' cried Jean. 'We'd better hurry!'

Then he caught sight of Coliche quietly pulling up lucerne in the field.

3

'Hey, your cow's doing some damage. Suppose anyone saw her . . . Just you wait, you stupid thing, I'll give you something else!'

'No, leave her alone,' said Françoise, stopping him. 'That land belongs to us. She knocked me down on our own land, damn her! All this side belongs to our family, as far as Rognes. Our piece goes from here to over there. The next piece belongs to Uncle Fouan and the one after that to my aunt, La Grande.'

They had started to walk, taking the narrow path which skirted the valley before plunging into the fields. The cow pulled on the rope as they followed her, neither of them saying any more, for they were lost again in the customary silence of peasants who can walk miles side by side without exchanging a word.

Down below, to their left, horse-drawn traps were driving rapidly along, one after the other, on their way to Cloyes, where the market did not open until one o'clock.

'I can see Uncle Fouan and Aunt Rose down there,' said Françoise, her eyes following a carriage no bigger than a walnut shell, flying along about a mile and a half away. 'They're going to see the notary.'

'Oh, yes,' replied Jean, 'I heard about that. So it's been decided then? The old man's going to divide his property between his daughter and his two sons?'

'Yes, it's been decided. They're all meeting today in Monsieur Baillehache's office.'

She was still watching the trap as it flew along the road.

'We're not worrying about it, it won't make any difference to us one way or the other. Buteau's in it, though. My sister thinks he might marry her when he's got his share.'

Jean began to laugh.

'That devil Buteau! We got on very well. He finds it easy enough to lie to the girls! But he can't do without them, and if kind words won't fetch them he turns tough.'

'He's a swine, that's what he is,' said Françoise firmly. 'You don't play that sort of dirty trick on your cousin, giving her a baby and then walking out on her.'

When they reached La Borderie, the big square farmyard, which was surrounded on three sides by cowsheds, sheep-pens, and barns, was deserted. Then a young woman came to the kitchen door; she was not tall but she had a bold pretty face.

4

'What's up, Jean, no dinner today?'

'Just coming, Madame Jacqueline!'

This was the daughter of Cognet, the Rognes road-mender, and she had always been called La Cognette; she had come to the farm when she was twelve to wash the dishes and had risen to the honoured rank of servant-mistress; now she insisted firmly on being treated as a lady.

'Oh, it's you, Françoise,' she went on. 'You've come for the bull. Well, you'll have to wait. The cowman's gone to Cloyes with Monsieur Hourdequin. But he'll soon be back, he should be here now.'

As Jean went into the kitchen she caught him round the waist, rubbing herself laughingly against him, unconcerned at being seen; she was a randy girl, sleeping with the master did not satisfy her, she wanted someone else as well.

Françoise was left alone and sat waiting patiently on a stone bench by the manure pit which took up a third of the yard. Half an hour later, when Jean reappeared, finishing a slice of bread and butter, she had not moved. He sat down beside her. The cow was getting restless, flicking her tail about and lowing.

'It's a nuisance the cowman hasn't come back.'

The girl shrugged her shoulders. She wasn't in a hurry. They fell silent again.

'Corporal,' she said, 'is your name just Jean?'

'No, Jean Macquart.'

'You don't come from these parts, do you?'

'No, I'm from the south, I come from a town there called Plassans.'

She raised her eyes and studied him, surprised that any-one could come from so far away.

'I left Italy eighteen months ago after Solferino,' he went on. 'I was discharged from the army and a friend brought me up here. I used to be a carpenter by trade but it didn't work out, various things happened, so I stayed on at the farm.'

'Oh,' she said simply, her big dark eyes never leaving him.

But at that moment Coliche lowed again, desperate with desire, and a hoarse snort came in answer through the closed door of the cowshed.

'Just imagine,' cried Jean, 'that devil Caesar heard her! Listen, he's talking in there. Oh, he knows his job all right,

5

you've only to bring a cow into the yard, he can smell her at once, he knows what's expected of him.'

He stopped short and then went on again.

'I think the cowman must have stayed with Monsieur Hourdequin. If you like I'll bring the bull out to you. We can manage it all right between us.'

'Yes, it's worth trying,' said Françoise, and she got up from the bench.

'Does your cow need tying up?' he asked, as he opened the cowshed door.

'Oh no, it's not worth it. She's quite ready, she won't budge an inch.'

Through the open door the cows could be seen in two rows against the sides of the shed; there were thirty of them, some lying in the straw and some crunching beetroot in their mangers. The bull, a black Friesian with white markings, stood in a corner, stretching his head forward, ready for his task.

As soon as he was untied Caesar came slowly out. But he immediately stopped, as though surprised by the fresh air and the daylight; he remained motionless for a moment, frozen in his tracks, his tail swinging nervously to and fro, his neck bulging, his outstretched muzzle sniffing the air. Coliche did not move, but turned her eyes towards him, lowing more softly. Then he came forward and rubbed against her, laying his head against her rump with a quick, rough movement; his tongue was hanging out, he pushed her tail aside with his snout and licked her down to her thighs; she let him do as he liked and did not move, although a shudder ran over her skin. Jean and Françoise stood by gravely, their hands hanging loosely as they waited.

When he was ready Caesar mounted Coliche, jumping on top of her so suddenly and heavily that the ground shook. She did not give way and he gripped her flanks firmly between his legs. But she came of a larger breed and she was so tall and wide that he couldn't serve her. He realized this, and tried to get higher up but couldn't manage it.

'He's too small,' said Françoise.

'Yes, just a bit,' replied Jean. 'It doesn't matter, he'll get in all the same.'

She nodded, but as she saw Caesar trying again and wearing himself out, she changed her mind.

6

'No, we'll have to help him. If he doesn't get right in it'll be wasted, she won't hold it.'

With an air of calm concentration, as though embarking on a serious job of work, she came forward. She was so engrossed that her face was immobile, her eyes looked darker than ever, and her lips were parted. She raised her arm firmly, took hold of the bull's member, and lifted it up. When he felt he was near the place Caesar summoned all his strength and with a single thrust he penetrated within as far as he could go. Then he withdrew. It was all over, he had driven the seed deep. The cow had remained as firm as the fecund earth when the seed is sown and she received the fertilizing sperm without moving. She had not even shuddered at the shock of encounter. The bull had come down again and the ground shook beneath his tread once more.

After removing her hand Françoise had kept her arm raised. Finally she lowered it.

'That's it, then.'

'A fine job,' replied Jean with an air of conviction, showing the satisfaction of a good worker who sees something done well and quickly.

It didn't occur to him to tell one of the coarse jokes that the farm boys usually brought out when the girls came with their cows like this. The child seemed to find it so straightforward and necessary that there was really nothing to laugh about. It was natural.

But Jacqueline had been standing at the door for a moment.

'Well,' she called out gaily, with her usual throaty, cooing laugh, 'you're handy enough! I suppose your boy friend doesn't know his way around?'

Jean burst out laughing but Françoise suddenly flushed scarlet. She tried to conceal her embarrassment and confusion, and while Caesar found his own way back to the stable and Coliche munched a tuft of oats which had grown in the manure pit, she searched in her pockets and finally brought out her handkerchief; she untied a knot and took out forty sous.

'There's the money,' she said. 'Goodbye!'

She set off with her cow and Jean, picking up his seedbag, followed. As he caught up with her and they went along the narrow path Jacqueline called out again in her mocking voice:

'No danger of you getting lost together, is there? The girl knows the way!'

This time neither of them laughed. They walked slowly and apart from the sound of their shoes knocking against the stones there was silence. Jean could see nothing of Françoise except the little black curls which escaped from her round cap over her childlike neck.

'She shouldn't tease other girls about men,' she said after they had walked a little way. 'I could have answered her back.'

She turned to Jean and stared at him.

'It's true, isn't it? They say she behaves as though she was Monsieur Hourdequin's wife already. Perhaps you know something about it, do you?'

This upset him, and he pretended to look stupid.

'Oh well, she does as she likes, that's her business.'

Françoise had turned her back and went on walking.

'Yes, that's true. I'm joking, for you're old enough to be my father, it doesn't matter what I say. But you see, since Buteau played that filthy trick on my sister I've made a vow that I'd rather cut my arms and legs off than take a lover.'

Jean nodded his head and they fell silent. When he reached his field, he stopped.

'Goodbye, then!'

'Goodbye,' replied Françoise. 'Thank you again.'

He was suddenly afraid and called out:

'What if Coliche starts all over again? Would you like me to come all the way home with you?'

She was already a long way off; she turned round and her voice reached him calm and clear across the silent countryside:

'Oh, no, it's not necessary, there's no danger now, she's had her fill.'

Jean tied his seed-bag round his waist and began to go down the field, scattering the seed continuously; he raised his eyes and watched Françoise disappear over the fields, looking very small behind the slow-moving cow, whose large body swayed from side to side. When he went back up again he could see her no longer, but as he came down he caught sight of her again, smaller than ever, so tiny that she looked like a dandelion flower, with her slim waist and her white cap. Three times he saw her, looking smaller each time;

when he looked for her again she must have turned in front of the church.

He sowed until dusk. He came and went in the fields with long regular steps, and as his seed-bag emptied the seed fertilized the earth behind him.

2

The house of Maître Baillehache, the notary at Cloyes, stood in the Rue Grouaise, on the left as you went to Châteaudun. That Saturday, in the room to the right of the vestibule which looked on to the street and served as an office, the junior clerk, a sickly pale-faced boy of fifteen, had raised one of the muslin curtains to watch the people passing by. The two other clerks, one old, pot-bellied, and very dirty, and one younger, gaunt, ailing and liverish, were both writing at a double desk of grimy deal which formed the sole furniture, along with seven or eight chairs and a cast-iron stove, which was never lit until December, even if it was snowing on All Saints' Day. The pigeon-holes along the walls, and the mouldering battered cardboard boxes stuffed with yellow files filled the room with a horrible smell of stale ink and old dust-laden papers.

Two peasants, a man and a woman, were seated side by side waiting patiently in respectful silence. The woman, who was thirty-four and very dark, her pleasant face marred by a large nose, sat with her work-worn hands folded over her velvet-trimmed black jacket, while her bright eyes penetrated into every corner, as she obviously brooded over all the deeds of property that slumbered there; the man, who was five years older, red-haired and placid, wearing black trousers and a long brand-new blue linen smock, sat with his round felt hat on his knees, while no hint of any thought illuminated his broad carefully-shaven terra cotta face, broken by large china-blue eyes which gazed out on the world with the fixed stare of a sleepy ox.

Then a door opened and Maître Baillehache, who had just lunched with his brother-in-law, the farmer Hourdequin, appeared; he had a very red face but still looked young in spite of his fifty-five years, with his thick lips and his slit-like eyes surrounded with wrinkles which endowed him with a perpetual smile. He wore pince-nez and had a nervous habit of plucking at his long grey side-whiskers.

'Oh, it's you, Delhomme,' he said. 'So old Fouan's decided to divide up his property, has he?'

The woman answered him.

'Oh yes, Monsieur Baillehache. We've all to meet here, so that we can come to an agreement, and for you to tell us what has to be done.'

'Very well, Fanny, we'll see . . . It's barely one o'clock, we must wait for the others.'

The clerks, who had not raised their heads, made their pens scratch more loudly than necessary while the Delhommes continued to wait in silence. Fanny had been lucky to marry an honest rich man who was in love with her, without even having a baby on the way first, and she did not expect her share from Old Fouan to be more than about eight acres. Her husband did not regret his marriage, for he could never have found a more efficient or energetic house-keeper, and in fact he allowed her to take the lead in everything; he himself had a limited intelligence, but he was so calm and straightforward that at Rognes he was often appointed as arbitrator in disputes.

At that moment the junior clerk, who was looking into the street, stifled a laugh behind his hand and whispered to the dirty fat old man beside him.

'It's Jésus-Christ!'

Fanny suddenly leant close to her husband.

'Listen,' she whispered in his ear, 'leave it to me . . . I'm very fond of father and mother, but I don't want them to rob us. And we have to watch Buteau and that rascal Hyacinthe.'

She was referring to her two brothers, for she had seen through the window that the elder one was arriving. His name was Hyacinthe, but he was known to everyone in the district as Jésus-Christ; he was a drunken good-for-nothing who during his military service had been sent to fight in Africa, and when he came back he had taken to wandering about the fields, refusing to do any regular work, living by poaching and stealing as though he were still holding to ransom a whole nation of frightened Arabs.

He came in now; he was a tall sinewy fellow of forty, at the height of his strength, with curly hair and a pointed beard that had grown long and unkempt, with the face of a ravaged Christ, a drunken Christ who raped girls and robbed passers-by on the highway. He had been in Cloyes all morning and was already drunk; his trousers were mud-stained, his smock covered with disgusting stains, and his ragged cap pushed back on his head. He was smoking a cheap black damp cigar which smelt foul. Yet he had fine eyes, and although they were watery now they revealed the malicious bantering humour and the open-heartedness of a cheerful scoundrel.

'So father and mother haven't arrived yet?' he asked.

When the thin, bilious-looking clerk shook his head angrily, he remained for a moment gazing at the wall, while the smoke rose from the cigar in his hand. He did not glance at his sister and brother-in-law and they did not appear to have seen him enter. Then without saying another word he left the room and waited on the pavement outside.

Barely five minutes later the old Fouan couple finally arrived, walking slowly and carefully. The father, who was seventy, had once been very sturdy, but now he was dried up and shrunken, for he had worked so hard, his passion for the land had been so fierce that his body was now bent as though ready to return to the earth he had coveted and pos-sessed so violently. But apart from his legs he was still vigorous and neatly dressed, with short white correctly-trimmed side-whiskers, while the long family nose gave a sharp expression to his thin face, with its leathery, deep-wrinkled skin. In his wake, never more than a foot behind him, came his wife, who was smaller and seemed to have remained plump, her stomach protruding with incipient dropsy; her face was the colour of oatmeal, her round eyes and mouth were drawn in tight with wrinkles like misers' purses. She was a stupid woman whose work as a house-keeper had reduced her to a docile beast of burden, and she had always trembled before the despotic authority of her husband.

'Oh, there you are!' cried Fanny, standing up. Del-homme also rose from his chair, and behind the old couple Jésus-Christ had reappeared, dawdling along without a word. He crushed out the end of his cigar and then put the stinking stub in one of the pockets of his smock.

'So we're all here,' said Fouan. 'Only Buteau's missing. He's never on time, the devil, never like anybody else.'

But as his father continued to grumble Buteau came in, looking lively and cheerful. He had a flattened version of the large Fouan nose, while his strong jawbones protruded like those of some carnivorous animal. His forehead receded, the top of his head was pointed in shape, and his cheerful laughing grey eyes already betrayed craftiness and violence. He had inherited his father's brutal greed and obstinate sense of possession, which were made even worse by his mother's avarice.

'Listen,' he replied, as the others grumbled at him, 'it's five leagues from La Chamade to Cloyes.'

Then they all began arguing and shouting in their loud piercing voices, discussing their private affairs just as if they had been at home. The notary heard the noise and opened the door of his office again.

'Are you all there? Come in then!'

Monsieur Baillehache sat down at his desk as though it were a court-room bench and opened the proceedings.

'So, Father Fouan, you've decided to share out your property during your lifetime between your two sons and your daughter?'

The old man did not answer, the others remained motionless, and there was dead silence.

'Isn't that so? I believe you've made up your mind,' repeated the notary at last, looking fixedly at old Fouan.

The old man turned round and looked at everyone.

'Yes, I think so, Monsieur Baillehache,' he replied haltingly. 'I mentioned it to you at harvest time and you told me to think it over. I've been thinking, and I see I must come to it in the end.'

He explained why, in broken sentences, interrupting himself continually. He had loved the earth like a woman who can kill, a woman for whom one commits murder. Neither wife nor children, nobody, nothing human: only the earth. And now he had grown old, he must pass his mistress on to his sons, just as his father had passed her on to him before, furious at his own impotence.

'The other day,' he went on, 'when Rose was making her cheeses, she fell in head first. Even going to market in the gig makes me feel worn out. And then, you can't take the earth with you when you die, you must give it up, you must give it up. Well, we've worked long enough, we want to die in peace, don't we, Rose?'

'We do indeed,' said the old woman, 'that's true, before God.'

Silence fell again, lasting a long time.

'Your reasons are sensible,' said Monsieur Baillehache. 'One is often forced to decide on making over one's property during one's lifetime. I should also add that it's an economical arrangement ·for families, for the taxes on inherited property are heavier than those on transferred property.'

Buteau, who so far had affected indifference, could no longer restrain himself.

'Is that really true then, Monsieur Baillehache?'

'Of course it is. You will save several hundred francs.'

The others became interested, and even Delhomme looked brighter, while the old people also shared the feeling of satisfaction. It was settled, the business was concluded, now that they knew it would cost them less.

'It only remains for me to make the customary observations,' added the notary. 'Many sensible people condemn the division of property and regard it as immoral, alleging that it destroys family ties. It is in fact possible to mention some shocking cases, sometimes children behave very badly, after the parents have given everything away . . .'

The two sons and the daughter listened to him openmouthed, their eyelids fluttering, their cheeks quivering.

'If dad sees things that way he'd better keep everything,' said Fanny, who was very sensitive.

'We've always done our duty,' said Buteau.

'We're not afraid of work,' declared Jésus-Christ.

Monsieur Baillehache silenced them with a gesture.

'You must let me finish. I know you're good children and honest workers, and in your case there's certainly no danger that your parents will regret it one day.'

He spoke without irony, repeating the smooth phrases that rose to his lips after twenty-five years of professional practice. But Rose Fouan, although she did not seem to understand, looked from her daughter to her two sons. She had brought all three of them up without affection, with the calculating coldness of a housekeeper who reproaches her children for eating too much while she is trying to economize; her expression softened only when her gaze rested on the eldest, this rascal who had inherited nothing from herself or her husband, strange bad stock who had sprung from nowhere, and perhaps that was why she made excuses for him and preferred him to the others.

'Now that you have decided upon the division,' the notary went on, 'we have to fix the conditions. Are you in agreement over the allowance to be paid?'

Immediately silence fell again and they all sat motionless. The tanned faces had assumed a rigid expression, the inscrutable gravity of diplomats about to assess the value of an empire. Then they glanced tentatively at each other, but still nobody spoke. The father had to explain the situation once again.

'No, Monsieur Baillehache, we haven't discussed it, we were waiting until we were all together here. But it's quite simple, isn't it? I own nineteen *setiers* of land, or nine and a half hectares, as they say nowadays. So if I rented it at a hundred francs a hectare, that would come to nine hundred and fifty francs altogether.'

Buteau, who was the least patient member of the family, jumped up from his chair.

'What! A hundred francs a hectare! Do you think we're fools, dad?'

And so the first argument about money began. Yes, the vineyard could be rented for fifty francs, but could Fouan ever have got that price for the twelve *setiers* of arable land, or for the six *setiers* of pasture, the meadows beside the river Aigre, where the hay was useless?

'Now, dad,' said Fanny reproachfully, 'you mustn't try to do us!'

'It's worth a hundred francs a hectare,' repeated the old man obstinately, slapping his thighs. 'I can let it for a hundred francs tomorrow if I want to . . . What do you think it's worth, then? Tell me what you think it's worth, will you?'

'Sixty francs,' said Buteau.

Fouan was beside himself; he stuck to his price and broke into exaggerated praise of his land, such good land which produced grain of its own accord, until Delhomme, who had remained silent so far, stated in a serious, straightforward way:

'It's worth eighty francs, not a sou more or less.'

The old man calmed down at once.

'Good, let's say eighty, I'm ready to make a sacrifice for my children's sake.'

But Rose's meanness led her to object; she tugged at his smock and uttered one word:

'No.'

Jésus-Christ remained indifferent. After the five years he had spent in Africa he was no longer attached to the land. He was desperately anxious only for one thing, to have his share and raise money on it. So he continued to sit there idly with a mocking, superior expression.

'I said eighty!' cried Fouan. 'Eighty! I've always been a man of my word. I swear it before God. Nine and a half hectares, let's see, that makes seven hundred and sixty francs, and in round figures that's eight hundred. So the allowance will be eight hundred francs, that's fair!'

Buteau burst out into violent laughter, while Fanny shook her head in protest, as though struck dumb. This time the old man was right, it was fair; but his children were roused, and carried away by their urgent desire to conclude the deal at the lowest possible cost to themselves. They revealed their ferocious meanness, haggling and swearing without a trace of honesty, like peasants buying a pig.

'Eight hundred francs!' sneered Buteau. 'So you want to live in comfort, do you? Eight hundred francs a year would feed four people. You'd better admit you're going to die of over-eating!'

Fouan did not lose his temper again. He found this haggling natural and faced the display of anger, which he had anticipated, fiercely pursuing his demands to the very end.

'Just a minute, that's not all: we'll keep the house and garden until we die, naturally. And then, since we won't have any more crops and the two cows will go, we want a cask of wine every year, a hundred bundles of firewood, ten litres of milk a week, as well as a dozen eggs and three cheeses.'

'Oh, dad!' moaned Fanny, heartbroken and shattered, 'oh, dad!'

Buteau took no further part in the discussion. He had leapt from his chair and was pacing up and down with jerky steps; he had even rammed his cap down in readiness to go. Jésus-Christ had risen too, alarmed at the thought that all these arguments might prevent the division from being made. Only Delhomme remained unmoved, with one finger placed against his nose, in an attitude of deep meditation and profound boredom.

Monsieur Baillehache then felt he must speed things up a little.

'You know, my friends, that wine and firewood, as well as cheese and eggs, are customary.'

Finally Delhomme indicated that he had something to say.

'I'm sorry, but what father's asking for seems fair. We could give him eight hundred francs, because he could rent his land for that . . . Only we don't see it that way. He's not renting us the land, he's giving it to us, and we have to work out what he and mother need to live on.'

'Exactly,' agreed the notary, 'that is the usual basis for these calculations.'

And then another interminable wrangle began. The daily life of the two old people was examined and laid bare, and their every need discussed. When the calculation was finished they began all over again, trying to find something else that could be left out, two shirts or six handkerchiefs per year, one centime out of the daily allowance for sugar.

In this way, paring things down again and again, going through every possible minute economy, they finally reached a figure of just over five hundred francs, which left the children in a state of restless fury, for they were determined not to go beyond a total of five hundred francs for everything.

Yet Fanny was getting exhausted. She was not really unkind, and had more pity than the men, for her feelings and her body had not yet been hardened by a harsh life in the open air. So she resigned herself to concessions and said they had better settle it. Jésus-Christ shrugged his shoulders, for he was very generous about money and was even overcome with drunken affection, ready to offer something on account from his own contribution, although he would never have paid it.

'Now,' asked his sister, 'can we settle for five hundred and fifty?'

'Of course we can,' he replied, 'the old people must have their bit of fun.'

His mother glanced at her elder son with an affectionate smile, while Old Fouan continued his struggle with the younger. He had given way only inch by inch, arguing over each reduction, insisting on certain figures. But anger was mounting beneath his cold obstinacy, as he saw his own flesh and blood so passionately determined to grow fat on *his* flesh, and suck his blood while he was still alive. He forgot that he had consumed his own father in the same way. His hands began to tremble.

'Bad seed that you are,' he muttered, 'to think we've brought you up and now you're taking the bread out of our mouths! I'm disgusted, I can tell you. I'd rather be rotting away in my grave already. So you're determined not to be decent about it, you won't give any more than five hundred and fifty?'

He was just about to agree when his wife again tugged at his smock.

'No!' she whispered.

'And that's not all,' said Buteau, after a moment's hesitation, 'what about the money you've got put by? If you've got money then surely you aren't going to accept ours?'

He had saved this up for the end, and looked at his father intently. The old man went very pale.

'What money?' he asked.

'The money you've invested, the money from the shares you've got hidden away?'

Buteau, who only suspected the secret hoard, wanted to be certain. One evening he had seen his father take a small roll of papers from behind a mirror. He had kept watch the next day and the days following, but he never saw anything again and the hole remained empty.

Fouan had gone white but now his anger finally broke out and he flushed scarlet. He stood up.

'So you've been going through my pockets, have you?' he shouted, with a gesture of fury. 'I haven't got a single sou invested. You've cost me too much for that, you devils! But what's that got to do with you, aren't I the master, aren't I your father?'

As he found his authority again he seemed to grow taller. For years everyone, his wife and his children, had trembled beneath the harsh tyranny of the head of the family. If they thought he was finished they were mistaken.

'Oh, go on, dad!' Buteau tried to sneer.

'Be quiet, you fool,' the old man went on, his hand still raised, 'be quiet or I'll hit you!'

The younger son stammered and shrank down on his chair. He had felt the swish of the blow, he was in the grip of childhood fears again, and raised his arm to defend himself.

'You needn't laugh, Hyacinthe. Lower your eyes, Fanny! I'll keep you in your place, I will, as true as the sun shines!'

He was on his feet, threatening, while everyone else was seated. His wife was trembling, as though she was afraid of receiving any misdirected blows. The children no longer moved, no longer breathed; they were subdued and tamed.

'Do you hear me, I want the allowance to be six hundred francs. Otherwise I'll sell my land, yes I will, I'll invest the money in an annuity, I'll get through everything and there won't be a thing left when I'm gone. Will you give me the six hundred francs?'

'Dad,' whispered Fanny, 'we'll give whatever you ask.'

'Six hundred francs, that's all right,' said Delhomme.

'I agree with what's agreed,' said Jésus-Christ.

Buteau gritted his teeth in resentment and simulated agreement by remaining silent. Fouan still dominated them, looking at them all with the hard eyes of a master who is obeyed. Finally he sat down.

'Well,' he said, 'that's settled, we agree.'

Monsieur Baillehache had been waiting for the quarrel to come to an end.

'Since you agree, that will do . . . Now that I know the terms, I'll draw up the deed . . . On your side, have the land surveyed and tell the surveyor to send me a note setting out how each share is to be made up. When you've drawn lots for them all we have to do is to add the number drawn after each name, and then we will sign.'

Outside, the family remained standing for a moment in the middle of the street.

'If you like,' said Old Fouan, 'we can do the survey on Monday, the day after tomorrow.'

They nodded in agreement and walked down the Rue Grouaise in groups a few paces apart.

3

The Fouans' house was the first one in Rognes, standing by the road which went from Cloyes to Bazoches-le-Doyen and passed through the village. On Monday morning Old Fouan rose early, at seven in the morning, to meet the others by the church, as arranged; as he left home he saw that his sister, La Grande, was already up, in spite of her eighty years, and was standing in the doorway of the next house.

La Grande was respected and feared by the family, not for her age but for her wealth. She still held herself very straight, and she was big-boned, very tall, thin, and tough; the blood showed through the skin of her long withered neck while her head and face were like those of some scrawny bird of prey. With her the family nose had become a terrible hooked beak and she had round, staring eyes; she wore a yellow scarf over her head, which was now completely bald, but she had kept every one of her teeth and her jaws could have crunched up stones. She never went out without her thorn stick, keeping it raised and using it only for hitting animals and people. She had been left a widow early in life with one daughter, but she had thrown her out, for the wretched girl had insisted on marrying, against her mother's wishes, a poor young man called Vincent Bouteroue; the girl and her husband had died of starvation, leaving a granddaughter, Palmyre, and a grandson, Hilarion, who were now thirty-two and twenty-four respectively, but La Grande remained unforgiving, she was letting them starve to death too and did not want to be reminded of their existence. Since her husband's death she had directed the cultivation of her land herself, owning three cows and a pig and employing one farm servant; they were all fed from the communal trough and everyone obeyed her orders, grovelling before her in terror.

When Fouan saw her at her door he went up to her, out of respect. She was ten years older than he was and he shared the admiration and deference of the entire village for her harshness, her avarice, her fierce possessiveness, and her zest for life.

'I wanted to tell you, La Grande,' he said. 'I've made up my mind, I'm going along to arrange the division of the property.'

She made no reply, but merely brandished her stick, clasping it firmly.

'I came to ask your advice the other evening. I knocked, but there was no answer.'

'You're a fool,' she shouted at him in her shrill voice. 'I've given you my advice! If you give up your land while you're still on your feet you're lazy and stupid. They could hold a knife to my throat and let me bleed to death, but I'd never do it. Let other people have what's mine, turn myself out for these wretched children? Never!'

'But when you can't plough any longer,' objected Fouan, 'when the land suffers . . .'

'Let it suffer, then! I'd go every morning and watch the thistles growing rather than give up an inch!'

As she drew herself up she looked like some fierce old moulting vulture. Then she tapped him on the shoulder with her stick, as though her words might make a deeper impression on him.

'Listen, remember this. When you've got nothing left and your children have got everything, they'll push you into the ditch, you'll end up like a tramp . . . And don't try knocking on my door then, I've warned you often enough! You'd like to know what I'd do, would you?'

He waited, uncomplaining, the submissive younger brother; then she went in, banging the door violently behind her.

'That's what I'd do,' she shouted. 'Go and starve in the street!'

Fouan stood motionless for a moment outside the closed door. Then he shrugged his shoulders in resignation and climbed the path which led up to the church. He noticed Delhomme and Jésus-Christ waiting, standing twenty yards apart. He went up to Delhomme and then Jésus-Christ joined them. They did not speak but all three of them looked at the path which ran along the edge of the plateau.

'There he is,' said Jésus-Christ at last.

It was Grosbois, the qualified surveyor, a peasant from the neighbouring village of Magnolles. His knowledge of reading and writing had ruined him, for when he was called from Orgères to Beaugency to take up surveying work he left his wife in charge of his own property and acquired such drunken habits on his continual journeys that he was never sober. He was very fat, hale, and hearty in spite of his fifty years, with a large red face covered with purplish spots, and although it was still so early he was already revoltingly drunk, for the night before he had been drinking heavily with wine-growers at Montigny, celebrating the division of an inheritance. But this did not matter, for the drunker he was the more lucid he became, he never made a mistake in his measurements or calculations. Everyone listened to him with respect, for he had the reputation of being extremely spiteful.

'Well,' he said. 'We're all here. Let's get on with it!'

They all set off, without waiting for Buteau, whom they had just seen standing motionless by the largest ploughed field in all the inheritance, at the spot known as Les Cornailles.

'Now,' Grosbois went on, taking a greasy notebook out of his pocket, 'I've already made a careful little plan of every piece of land, as you asked me to, Father Fouan. We now have to divide the whole lot up into three sections, and we're going to do it all together, my friends. That's so, isn't it? Just tell me how you want it done.'

The five men, who were dressed in their best clothes for this important occasion, said nothing. As they stood by the field, in the midst of this endless space, they stared dreamily before them, like sailors who live in solitude on the vast oceans.

'Everything must be divided into three,' said Buteau at last.

Grosbois nodded and an argument began. His contacts with the big farms had led him to take progressive views, and he sometimes disagreed with clients who were small property-owners, saying that he was opposed to unlimited division of the land. The only reasonable thing was to come to an agreement and not slice up a field as though it were a cake. It was a murderous thing to do. If one of them would be satisfied with the arable land another could have the pasture—in short the three shares could be made equal and ownership would be decided by drawing lots.

Buteau, who was still young enough to laugh easily, treated the whole thing as a joke.

'Suppose my share is all pasture, what would I have to eat? Grass? Oh no, I want something of everything, some hay for the cow and the horse and some wheat and wine for myself.'

Fouan, who was listening, nodded his assent. From father to son land had always been handed down and divided up like this; as new acquisitions and marriages followed, the strips were rounded out again.

The surveyor, with the support of Fouan and Delhomme, wanted to divide the land into three strips running parallel to the Aigre valley, but Buteau insisted that the strips should run at right angles to the valley, for he alleged that the arable land became thinner towards the slope. In this way everyone would have an equal share of poor ground, whereas the other method would mean that the third strip would be poor throughout. But Fouan became angry, swearing that the depth of good soil was the same everywhere, and reminded them that the former division between himself, his brother Mouche, and La Grande, had taken place in the way he had indicated, which was proved by the fact that Mouche's five acres would run along the edge of this third strip. Then Delhomme made a remark that decided them—even admitting that this strip was less good, its value would go up as soon as it was decided to build the road which was to run alongside the field at this spot.

'Oh, yes,' cried Buteau, 'the famous road going direct from Rognes to Châteaudun, passing through La Borderie! You can wait a long time for that!'

But in spite of his insistence they ignored him, and he grumbled, clenching his teeth.

They all became absorbed in watching Grosbois establish the dividing lines; they kept a sharp eye on him, as though they suspected him of trying to cheat and make one part a centimetre larger than the others. Fouan stood with arms dangling, and watched his property being cut up without saying a single word.

Buteau instinctively bent down and took up a handful of soil, bringing it close to his face, as though he were about to taste it. Then, wrinkling his nose with a smug expression, he seemed to pronounce it the best soil of all; after watching it run through his fingers he said that if they let him have this strip he would agree to their plan, but if they didn't, he would insist on a division being made. Delhomme and Jésus-Christ were irritated and refused, saying they wanted their share too. And so all the plots were divided up, for in this way they were certain that no one could have something that the other two hadn't got.

'Let's go to the vineyard,' said Fouan.

They turned behind the church and passed quickly alongside the former presbytery, and then made their way down among the close-set vine-slips, planted in chessboard formation. As they crossed a patch of rocky ground covered with bushes, they heard a shrill voice shouting from a hole:

'Father! It's started to rain, I'm taking the geese out!'

It was Boldie, Jésus-Christ's daughter, a girl of twelve, with tangled fair hair, as thin and wiry as a holly branch. Her large mouth was twisted to the left and her green eyes were so fearless that she might have been taken for a boy. Instead of a dress she wore one of her father's old smocks tied round her waist with a piece of string.

This wild girl's mother had been a tramp-woman whom Jésus-Christ had picked up by a ditch after a fair and installed in his hideout, causing a terrible scandal in Rognes. For three years the pair had quarrelled bitterly, and then one evening during harvest time the slut had left just as she had arrived, going off with another man. The child, who was scarcely weaned, had grown up as tough as a weed, and ever since she had been able to walk she had done the cooking for her father, whom she feared and loved.

'Go and make dinner, or you'll be in trouble,' said Jésus-Christ angrily. 'And lock the house up properly, you careless thing, or thieves will get in!'

Buteau uttered a derisive laugh, while Delhomme and the others could not help laughing either, for the idea of Jésus-Christ being robbed struck them as very funny. The house was an old cellar, consisting of three walls in the ground, a real fox's lair, surrounded with heaps of fallen stones and roofed by a clump of old lime trees. It was all that remained of the Château, and when the poacher had taken refuge there after a quarrel with his father, he had to build a fourth wall of loose stones to close off the cellar. He left two openings in it, a window and a door. Brambles hung down over the wall and a big wild rose bush concealed the window. Everyone in the district referred to the place as the Château.

It began to rain again. Fortunately the vineyard was close by and it was divided into three sections quickly without any further argument. All that was left now was the division of the eight acres of pastureland down beside the river Aigre, but at that moment the rain began to fall so heavily that as they reached the entrance gate to a neighbouring house the surveyor suggested they should go in.

'Why don't we shelter at Monsieur Charles' place for a while?'

Fouan stopped, hesitating, for he was full of respect for his brother-in-law and his sister, who, after making a fortune, were living a retired life on this bourgeois estate.

'Oh, no,' he murmured, 'they lunch at twelve, we'd disturb them.'

But Monsieur Charles had come to the top of the steps to look at the rain from under the awning. He recognized them and called out to them.

'Come in, come in!'

Then, as they were all drenched, he shouted to them to go round to the kitchen, saying he would join them there. He was sixty-five, a fine figure of a man, clean-shaven, with heavy-lidded, lack-lustre eyes and the solemn sallow face of a retired magistrate. He was wearing a blue lined jacket, fur-lined slippers, and a clerical skull-cap which gave him a dignified air, as though he had spent his life performing work of a delicate nature in an authoritative manner.

Laure Fouan was a dressmaker at Châteaudun when she married Charles Badeuil, who at that time kept a little café in the Rue d'Angoulême. The young couple were ambitious and since they wanted to make money quickly, they left for Chartres. But at first nothing went well, and money seemed to slip through their fingers; in vain they tried another café, a restaurant, even a shop where they sold dried fish. They despaired of ever being able to put anything by when Monsieur Charles, who was very enterprising, thought of buying one of the brothels in the Rue aux Juifs, which had fallen into disrepute because it lacked staff and had become extremely dirty. At one glance he summed up the situation, the needs of Chartres, and the gap to be filled in an administrative centre which lacked a respectable establishment offering both safety and comfort of a type in keeping with contemporary progressive standards. From the second year No. 19, which had been redecorated, adorned with curtains and mirrors, and provided with a well-selected staff, acquired such a good name that the number of girls had to be increased to six. The army officers, the civil servants, in fact the entire local society, no longer patronized any other place. And this success was maintained, thanks to Monsieur Charles' iron control and his paternal, unwavering management. Madame Charles also revealed herself to be extraordinarily active and kept an eye on everything, missing nothing, wasting nothing, and yet capable of tolerating when necessary small thefts from rich clients.

In less than twenty-five years the Badeuils saved three hundred thousand francs; then they began to think of fulfilling the dream of their lifetime, an idyllic old age spent in the heart of the country, among trees, flowers, and birds. They discovered, with affectionate satisfaction, that their daughter, Estelle, although she had been brought up in quite a different atmosphere, proved herself an outstanding organizer for the establishment, compensating fortunately for the laziness of their son-in-law, who was totally lacking in administrative ability. They had retired to Rognes five years previously, and looked after their little grand-daughter Elodie, who like her mother, had been placed in the convent at Châteaudun to be educated by the Sisters of the Visitation, according to the strictest moral principles.

When Monsieur Charles came into the kitchen, where a young maid was beating eggs for an omelette and keeping an eye on a dish of larks cooking in butter, everyone, even Old Fouan and Delhomme, took their hats off and appeared extremely flattered to shake the hand he offered them.

He told the maid to get some glasses out while he went down to the cellar himself to find two bottles of wine. The others all turned towards the stove where the larks were frying and relished the good smell. They drank appreciatively, rolling the wine over their tongues.

'My God, this isn't local wine! It's splendid!'

'Another glass . . . your health!'

'Your health!'

As they were putting down their glasses Madame Charles appeared, a respectable lady of sixty-two, wearing her snow-white hair in plaits. She had the heavy features and large nose of the Fouan family, but her skin was pale pink and she had the peaceful sweet face of an old nun who had lived her life in some shadowy cloister. Her grand-daughter Elodie, who was at Rognes for two days on holiday, followed her, huddling against her in terrified, clumsy silence. She was anaemic and too big for her twelve years, with the flabby, puffy ugliness and thin colourless hair caused by her poor blood, and so repressed by her education as an innocent young maiden that she was reduced to imbecility.

'Oh, good morning,' said Madame Charles, shaking hands with her brother and her nephews in a slow and dignified fashion, to mark the distance between them.

Monsieur Charles was impatient now, for he was upset at seeing the larks getting overcooked, while the maid was tired of beating the eggs and stood waiting, her arms dangling by her sides.

'It's lunch-time now . . . well, I hope we meet again soon. It's stopped raining now.'

Regretfully they went out, going down towards the Aigre, along paths which had been transformed into torrents. They had reached the eight acres of meadowland which had to be divided when the rain began to pour down again.

But this time they went on obstinately, although they were dying of hunger, for they wanted everything to be settled. Only one argument held them up, for the third section of land had no trees on it, while the other two each contained part of a small wood. But finally everything seemed in order, and the division was accepted. The surveyor promised to send some notes to the lawyer so that he could prepare the deed, and it was decided that lots would be drawn the following Sunday, at Old Fouan's house, at ten in the morning.

4

As it happened, the following Sunday was November 1st, All Saints' Day. The clock was just about to strike nine when the Abbé Godard, priest at Bazoches-le-Doyen, who also officiated in the ancient parish of Rognes, reached the top of the pathway that came down to the small bridge over the Aigre.

Rognes, which was smaller now than it had been in the past, its population reduced to barely three hundred, had had no parish priest for several years, and did not appear anxious to have one, with the result that the village constable had been installed in the presbytery, which was now half in ruins.

Every Sunday therefore the Abbé Godard walked the two miles from Bazoches-le-Doyen to Rognes. He was short and fat, so thick-necked that he had to walk with his head thrown back, and forced himself to take this exercise for the good of his health. This Sunday however, he realized he was late, and he was puffing terribly, his mouth wide open, while his apoplectic face looked so fleshy that his little snub nose and his small grey eyes could hardly be seen. The over-cast sky was full of snow but in spite of the early cold spell which had followed the showery week, he carried his three-cornered hat in his hand and walked bare-headed, revealing his thick tangled red hair with its tinge of grey.

The road came down steeply and there were only a few houses built along the left bank of the Aigre before the stone bridge. The Abbé passed through this outpost at a tempestuous speed. On the right bank the village began; a double row of houses looking on to the road, while others were built up on the hillside. Just over the bridge stood the Mairie and the school, an old white-washed barn with an additional storey built on to it. After hesitating for a moment the Abbé peeped into the empty vestibule; then he turned round, and his glance seemed to penetrate through two taverns that stood opposite. He was just deciding to take a steep alleyway between them which led up to the church, when he caught sight of an old peasant and stopped.

'Oh, it's you, Father Fouan . . . I'm in a hurry. I wanted to come and see you . . . Now what are we going to do? Your son Buteau can't leave Lise in this situation, she's so far gone her big belly's obvious to everyone . . . She's a Maid of the Virgin, it's an absolute scandal!'

The old man listened to him in respectful silence.

'Well, Father, what can I do about it, if Buteau's still obstinate? And then the boy's right, really, you can hardly marry at his age if you've got nothing.'

'But there's a baby coming!'

'Yes, that's so, but it hasn't come yet. You never can tell. And a baby's not much encouragement when you can't buy a stitch of clothing for him.'

He spoke sagely, like an old man who has seen life.

'Besides,' he added, in the same quiet way, 'things may work out. I'm dividing up my property. We're drawing lots later on, after Mass. Then, when Buteau has his share, I hope he'll see his way to marrying his cousin.'

'Good,' said the priest. 'That satisfies me. I rely on you, Father Fouan.'

A peal of bells cut him short.

'That's the second bell, isn't it?'

'No, Father, the third.'

'Good heavens, that wretch Bécu is ringing without waiting for me.'

27

At last he reached the sacristy where he found Delphin and Nénesse pushing each other about in some game while preparing the burettes for the altar. The former was Bécu's son, aged eleven, a cheerful sunburnt boy who was already robust and loved the earth so much that he left his school-books for the plough. Ernest, the Delhommes' eldest son, who was known to everyone as Nénesse, was an idle, thin, fair-haired boy of the same age who always carried a mirror in his pocket.

'Come on, we must be quick,' repeated the priest, urging them on.

He rushed through Mass, gabbling the Latin and hurrying the Ritual. He did not go up to the pulpit for the sermon but sat on a chair in the centre of the choir where he began to drone away, forgot what he was saying, and gave up any attempt to disentangle himself. Eloquence was his weak point, words would not come, he stammered and stuttered without ever being able to finish a sentence, which explained why the Archbishop had forgotten him for twenty-five years in the little parish of Bazoches-le-Doyen. He hurried through the rest; the bells for the elevation rang out like electric signals gone mad, and then he dismissed his congregation with an *Ite, missa est* like the crack of a whip.

Free at last, the Abbé was rushing out when he found himself face to face with the Charles family. His face broke into a broad smile, he swept off his hat, Monsieur Charles bowed regally and Madame greeted him politely. But it was ordained that the priest would not leave for he had not reached the far side of the square when he met someone else and stopped. This was a tall woman of thirty or so, who looked at least fifty, with her thin hair, flat features, and her yellow, flabby face. She looked bent and exhausted by heavy work, and was staggering along trying to carry a big bundle of firewood.

'Palmyre,' he asked, 'why didn't you come to Mass? It's All Saints' Day. It's very wrong of you.'

'I know, Father,' she groaned, 'but what can I do? My brother's cold, it's freezing at our place, so I came to collect this along the hedgerows.'

'So La Grande's still as hard-hearted as ever?'

'Indeed, yes. She'd die rather than throw us a loaf or a log of wood.'

And in her mournful voice she repeated their story, how

28

their grandmother had thrown them out, and how she and her brother had been forced to live in an old abandoned stable. Poor Hilarion, who was bandy-legged, his mouth twisted by a hare-lip, was without malice and so stupid in spite of his twenty-four years that nobody wanted to give him work. So Palmyre worked for him, nearly killing herself, and she cared passionately for her crippled brother with courageous maternal affection.

As he listened the Abbé Godard's fat sweaty face was transfigured by an exquisite kindness, his angry little eyes glowed with love and his large mouth looked sad and gracious. This terrible grumbler, who was continually carried away by a storm of violence, had a passionate love for the poor and gave them everything, his money, his linen, and his clothes, to such an extent that in the whole of the Beauce there was no priest to be found whose cassock was so rusty or so much darned.

He searched his pockets and gave Palmyre a five-franc piece.

'Here, hide it, I haven't got any for anyone else. And I'll have to speak to La Grande again, she's too hard on you.'

In the meantime the church square had emptied and Fouan and Rose had just gone down to their house again where Grosbois was already waiting. Just before ten o'clock Delhomme and Jésus-Christ arrived in their turn, but they waited in vain for Buteau, until noon. He had to be different, confound him. He could never be on time. He must have stopped somewhere on the way to have dinner. They wanted to proceed without him, but they were secretly afraid of his awkward character and decided to draw lots only after the meal, at about two o'clock. Grosbois accepted a piece of bacon and a glass of wine from the Fouans, finished the bottle, opened another, and lapsed into his usual drunken state.

Buteau had still not arrived at two o'clock. Then Jésus-Christ, who wanted some of the drink that the village was drowsily enjoying on this fête-day Sunday, went past the door of Macqueron's tavern and tried hard to look in. His attempt was successful, for the door was thrown open and Bécu appeared, shouting:

'Come in, you old villain! I'll buy you a drink!'

At about five o'clock the door was roughly pushed open

and Buteau appeared with Jean behind him. He caught sight of Jésus-Christ.

'I'd have wagered a whole franc!' he cried. 'Don't you give a damn for us? We're all waiting for you!'

'You ruddy joker,' replied the drunkard, spluttering cheerfully. 'I'm waiting for *you*! We've been hanging around for you ever since this morning.'

Buteau had stopped at La Borderie where Jacqueline, whom he had taken to bed in the hay when he was fifteen, had made him stay and eat buttered toast dipped in wine. Since Farmer Hourdequin had gone to lunch in Cloyes after Mass they had enjoyed themselves for a long time, and the two men had stuck together, until they reached Rognes.

Jésus-Christ rose unsteadily from his chair and followed his brother, his eyes brimming over with kindness.

'Wait here,' said Buteau to Jean, 'then come and join me in half an hour's time. You know you're eating with me at father's house.'

When the two brothers entered the Fouans' house, everyone was present. Old Fouan was on his feet, looking at the floor. Rose sat by the table in the middle of the room, knitting mechanically. Opposite her sat Grosbois, who had eaten and drunk so much that he had dozed off, his eyes half open. Further away, Fanny and Delhomme, seated on two low chairs, were waiting patiently.

Looking strange in this smoke-grimed room with its cheap old furniture and its few utensils worn away by cleaning, a sheet of blank paper, an inkwell, and a pen lay on the table beside the surveyor's hat, a huge black hat which had grown rusty after being carried about and worn for ten years in rain and sunshine. Night was falling, and as the last gleams of faint light filtered through the narrow window, the flat-brimmed urn-like hat assumed a remarkable importance.

Grosbois, who was on the job in spite of being drunk, woke up.

'Now we're all there . . . as I was telling you, the deed is ready. I saw it yesterday at Monsieur Baillehache's office. Only the numbers of the lots have been left blank, after your names . . . so we'll draw them now, then the notary only has to write them in, so that you can sign the deed there on Saturday.'

He shook himself and raised his voice.

'Now, I'm going to prepare the slips of paper.'

The young people moved quickly nearer, without attempting to conceal their distrust. They stood over him and watched every movement he made, as though he was a trickster capable of spiriting away the shares. He had the trembling hands of an alcoholic, and with his flabby fingers he now cut the sheet of paper in three; then on each piece he wrote a huge figure, 1, 2, 3, with heavy strokes. Everyone looked over his shoulder and followed his pen, while the father and mother themselves nodded their heads, for they were pleased to see that there would not be any trickery. The slips of paper were folded slowly and thrown into the hat.

A solemn silence fell.

'You must make up your minds now,' said Grosbois after two long minutes. 'Who's going to begin?'

Nobody moved. It was growing darker, and the hat seemed to loom larger through the dusk.

'Do you want to go by age?' suggested the surveyor. 'Come on Jésus-Christ, you're the eldest.'

Jésus-Christ came forward cheerfully, but he lost his balance and almost fell flat. He had plunged his fist into the hat with a violent effort, as though he was going to take out a block of stone. When he took out one of the papers he had to go to the window to read it.

'Two!' he cried. And he apparently found this figure exceptionally funny for he was convulsed with laughter.

'Your turn, Fanny,' called Grosbois.

When Fanny's hand touched the bottom she did not hurry. She rummaged about, moved the slips round and weighed them, one after the other.

'You've no right to choose,' said Buteau furiously. He was so tense he could hardly breathe, and when his brother had drawn No. 2 he had turned pale.

'Oh, why not?' replied Fanny. 'I'm not looking, surely I can feel them.'

'Come on,' her father murmured, 'they're all the same, no piece is heavier than any other.'

Finally she made up her mind and rushed to the window. 'One!'

'Well, Buteau's got No. 3,' Fouan went on. 'Draw it, my boy.'

In the gathering darkness the others had not seen how the younger son's face had fallen.

31

'Never!' he shouted in anger.

'What?'

'If you think I'll accept that, well I won't! It's lot No. 3, isn't it? The bad one! I told you plain enough I wanted it divided up differently. Oh no, you can't treat me like dirt! Do you think I can't see through your tricks? Surely the youngest should have drawn first? Oh no, I'm not going to draw, because you're cheating!'

His father and mother watched him rave, stamping his feet, and striking the table with his fists.

'My poor boy,' said Rose, 'you've gone mad.'

'Oh, mother, I know you've never loved me. You'd flay the skin off my body to give it to my brother . . . you'd destroy me between you . . .'

Fouan interrupted him harshly. 'That's enough now. Are you going to draw?'

'I want it done again.'

But everyone objected. Jésus-Christ and Fanny clutched their slips of paper as if someone were trying to wrest them out of their hands. Delhomme said that the draw had been quite fair; Grosbois was very hurt and threatened to go if he was suspected of being dishonest.

'Well then, I want dad to add to my share a thousand francs out of the money he's got hidden away.'

The old man was taken aback for a moment and could not speak. Then he stood up and came forward threateningly.

'What did you say? Do you really want to kill me, you scoundrel? You can knock the house down, you won't find a penny. For God's sake take the slip, or you'll get nothing!'

An embarrassed silence fell once more. Now the huge hat formed an obstruction, standing there with the one slip of paper in the bottom that nobody would touch. The surveyor, in order to bring things to an end, advised Fouan to draw it himself. And the old man gravely drew it out and went to the window to read it, as though he did not know what number it was.

'Three! You've got the third lot, do you hear? The deed's ready. Monsieur Baillehache won't change anything in it, for what's done can't be undone, and since you're sleeping here I'll let you think it over tonight . . . It's settled now, let's say no more about it.'

Buteau could not be seen through the darkness and made

no reply. The others gave their approval loudly, while their mother decided to light a candle and lay the table.

At that moment Jean was coming to join his friend. He noticed two shadowy forms, standing with their arms round each other, watching from the deserted, dark roadside, what was going on in the Fouan's house. Feather-light flakes of snow were beginning to drift across the slate-grey sky.

'Oh, Monsieur Jean,' said a soft voice, 'you frightened me.'

Then he recognized Françoise, seeing her oval face and full lips below her hood. She was nestling against her sister Lise, clasping her round the waist. The two sisters adored each other and they could always be seen like this, their arms round each other's necks. Lise was the taller, a pleasant-looking girl although she had large features, while her plump body was beginning to swell; but she was still cheerful even in her misfortune.

'So you're spying, are you?' asked Jean gaily.

'Good heavens!' she answered. 'What's going on in there matters to me—if only I knew whether it would make Buteau decide!'

Françoise affectionately placed her other arm over her sister's bulging stomach.

'If he's allowed to, the swine! When he's got his land perhaps he'll want a girl with more money.'

PART TWO

1

It was four o'clock and the sun was just rising, with the rosy light of early May. As the sky grew bright the farm buildings at La Borderie still slept half in darkness; three long buildings round three sides of the huge square farmyard, the sheep-pen at the far end, the barns on the right, the cowshed, the stable, and the house on the left. The fourth side was closed by a carriage gate secured by an iron bar. Only a big yellow cock perched on the manure heap greeted the day with a resounding trumpet call. A second cock replied, then a third. The call was taken up from farm to farm and echoed from one end of the Beauce to the other.

That night had been like most other nights: Hourdequin had gone to Jacqueline in her bedroom, the little servant's bedroom that he had allowed her to decorate with flowered wallpaper, cambric curtains, and mahogany furniture. Her hold over him was growing, but every time she tried to share his dead wife's room with him she was greeted with a fierce refusal for, as a last mark of respect, he kept the marriage chamber unsullied. Jacqueline was deeply hurt, for she realized she would never be the true mistress until she slept in the oak bed with its red cotton hangings.

She woke up with the first light and lay on her back, her eyes wide open, while the farmer still snored beside her. In the provocative warmth of the bed her dark eyes took on a dreamy look and a shudder ran through her slim attractive body. She hesitated for a moment; then she made up her mind, lifted up her nightshirt and climbed over her master with such light, agile movements that he felt nothing. Silently, her hands feverish with sudden desire, she put on a petticoat, but she knocked against a chair and Hourdequin opened his eyes in his turn.

'Getting dressed? Where are you going?'

'It's the bread. I'm worried, I'm going to look at it.'

Hourdequin went to sleep again, muttering to himself, surprised at her excuse and pondering about it dimly, even in his heavy drowsy state. What an odd idea! There was no

34

need for her to look at the bread at this time of day. Then he awoke with a start, suspicion jabbing at his brain. He saw she was no longer there and in his dazed state he looked vaguely round the maid's bedroom, which contained his slippers, his pipe, and his razor. The slut was craving for one of the farmhands again!

Hourdequin, square-shouldered, with a broad brick-red face, had always played the dominating male with his maidservants; even when his wife had been alive he had slept with them all in a natural, unthinking way, as though it were the right and proper thing. The daughters of poor peasants who take up dressmaking sometimes escape, but a girl who goes to work on a farm can never avoid men, either the farmhands or the master. Madame Hourdequin was still alive when Jacqueline was taken on at La Borderie, out of charity. Cognet, her father, was an old drunkard who beat her incessantly; she was such a skinny little wretch that her bones stuck out through her ragged clothes, and she was regarded as so ugly that the children booed at her. She did not look fifteen, although she was nearly eighteen. She helped the kitchen-maid and was treated like a drudge, doing the washing-up and cleaning out the farmyard and the animals, which made her filthy from head to foot. But after Madame Hourdequin's death she began to look a little brighter. All the farm servants took her to bed in the hay, and every man who came to La Borderie was her lover for a time.

One day when she went down into the cellar with the master he felt he would like a taste of this ugly girl, although he had looked down on her previously, but she defended herself furiously, scratching and biting until he was forced to let her go. From that moment her fortune was made. She resisted him for ten months, and finally yielded inch by inch. She was promoted from the yard to the kitchen and became an official servant. Then she engaged a young girl to help her, and after that, like a real lady, she had a maid to wait on her. The former slut had developed into a dark-skinned girl with a pretty delicate face and firm breasts, with the strong sinewy limbs of women who are deceptively slim. She revealed herself to be an extravagant coquette and drenched herself with perfume, although she was never really clean. Hourdequin had reached the critical age of fifty-five and now he was in her power. He hungered physically for Jacqueline, just as men hunger for food and drink.

35

When she wanted to be really nice to him she would embrace him with kittenish caresses and let him have his fill in a shameless unscrupulous way, showing no distaste, going further than girls usually dare; and to get an hour like this he would humiliate himself and beg her to stay, after quarrels and fierce clashes of will during which he threatened to kick her out.

He had struck her again the previous day, for she had made a scene, saying she wanted to sleep in the bed where his wife had died; then she had refused his advances all night, and whenever he came near her she had slapped him, trying to increase his desire through enforced abstinence and in this way obtain more hold over him than ever. She amused herself all the time with the farmhands, but rationed him. And so that morning in the damp room, in the rumpled bed where he could still smell the warmth of her presence, he was overwhelmed again with anger and desire. He had suspected for some time that she was being continually unfaithful. He leapt out of bed.

'You bitch!' he said aloud. 'Wait till I catch you!'

He dressed quickly and went downstairs.

Jacqueline had gone rapidly through the silent house where the first light of dawn was just beginning to penetrate. As she crossed the yard she suddenly hesitated, for she caught sight of old Soulas, the shepherd, who was already up. But her desire was too strong for her, and she went on, deciding to ignore him. She avoided the stable with its fifteen horses, where four of the waggoners slept, and went to the end into the loft where Jean slept on the straw under a blanket without any sheets. She embraced him as he lay asleep and trembled as she closed his mouth with a kiss.

'It's me, you silly boy!' she said breathlessly in a low voice. 'Don't be frightened. Quick! Quick! Let's hurry!'

But he was afraid. He never wanted it here in his bed for he was frightened of being caught. The ladder to the hayloft stood nearby and they climbed up it, left the trap-door, and went straight down on the hay.

'Oh you silly, silly boy!' Jacqueline repeated, and in her delight her voice cooed softly in her throat as though it rose from the depths of her body.

Jean Macquart had been at the farm for nearly two years. When he came out of the army he happened to come to Bazoches-le-Doyen with a friend who was a carpenter like himself, and he had taken work with his friend's father, a small village contractor who employed two or three men. But his heart was no longer in his work, for the seven years of military service had blunted the edge of his skill and destroyed him with the result that he was now so uninterested in his saw and plane that he seemed another man. He no longer recognized himself! He had not become lazy, but regimental life had broadened his mind. Politics, for instance, which had previously bored him, now interested him and led him to think about equality and fraternity. He had become used to time-wasting habits, the dreary, idle guard duties, the dull life of the barracks, the savage scramble of war. Then the tools would fall from his hands; he thought of his campaigns in Italy and he was overcome by a great need for rest, a desire to stretch out and forget himself on the grass.

One morning his employer installed him at La Borderie to do some repairs. There was a good month's work, bedrooms to be floored, doors and windows everywhere that needed reinforcing. He was so happy there that he made the work last six weeks. In the meantime his employer died, and the son, who was now married, went to settle down in his wife's home district. Jean stayed at La Borderie, where there was always some rotten wood to be replaced, and earned his keep by working. Then, as harvest time came, he gave a hand and stayed on six weeks longer. In the end, when the farmer saw that Jean had taken to the land so well, he kept him on for good. In less than a year the former artisan became a good farm-worker, driving waggons, ploughing, sowing, and reaping in the peaceful atmosphere of the land, where he hoped to satisfy at last his search for quiet. No more sawing and planing! He seemed born to work in the fields, with his slow, careful ways, his love of orderly work, and the ox-like temperament he had inherited from his mother. At first he was delighted and was able to enjoy the countryside in a way that peasants never can, and he enjoyed it, too, through what he remembered of sentimental books and the ideas of simplicity, virtue, and perfect happiness that can be found in little moral tales for children.

To be honest, he enjoyed life at the farm for another reason. When he was repairing the doors, Jacqueline had come and sprawled among the wood shavings. She had led him astray first, for she had been fascinated by this big strong-limbed man whose large regular features indicated true maleness and reliability. He gave in to her and went on doing so, for he was afraid to look a fool, and also because he in his turn was tortured by desire for this vicious creature who knew how to rouse men. Deep within him his natural honesty rebelled. It was bad to sleep with Monsieur Hourdequin's mistress, for he owed the farmer a debt of gratitude. Obviously, he would reason with himself, she was not the master's wife, she was just his bit of stuff: and since she deceived him at every turn, Jean might just as well have this pleasure as any other man; but these excuses did not prevent him from feeling more uneasy as he saw the farmer's growing attachment to her. It was bound to end badly.

Lying in the hay, Jean and Jacqueline held their breath; he listened carefully and heard the ladder creaking. He leapt to his feet and, at the risk of his life, he let himself drop through the hole that was used for passing the hay down. At the same moment Hourdequin's head appeared on the other side, level with the trap-door. He saw simultaneously the shadow of the man as he escaped, and the woman's naked belly. She was still sprawling on the floor with her legs apart. She began to get up, and he was seized with such fury that he did not go down to find out who her lover was, but knocked her down instead, with a blow that would have felled an ox.

'You whore!'

'It's not true!' she screamed, denying the evidence with a cry of rage.

He refrained from kicking her in the stomach and digging his heels into the exposed nakedness of a creature on heat.

'I saw him. Admit it's true, or I'll kill you!'

'No, no, it's not true!'

Then when she had finally got to her feet and pulled her skirt down, she became insolent and provocative, determined to use her all-powerful influence.

'Anyway, what's it got to do with you? I'm not your wife. You won't let me sleep in your bed, so I'm free to sleep where I want to.'

She laughed in her cooing dove-like way, as though making a mockery of passion.

'Now then, get out of the way, let me get down. I'll go away tonight.'

38

'You'll go now!'

'No, this evening. Wait a bit and think it over.'

He remained there, trembling, beside himself, not knowing which man to accuse. He no longer felt strong enough to throw her out at once, but how cheerfully he would have got rid of the man! Yet where could he find him now? He had gone straight up to the hayloft, for he had seen the open doors, but he had not looked at the beds. When he came down again the four waggoners were getting dressed in the stable, and so was Jean in his loft. Which one of the five had it been? It could have been any of them, perhaps even all five in a row, but he hoped the man would give himself away.

He gave his orders for the morning, sending nobody out into the fields. He did not go out himself; he clenched his fists and wandered round the farm, glancing suspiciously about him and longing to knock somebody down. As he finished his tour of inspection at the sheep-pen, Hourdequin thought of questioning Soulas the shepherd. This old man of sixty-five had been at the farm for half a century, but had saved no money, for his drunken slut of a wife had spent everything. He had at last just had the pleasure of burying her. He was afraid he would soon be dismissed because of his age. Perhaps his master would help him, but who was to know if the master would not die first? Did they ever give you anything for tobacco and a drop of wine? Moreover, he and Jacqueline were at daggers drawn. He detested her with the hatred of a jealous old retainer, and had been disgusted by the rapid rise of this latecomer. Now, when she gave him his orders, the thought that he had seen her dressed in rags and working in filth infuriated him. She would certainly have sacked him if she had felt strong enough. This made him careful, for he wanted to keep his job, and he avoided any conflict with her, although he felt certain that the master would be on his side.

The sheep-pen at the end of the yard took up the whole building, measuring about twenty yards, where the eight hundred sheep were separated from each other only by hurdles. The ewes were kept in one place in various groups, the lambs in another, and the rams further on. The rams were castrated when they were two months old, and brought up to be sold, while the ewes were kept in order to replenish the flock while the oldest among them were sold every year.

The rams served the young ewes at fixed dates; they were Dishleys crossed with Merinos, proud creatures with a stupid gentle look, heavy heads, and the large round noses of passionate men. There was a suffocating stench in the sheep-pen, the smell of ammonia which rose from the litter, old straw which was covered with a fresh layer only every three months. Along the walls were racks which enabled the mangers to be raised as the layer of dung became thicker. Yet some air came through the big windows, and the floor of the hayloft up above was made of movable planks, some of which were removed when the store of fodder became low: and the living heat of this soft warm fermenting layer was thought necessary for keeping the sheep in good health.

As Hourdequin pushed open one of the doors he caught sight of Jacqueline going out through another. She had thought of Soulas, too, and she was anxious, for she was sure he had seen her with Jean. But the old man had remained unmoved, without apparently understanding why she was being so considerate to him, which was unlike her! When the farmer saw the young woman going out of the sheep-pen, where she never went, his uncertainty was increased.

'Well, Soulas,' he asked, 'any news this morning?'

The shepherd was very tall and thin, with a long wrinkled face, and looked as though he had been hacked out of a piece of knotted oak with a billhook.

'No, Monsieur Hourdequin,' he replied slowly, 'nothing at all, except that the sheep-shearers are coming and they'll be starting work soon.'

When Hourdequin went back across the yard he noticed that Jacqueline had stayed there listening nervously to what was being said in the sheep-pen. She was pretending to look over her six hundred head of poultry, hens, ducks, and pigeons, which were flying about, cackling and scratching in the manure-pit, and making a continual din. When the little swineherd upset a bucket of clean water he was taking to the pigs, she relieved her nerves somewhat by boxing his ears, but one glance at the farmer reassured her—he knew nothing. The old man had held his tongue. She became more insolent still.

During the midday dinner, therefore, she behaved with provocative gaiety. They ate in the kitchen, a huge room furnished with a long table and two benches. The only sign of progress was a cast-iron stove which stood in a corner of the vast hearth. There was an oven at the back with a gaping black mouth, and the old saucepans hung in gleaming straight rows along the smoke-grimed walls. The kitchen-maid, a fat ugly girl, had baked that morning and a good smell of warm bread rose from the breadpan which had been left open.

'Is your stomach bunged up today?' asked Jacqueline boldly as Hourdequin came in last.

Since the death of his wife and daughter, he had taken his meals with the servants to avoid eating alone. He sat on a chair at one end of the table while the servant–mistress sat at the other. They were fourteen to table and the maid served them. The farmer sat down without replying and Jacqueline said she would see about the food, which consisted of slices of toasted bread crumbled into a soup tureen and then sprinkled with wine sweetened with treacle. She asked for another spoonful, pretending she wanted to spoil the men, and made jokes which caused loud laughter. Each of her remarks had a double meaning, reminding them all that she was leaving that night; you met, you parted, and the one who was left behind would be sorry he hadn't dipped his fingers in the sauce just once more. The shepherd ate with his usual stupid expression, while the master remained silent and did not seem to understand either. Jean, in order not to give himself away, was forced to laugh with the others, in spite of his uneasiness, for he didn't care for the part he had been playing in this business.

After lunch Hourdequin gave his orders for the afternoon. He was worn out now, his ears buzzed after his sudden fury, and he felt depressed; he began to wander about helplessly, trying to forget his wretchedness. The sheep-shearers had begun work under one of the barn roofs in the corner of the yard. He stood in front of them and watched.

There were five of them, tall, thin, and sallow-faced, squatting down as they worked with their big gleaming steel shears. The shepherd brought the sheep along with their forefeet tied together, which made them look like skin bottles, and laid them down on the beaten earth floor where they could do no more than raise their heads and bleat. When one of the shearers got hold of a ewe she became quiet and relaxed, looking huge in her thick woolly coat with its outer layer of black grease and dust. Then, as the shears moved rapidly over her, the animal emerged from her fleece like a naked hand from a dark glove, all pink and clean among the golden snowy wool next to her skin.

That day, when he went outside, Hourdequin remembered his son, the captain. The two of them could have worked so well together! But he thrust aside the memory of this silly man who preferred to trail a sword about. He had no more children, he would die a solitary man. Then he cut across the ploughed fields to glance at the work of his two ploughmen. The soil clung to his feet, he could feel its rich fertility as though the earth wanted to hold him fast in an embrace, and the earth possessed him again completely; he recovered the virility of the time when he was thirty, his strength and happiness. Earth was the only woman: there were no others. Women like Jacqueline did not matter; they were all the same, dishes from which everyone could eat; you had to put up with them, provided they were reasonably clean. He found this excuse for his shameful need of the slut so convincing that in the end it cheered him up. He walked for three hours, and joked with a servant-girl from another farm who was riding back from Cloyes on a donkey, showing her legs.

When Hourdequin returned to La Borderie he noticed Jacqueline in the yard saying goodbye to the farm cats. There was always a whole troop of them, twelve, fifteen, twenty—nobody knew the exact number, for the cats had their kittens in holes hidden in the straw and reappeared with five or six walking behind them. Next she went up to the kennels of Emperor and Massacre, the two sheepdogs, but they hated her and growled at her.

In spite of these farewells to the animals dinner passed as it did every day: the master ate and talked in his usual way. Then, as the day came to an end, there was no question of anyone leaving. Everybody went to bed and darkness enveloped the silent farm.

That very night Jacqueline slept in the late Madame Hourdequin's bedroom. It was a fine room, and a big bed with red hangings stood in an alcove. There was a wardrobe, a round table, an armchair in the Voltaire style, and over a small mahogany desk hung the medals won by the farmer at agricultural shows, gleaming in their glass case. When La Cognette, in her nightgown, climbed up into the marriage bed she stretched her arms and legs wide apart as if she wanted to possess it completely, and she laughed her turtle-dove laugh.

Next morning, when she tried to throw her arms round Jean's neck, he pushed her away. If it was going to turn serious this was not right, and he did not want any more of it.

2

A FEW days later Jean was returning on foot one evening from Cloyes and when he was about a mile from Rognes he noticed a peasant's cart going along in front of him. There was something strange about it. The cart seemed empty, there was nobody on the seat, and the horse, left to its own devices, was returning slowly, apparently sure of the way, back to the stable. The young man soon caught up. He stopped the cart and climbed up to look in. A man was lying in the bottom, a short, fat, old man of sixty; he had fallen backwards and his face was so red that it looked black.

Jean was so surprised that he began to speak aloud.

'My goodness! Is he asleep? Is he drunk? Why, it's Old Mouche, the father of those two girls! Good heavens, I think he's done for! What a business!'

Mouche had been stricken with an apoplectic fit, but he was still breathing in short painful gasps. Jean stretched him out and raised his head, then got on to the seat and whipped up the horse, taking the dying man home at a gallop, for he was afraid he might pass away any moment.

When he reached the square in front of the church he noticed Françoise, who was standing at the door of her house. She was astonished to see Jean driving their horse and cart.

'What's happening?' she asked.

'Your father's not well.'

'Where?'

'There, look!'

She climbed up on the wheel and looked. When she saw the purple mask-like face with one side contorted as though it had been drawn violently upwards, she was horrified, as though she did not understand. Night was falling and a

43

great tawny cloud coloured the sky yellow, lighting up the dying man in a fiery glow.

Then all at once she broke into sobs and ran off to tell her sister.

'Lise! Lise! Oh heavens!'

Left on his own Jean hesitated. He could not leave the old man at the bottom of the cart. There were three steps down to the house from the square, and he realized it was difficult to go down into this dark entrance. Then he saw that on the side facing the road, to the left, another door opened into the yard at ground level. He loosened the horse, who went in of its own accord and stopped in front of the stable near the cowshed where there were two cows.

But now Françoise and Lise ran up together. Lise's baby had been born four months previously, and in her fright she was still holding him in her arms, for she had been taken by surprise just as she was feeding him. He was howling too.

'Dad!' the two girls called out tearfully, 'won't you say something? Tell us what's the matter. Heavens, is it something in your head? You can't even say anything! Dad, please answer us!'

'Get down,' said Jean sensibly, 'we'd better take him out.'

They did not help him, but only cried more loudly. Fortunately, a neighbour, La Frimat, heard the noise and finally came along. She was a tall, bony, dried-up old woman who for two years had been looking after her paralytic husband, and kept them both alive by cultivating the small plot of ground they owned, working as doggedly as some beast of burden. She was not upset, and seemed to treat this incident as normal. She helped like a man. Jean got hold of Mouche by the shoulders and pulled him until La Frimat could take hold of his legs. Then they carried him into the house.

'Where shall we put him?' asked the old woman.

Françoise lit a candle. La Bécu arrived, the policeman's wife, who had no doubt picked up the news somehow, informed by that secret system which can circulate news right round a village in the space of a minute.

'What's the matter with him, poor dear man? Oh, I see, the blood's begun to run the wrong way in his body. Quickly, sit him on a chair.'

But La Frimat advised differently. A man who cannot stand up cannot sit down either; the best thing would be to lay him on one of his daughters' beds. At the height of the discussion Fanny appeared with her son Nénesse. She had heard the news while buying vermicelli at Macqueron's and had come to see, for she was upset on behalf of her young cousins.

'Perhaps we should sit him down,' she declared, 'so that the blood can circulate.'

Then Mouche was dumped on a chair near the table where the candle was burning. His chin fell on his chest, his arms and legs hung down loosely. His left eye had opened, for this side of his face was pulled out of shape, and his breathing came through the corner of his twisted mouth more loudly, with a whistling sound. Silence fell, for death was pervading the damp room with its beaten-earth floor, its stained walls, and great black chimney-piece.

Jean went on waiting awkwardly while the two girls and the three women looked at the old man.

'I'll willingly go and fetch the doctor,' he said.

La Bécu nodded her head, but none of the others replied. If he was going to be all right why spend money on the doctor? And if he was dying, what could the doctor do?

They forced the old man to take a cup of lime tea by placing a spoon between his clenched teeth. Then they rubbed his head with eau-de-Cologne, but he got no better. They began to despair. His face had gone even blacker; they had to lift him up on the chair again for he had slumped down and looked as though he would fall flat on the ground.

'Oh!' said Nénesse, going back to the door, 'it's going to rain like nothing on earth. The sky's a very queer colour.'

'Yes,' said Jean, 'I saw a nasty-looking cloud coming up. But it doesn't matter,' he said as though returning to his earlier idea, 'I'll go and find the doctor if you want me to.'

Lise and Françoise looked at each other anxiously. Finally the latter made the decision, with the generosity of youth: 'Yes, yes, Corporal, go to Cloyes and find Monsieur Finet. We won't have it said that we didn't do everything we ought to.'

In the confusion the horse had not even been unharnessed and Jean had only to jump in the cart. From the house the others heard the jangle of metal and the rattling of the wheels over the bumpy road. Then La Frimat mentioned the priest, but the others indicated that they were going to enough trouble as it was.

Ten o'clock struck on the painted wooden cuckoo clock. They were surprised: to think they had been there for more than two hours without getting any further! None of them spoke of going, for the sight fascinated them, and they wanted to watch until the end. They had not lit another candle and did not even trouble to snuff the one that was burning. It was not very cheerful, this poor, bare, dark, peasant's kitchen, with the sound of the death-rattle coming from the body hunched up by the table.

All at once, half an hour after Jean had left, Mouche fell over and slid down flat on the floor. He was no longer breathing, he was dead.

'What did I tell you!' said La Bécu bitterly, 'but you would go and get the doctor!'

Françoise and Lise burst into tears again. Instinctively they threw their arms round each other's necks in deep sisterly affection.

'My God!' they repeated brokenly again. 'Now there's only the two of us left. It's all over, only the two of us now. What's going to become of us? Oh heavens!'

But they could not leave the dead man on the floor. La Frimat and La Bécu did what was essential in a few moments. Since they did not dare move the body they took the mattress off one of the beds, carried it into the room, and stretched Mouche out on it, covering him with a sheet up to his chin. In the meantime Fanny had lit the candles in two other candlesticks and placed them on the floor like wax tapers, one to the right and one to the left of the dead man's head. This would do for the time being. But the left eye, which had been closed three times, persistently kept on opening again and seemed to watch them all from the contorted purple face which formed such a sharp contrast to the white sheet.

Midnight struck and La Bécu raised her voice:

'And what about Monsieur Finet? I ask you! There's plenty of time to die with someone like him. It's taking more than two hours to bring him from Cloyes!'

A strong gust of wind came in from the open yard door and blew out the candles on both sides of the corpse. This frightened them all, and as they lit them again the storm wind blew once more, fiercer this time, while a long drawn-out howling sound rose louder and louder from the black depths of the countryside. It sounded like the approach of a plundering army accompanied by the cracking of branches and the moaning of the devastated fields. The women ran to the threshold: they saw a copper-coloured cloud flying and twisting over the livid sky, then suddenly there was a crackling as of musketry and a violent rain of lacerating shot fell bouncing at their feet. Then a cry of utter despair rose to their lips.

'It's hail! It's hail!'

The colour left their faces as they watched the terrible scourge, dazed with horror. It lasted barely ten minutes. There were no claps of thunder but huge blue flashes of lightning played incessantly over the surface of the earth in broad phosphorescent furrows. The night was no longer dark, the hailstones illuminated it with countless streaks of faint light as though showers of glass were falling. The noise became deafening, like a volley of shot, or a train running at full speed over an iron bridge. A furious wind blew and the hailstones fell at an angle, cutting through everything and piling up in a white layer on the ground.

'It's hail! Good heavens! Oh, how terrible! Look, hailstones the size of a hen's egg!'

They did not dare venture into the yard to pick them up. The hurricane became even more violent; breaking every pane in the window and acquiring such force that one hailstone broke a jug, while others rolled right up to the mattress where the dead man was lying.

'Less than five of them to a pound!' said La Bécu, weighing them in her hand.

Fanny and La Frimat were quite desperate.

'Everything's ruined! It's terrible!'

Then it was over. The sound of the disaster could be heard rushing further away and a sepulchral silence fell. The sky behind the cloud had become as black as ink. Fine close rain was falling silently. All that could be seen on the ground was the thick layer of hailstones spread out like a white sheet which seemed to emit a faint light of its own, like millions of nightlights stretching as far as the eye could see.

Nénesse rushed outside and came back with a real icicle the size of his fist, irregular and jagged in shape. La Frimat could no longer stand still and could not resist her urge to go and see.

47

'I'm going to find my lantern,' she said. 'I must look at the damage.'

Fanny controlled herself for a few minutes longer. She continued to moan about it. Oh, how terrible it was! The damage it had done to the vegetables and fruit trees! The wheat, oats, and barley had not grown tall enough to have suffered much, but the vines, oh, the vines!

'Well, girls,' she said, in the end. 'I'm going to borrow one of your lanterns. I'll run over to our vineyard.'

La Bécu, who owned no land, did not really care. She sighed and called on heaven for help, out of sheer habit, for she was always complaining. But curiosity took her to the door time after time, and when she noticed that the village was full of light, she stood there firmly, full of curiosity. Through a gap in the boundary between the cowshed and an outhouse you could see the whole of Rognes. The hailstorm had woken up the peasants; everyone was equally impatient to see their fields, and since they were too worried to wait for the daylight, the lanterns came out one by one, more and more of them running and dancing about.

So Lise and Françoise were left alone with their father's body. The rain went on and weak gusts of damp wind ran over the ground, causing the candles to flicker. The girls should have closed the door but neither of them thought of it, for they too had been shaken by the tragedy outside in spite of the sorrow in their own house. Was it not enough, then, to have death in one's home? God had ruined everything; nobody even knew if they had a crust of bread left to eat.

'Poor father,' murmured Françoise, 'he'd have been so upset! It's a good thing he didn't see it.'

Her sister took the second lantern.

'Where are you going?'

'I'm thinking of the peas and beans. I'll be back in a moment.'

Lise crossed the yard in the rain and went into the kitchen garden. Françoise was left alone with the old man, yet she still stood at the threshold, terribly upset as she saw the lantern moving backwards and forwards. She thought she could hear moaning and crying, and her heart sank.

'Tell me,' she cried, 'what's happened? What's the matter?'

No voice answered her: the lantern danced about madly.

'Are the beans down? Tell me? Are the peas spoilt? Good heavens, what about the fruit and the lettuces?'

Then a cry of distress reached her and she made up her mind. She lifted her skirts and ran through the rain to her sister; the dead man was abandoned, lying in the empty kitchen, stiff beneath his sheet between the two pathetic little smoky candles. The left eye remained obstinately open and stared at the old ceiling joists.

The district had suffered terrible damage. Everyone was complaining bitterly about the disaster, for the wavering lights of the lanterns showed them what had happened. The trees had suffered most: the smaller branches and the fruit looked as though they had been cut with knives, while the trunks themselves had been bruised and their sap was trickling out through holes in the bark.

The vine-stocks seemed to have been scythed down and the clusters of blossom lay on the ground along with splinters of wood and tendrils. Not only this year's harvest was lost, but the stumps which had now been stripped bare would decay and die. Nobody felt the rain. A dog howled loudly and women burst into tears as though they were standing by an open grave.

On the mattress in the kitchen the abandoned Mouche was still gazing at the ceiling with his staring eye, when two carriages stopped in front of the door. Jean was at last bringing Monsieur Finet, having waited nearly three hours for him at his house; he had come back in the cart while the doctor had taken his own gig.

The latter, a tall, thin man, his face jaundiced by thwarted ambition, pushed his way into the house. At heart he hated his peasant patients and blamed them for his own mediocrity.

'Hullo! Isn't there anyone here? Is he better?' Then he noticed the corpse. 'No, it's too late. I told you I didn't want to come. It's always the same story: they call me in when the patient's dead.'

This unnecessary disturbance in the middle of the night made him angry; Lise and Françoise came in just then and he lost his temper completely when he learnt that they had waited two hours before sending for him.

'You've killed him yourselves! It's ridiculous to give eau-de-Cologne and lime tea in a case of apoplexy! And then there was nobody with him! You could be sure he wouldn't run away.'

49

'But, Monsieur,' stammered Lise in tears, 'it was because of the hail.'

Monsieur Finet became interested now and calmed down. Had there been a hailstorm? Through living with peasants he had come finally to share their feelings. Jean had joined him and they were both amazed, for on the way from Cloyes they had not seen any hail at all. Some people had been spared and some ruined, only a few miles from each other. What rotten luck if you happened to be on the wrong side! Then Fanny came back with the lantern, followed by La Bécu and La Frimat, and all three of them poured out details about the terrible things they had seen.

'It's a tragedy, a great tragedy,' said the doctor gravely. 'There's nothing more tragic for the countryside.'

He was interrupted by a kind of muffled bubbling sound. It came from the dead man, who had been forgotten between the two candles. Everyone fell silent and the women crossed themselves.

3

A month went by. Françoise was entering on her fifteenth year and her sister Lise was ten years older. Old Fouan had been appointed guardian to Françoise and persuaded the two sisters to lease their land, with the exception of a small stretch of pasture, to their cousin Delhomme, so that the fields would be well cultivated and looked after. Now that the two girls were left on their own, with no father or brother in the house, they would have been led to the ruinous expense of employing a servant, as labour was becoming more costly. Delhomme, moreover, who was only doing them a service, agreed to end the lease as soon as the marriage of either girl made it necessary to divide the land they had inherited.

Lise and Françoise also allowed their cousin to have their horse, which they no longer needed, but they kept the two cows, Coliche and Blanchette, as well as the donkey, Gidéon. Lise undertook to maintain the small kitchen garden, while Françoise would look after the animals. This would still give them plenty to do, but they were in good health, thank heavens, and they would win through in the end.

The first weeks meant very hard work, for they had to make good the damage caused by the hail, dig over the garden and plant vegetables again. This led Jean to help them. Ever since he had brought home their dying father he felt closer to the two girls; the day after the funeral he had come to see how they were; then he returned to chat, and gradually became a helpful friend until one afternoon he took the spade out of Lise's hands and finished digging over a section of ground. From that day the sisters regarded him as a friend and all his free time away from the farm was spent with them. He belonged to the household now; he was at home in the old Fouan house, built by some ancestor three centuries earlier and now the centre of a kind of family cult.

Jean felt happy there and did not wonder what made him keep coming back. The cheerful buxom Lise always gave him a warm welcome. Although she was only twenty-five she was looking older and plainer, especially since her baby had been born, but she had firm strong arms, and she worked with such hearty energy, shouting and laughing all the time, that it was fun to watch her. Jean treated her like a woman, but her sister, who was only fifteen, seemed to him still a child. Françoise, who had not yet lost her looks through heavy work in the open air, was still pretty, with her oval face and low obstinate forehead, her dark mysterious eyes and her thick lips with their shadowy outline of early down. Although she was regarded as a child she was a woman already, and, as her sister said, a man needn't get too close to give her a baby. Lise had brought her up after their mother's death. This was the reason for their great affection, which was expressed in an open boisterous way by the older girl, while the younger one remained passionate and restrained. Françoise was known to be extremely self-willed. Injustice made her furious. Whenever she said, 'This is mine and this is yours' she would never have taken back her words under pain of death, and moreover she adored Lise because she thought she ought to adore her. She was reasonable, very sensible, without any evil thoughts, and only tormented by her active blood which made her somewhat greedy and lazy. One day she too began to talk familiarly to Jean, regarding him as a kind friend much older than herself; he played with her, and sometimes teased her, telling lies on purpose, or defending unjust opinions for the pleasure of watching her turn speechless with rage.

One hot Sunday afternoon in June Lise was working in the kitchen garden, weeding the peas. Jules, the baby, had been put down under a plum tree and had gone to sleep. The burning sun was shining straight down on Lise and she was breathing hard, bent double as she pulled out the weeds, when she heard a voice over the hedge.

'What's this? No rest, even on Sunday?'

She recognized the voice and stood up, her arms red, her face flushed, yet smiling all the same.

'Good heavens, work doesn't do itself, no more on a Sunday than on a week day!'

It was Jean. He went along the hedge and came into the yard.

'You leave it to me. I'll get your work done quickly for you.'

But she refused, saying she had nearly finished, and then if she didn't do that she would be doing something else. There was no time to hang about. Although she got up at four o'clock and did her sewing in the evening by candlelight she never seemed to get to the end of the work.

In order not to upset her, Jean sat down in the shade of the nearby plum tree, taking care not to sit on Jules. He watched her bending down again with her hips in the air, pulling down her skirt, which worked up and revealed her plump legs, while her breasts almost touched the ground.

'It's a good thing you're so well built,' he said.

She was rather proud at this and laughed complacently. He laughed, too, admiring her sincerely and finding her as strong and hard-working as a boy. With her hips in the air, her calves strained as she knelt down to the work, she sweated with the smell of some creature on heat, yet he felt no dishonourable desire: he felt only that with such limbs she would be able to get through a lot of work. He was sure that in a home a woman of this build could work as well as her man.

Some association of ideas must have taken place in his mind, for involuntarily he blurted out a piece of news that he had firmly intended not to mention.

'I saw Buteau yesterday.'

Slowly Lise stood up, but she had no time to question

him, for Françoise, who had recognized Jean's voice, came up from her dairy at the end of the cowshed, her naked arms white with milk.

'You saw him?' she exclaimed angrily. 'He's a swine!'

Her antagonism was growing; whenever she heard her cousin's name mentioned she was carried away by righteous indignation as though she was responsible for avenging some personal insult.

'He *is* a swine,' said Lise calmly, 'but saying so doesn't get us anywhere now.'

She put her hands on her hips.

'Well, what has Buteau got to say?' she asked seriously.

'Nothing,' said Jean, who was embarrassed now and sorry that he had let his tongue run away with him. 'He spoke of his own affairs, because his father's telling everyone he's going to disinherit him. Buteau says he's got plenty of time because the old man's quite healthy, and in any case he doesn't care a damn.'

'Does he know that Jésus-Christ and Fanny have both signed the deed all the same, and taken over their shares?'

'Yes, he knows, and he knows too that Old Fouan has leased the share that Buteau didn't want, to Delhomme. He knows that Monsieur Baillehache was furious, and even swore he'd never allow lots to be drawn again without getting the papers signed first. Oh yes, he knows it's all over.'

'But didn't he say anything?'

'No, nothing.'

Silently Lise bent down, moved about for a moment and pulled out some more weeds, revealing only her spreading buttocks: then she turned round, and with her head still lowered she added:

'Shall I tell him something, Corporal? Well, I can keep Jules on my own.'

'Well, yes, I think you're right.'

He looked at Jules, whom he had forgotten. The baby, in his swaddling-clothes, was still asleep and the light fell full on his little motionless face. This child was the cause of all the trouble. Otherwise, why shouldn't *he* marry Lise, since she was free? This idea had come to him all at once as he watched her working. Perhaps he loved her; perhaps it was the pleasure of seeing her that brought him to the house, but he was surprised all the same, for he had felt no desire for her, and had never even played with her, as he played with

Françoise, for example. And just then, as he raised his head, he saw the younger girl standing upright in the sunshine, her face so furious, her eyes so bright with passion, that he was amused all the same, and felt more cheerful, in spite of his disturbing discovery.

But at that moment a strange trumpet-call was heard.

'Oh, it's Lambourdieu!' cried Lise, leaving her peas. 'I want to order a hood from him.'

On the road beyond the hedge appeared a little man with a trumpet, walking in front of a big long carriage drawn by a grey horse. It was Lambourdieu, who kept a large shop in Cloyes, and had gradually increased his trade in novelties by selling knitwear, haberdashery, shoes, and even iron-mongery—a complete bazaar that he took round from village to village within a radius of five or six leagues.

He took the order for the hood.

'Wouldn't you like some nice scarves in the meantime?' he added. He took out a box full of red scarves with dazzling gold patterns, and brandished them in the sunshine.

'Three francs,' he said. 'I'm giving them away! You can have two for a hundred sous.'

Lise and Françoise took them over the hawthorn hedge where Jules' nappies lay drying, and held them in their hands, longing to buy them. But they were sensible girls and did not need them, so what was the point of spending the money? Just as they were giving them back, Jean decided all at once that he wanted to marry Lise, in spite of the baby, and so, to hurry things up, he shouted:

'No, no, keep it, I'll give it to you! I'll be upset if you don't. It's a token of friendship, you know.'

He had said nothing to Françoise, but as she was still holding out her scarf to the shopkeeper he noticed her expression and felt a stab at his heart, for he thought she had grown paler and her mouth drooped.

'Keep yours too, you silly girl! I want you to, there's no need to pull a face about it!'

The two sisters were won over, although they said no and laughed. Lambourdieu had already stretched out his hand over the hedge to take the money, and off he went again, his horse pulling the long carriage behind him, while the raucous trumpet fanfare faded away along the winding road.

A week passed, and Jean was overwhelmed with such

deep shyness that he no longer dared to speak to Lise. He did not regard his idea as a bad one; when he thought it over, on the contrary, he had realized its advantages more clearly. On both sides it could only mean improvement. He possessed nothing, but she was encumbered by her child; this meant that they were equal. He made no grasping calculations, but tried to look at the whole thing reasonably, as much for her happiness as for his own. And then, marriage would force him to leave the farm, which would free him from Jacqueline, whom he had been seeing again, enjoying their encounters out of sheer weakness. He had made up his mind, then, and he was now waiting for an opportunity to speak, but he was trying to find the right words, for even military life had left him a coward as far as women were concerned.

One day, finally, Jean slipped away from the farm about four o'clock, determined to say something. This was the time Françoise took her cows out to pasture for the evening, and he had chosen to go then so that he could be alone with Lise. But he was immediately put out, for La Frimat had come round unexpectedly, like a well-meaning neighbour, and was just helping Lise to do the washing in the kitchen. She was not much use, but she talked, and every five minutes she lifted the bucket which had been placed to catch the continual drips from the washing, and emptied it into the cauldron.

Jean waited patiently, hoping she would go. But she stayed, talking of her poor paralysed husband who could now only move one hand. It was a terrible affliction. They had never been rich, but when he could still work he rented land and made it pay, while now it took her all her time to look after a small patch of ground which belonged to them.

She began to relate, too, all the gossip in Rognes about Jean himself. At first the people had hated him because he was an artisan who sawed and planed wood instead of ploughing the earth. Then, when he had taken to the plough in his turn, they had accused him of coming to take the bread out of their mouths in a district which was not his own. Nobody knew where he came from. He must have committed some crime in his home town if he daren't even go back there. They knew, too, that he was carrying on with Jacqueline, and said that one fine day the two of them would put old Hourdequin to sleep with a bedtime drink and would rob him.

'Oh, the swine!' muttered Jean, white with fury.

Lise, who was drawing a jug of boiling water from the cauldron, began to laugh at the mention of Jacqueline, for she sometimes teased Jean about her, too.

'Well,' continued La Frimat, 'since I've begun I might as well go on. There's no end to the horrible things they say about you since you've been here. Last week you gave these two girls some scarves, and they wore them at Mass yesterday. It's disgusting: they swear you sleep with both of them.'

Then all at once Jean, trembling but resolved, stood up.

'Well, Mother,' he said, 'I'm going to reply in front of you. It doesn't worry me. Yes, I'm going to ask Lise if she'd like to marry me. Are you listening, Lise? I'm asking you, and if you say yes, I'll be very pleased.'

At that moment she was emptying her jug into the washtub, but she did not hurry, and carefully finished soaking the linen. Then she became serious and, her arms naked and damp with steam, she looked him in the face.

'So you're serious then?'

'I'm very serious.'

She did not seem at all surprised. It was quite natural, only she was not saying yes, or no; there must be something that was holding her back.

'You mustn't say no because of Jacqueline,' he went on, 'because Jacqueline . . .'

She stopped him with a gesture, for she knew very well that the games at the farm meant nothing.

'It's true as well that I can bring you nothing except what I stand up in, while you own this house and your land.'

Again she made a gesture indicating that in her position, with a child, she thought as he did that things evened themselves out.

'No, no, it's not that at all,' she said finally. 'It's Buteau.'

'But he doesn't want to marry you!'

'That's quite true, and we're not friends any more, for he's behaved too badly. But all the same, we must ask him.'

Jean thought this over for a good moment.

'If you want to,' he said sensibly, 'that's how it should be because of the child.'

And La Frimat, who had also been seriously emptying the bucket of drips back into the cauldron, thought that she should approve this move, although she was favourably in-clined towards Jean, who was straightforward, and neither obstinate nor rough At that moment they heard Françoise coming home with the two cows.

'Lise!' she called. 'Come and see. Coliche has hurt her foot.'

They all went out, and Lise, when she saw the animal limping along, its left forefoot bruised and bleeding, flew into a rage, one of those outbursts which she used to inflict on Françoise when she behaved badly as a child.

'So you've been careless again, have you? I suppose you went to sleep in the grass as you did the time before?'

'No, I didn't, really I didn't. I don't know what she did. I fastened her to the stake and she must have caught her foot in the rope.'

'Be quiet, you liar! You'll kill my cow for me one day!'

Françoise's dark eyes blazed, and she went very pale.

'Your cow! Your cow!' she stammered angrily. 'You could say "our cow".'

'What d'you mean, "our cow"? How could a kid like you own a cow?'

'I do. Half of everything here belongs to me. I've a right to half of it and I can make a mess of it if I want to.'

The two sisters glared at each other fiercely; after all their years of affection this was the first bitter quarrel, with the violent division into 'yours' and 'mine'. Lise was angry at the younger girl's rebelliousness, and François was violent and obstinate in the face of such injustice. The elder girl gave way and went back into the kitchen to stop herself from striking her sister. And when Françoise, after taking her cows back to the shed, reappeared and came to the bread-pan to cut herself a slice of bread there was a silence.

But Lise had calmed down now. The sight of her sister in this tense sulky state upset her. She spoke first, for she wanted to close the incident by a piece of unexpected news.

'You'll never guess! Jean wants me to marry him. He's asked me.'

Françoise, who was eating as she stood in front of the window, remained indifferent, and did not even turn round.

'What does that matter to me?'

'You'll have him for your brother-in-law, so I want to know if you like him.'

She shrugged her shoulders.

'If I like him? It makes no difference. He or Buteau, as long as I don't have to sleep with either of them! What d'you want me to say? I don't think it's very nice.' And she went out to finish her bread in the yard.

'Well,' said Lise, 'we'll leave it like that, Corporal. I'm not saying no, and I'm not saying yes. Haytime's coming, I'll be seeing our family. I'll ask them, and I'll know what I ought to say, then we'll decide something. Is that all right?'

'That's all right.'

He held out his hand and shook hers. Her entire body was damp with steam, giving off a good housewifely smell, the smell of wood-ash scented with orris-root.

4

LISE had gone to the Fouans' house, but she was afraid there was nobody there, for it seemed so deserted. Rose had got rid of her two cows, the old man had just sold his horse, so there were no more animals, there was no work, no movement in the empty buildings and yard. Yet the door gave way as she touched it, and when Lise came into the room that was dark and silent in spite of the cheerful hay-making outside, she found Old Fouan standing up, just finishing a piece of bread and cheese, while his wife sat watching him, doing nothing.

'Good day to you, Aunt. Are things going well with you?'

'Oh yes,' replied the old woman, her face lighting up with pleasure at this visit. 'Now that we're idle folk we've got nothing to do but enjoy ourselves from morning to night.'

Lise also wanted to be nice to her uncle.

'I can see you've still got a good appetite,' she said.

'Oh, it's not because I'm hungry,' he replied. 'It's just that eating something keeps me busy. It helps to pass the time.'

He looked so miserable that Rose immediately began to exclaim again how happy they were now that they had no more work to do. They had certainly earned the rest, and it wasn't too soon. It was nice to watch other people working, and to enjoy their income coming in, getting up late, twiddling their thumbs, not caring whether it was hot or cold, having no worries. Oh yes, it was a big change for them. They really felt they were in paradise. Yet their forced happiness and the feverish excitement of their talk barely concealed the underlying boredom, the torture that idleness inflicted on these two old people now that their limbs were suddenly still, and as they rested seemed to go wrong like old machines thrown on the scrap-heap.

Finally, Lise decided to take the plunge and tell them why she had come.

'Uncle, I heard you met Buteau the other day.'

'Buteau's a filthy swine!' cried Fouan in a sudden rage, interrupting her before she could finish. 'If he hadn't been so damned obstinate, I'd never have had this trouble with Fanny.'

It was the first sign of hostility between himself and his children, and he had kept it secret; but now all his bitterness rose to the surface. When he had entrusted Buteau's share to Delhomme he had intended to let it at eighty francs a hectare, but Delhomme only expected to pay a double allowance, two hundred francs for his own share, and two hundred for the other. This was a fair arrangement and the old man was furious at being in the wrong.

'What trouble?' asked Lise. 'Aren't the Delhommes paying you?'

'Oh yes,' replied Rose. 'Every three months, exactly at noon, the money's put there on the table. Only there are ways of paying, you know, and father has his feelings; he'd like them to be polite about it, at least. Fanny comes in as though she was going to the bailiff because someone was robbing her.'

'Yes,' added the old man, 'they pay, and that's all. I don't think it's enough, myself. I'd like to have a little respect. Money doesn't let them off everything, does it? We're just like creditors, that's all. But still, we mustn't grumble. If only they all paid!'

He broke off and an embarrassed silence fell. This reference to Jésus-Christ, who had never paid a penny, drinking away his share and mortgaging it piece by piece, broke his mother's heart, for she was always ready to defend this rogue, who was her favourite. She trembled as she saw another wound opened, and hastened to reply.

'Don't eat your heart out over silly things. Since we're satisfied, why worry about the rest? Enough's enough!'

59

So Lise was able to go on.

'I would like to know what Buteau is thinking of doing about me and his child. It can't be said I've bothered him. It's time he made his mind up now.'

The two old people were silent. Lise questioned old Fouan directly.

'Since you saw him he must have mentioned me. What did he say?'

'Nothing. He simply didn't say a word, and my goodness, there isn't anything to say! The priest is always bothering me and asking me to fix things up, but nothing can be done as long as the boy refuses to take his share!'

Lise was very doubtful, and thought it over.

'Do you think he will accept it one day?'

'It's still possible.'

'And do you think he might marry me?'

'He might.'

'So d'you advise me to wait?'

'Good heavens! That's up to you. Everyone should do as they want.'

She was silent, for she was not keen to mention Jean's proposal, but did not know how to get a definite answer without doing so. Then she made one last effort.

'You must understand. I'm fed up with this, not knowing what's going to happen. I must have yes or no. Uncle, couldn't you go and ask Buteau? Please!'

Fouan shrugged his shoulders.

'In the first place, I'll never speak to the swine again. And then, girl, you're silly! Why go and make him say no? That obstinate boy will always say no. Give him the chance to say yes one day if he wants to.'

'Yes, that's it,' said Rose simply.

Lise could get nothing more definite out of them. She left them and closed the door, while the room fell silent once more and the house looked empty.

In the fields beside the Aigre Jean had begun work on the first haystack with the help of two girl haymakers. Françoise was building it up. Standing in the middle on a heap of grass she took the fork-loads of hay handed up by Jean and Palmyre, and arranged them in a circle. Gradually the stack grew higher and bigger, while she still remained in the middle, putting more hay beneath her feet in the hollow where she stood, as the wall around her mounted up to her knees. The stack was taking shape and it was already over six feet high. Palmyre and Jean both had to stretch out with their forks, and there was plenty of loud laughter, for the open air made them happy and they shouted out nonsensical jokes to each other among the good smell of the hay. Françoise in particular seemed in her element, her kerchief had slipped off, the sun beat down on her bare head and her hair was flying loose, full of grass, as the moving heap of hay submerged her up to the thighs. Her naked arms plunged down on every bundle thrown from below, and she was covered with a shower of grass. She kept on disappearing, pretending to be shipwrecked on the tide.

'Oh! It's pricking me!'

'Where?'

'Under my skirt, up here!'

'It's a spider. Stand still and keep your legs together!'

Then they laughed even louder, and told each other dirty jokes which made them scream with laughter.

Delhomme, in the distance, became anxious and turned his head a moment, although he did not stop swinging his scythe backwards and forwards. That girl could not be doing very much work if she was playing like that! Girls were spoilt nowadays, they only worked to amuse themselves. He went on laying the grass low with a rapid cutting movement, leaving a wake behind him through the hay. The sun was going down towards the horizon and the hay-makers were clearing more and more space in the fields.

'Good!' cried Jean. 'One of the boys has gone off to sharpen his tool again. There's a lady knife-grinder waiting for him over there!'

'Isn't he dirty-minded!' said Palmyre again, who was so unused to laughing that she began to choke.

Then Jean teased her.

'To think you've got to the age of thirty-two and you've never looked on the other side of the fence!'

'No, never!'

'You mean to say you've never been with a boy? You've never had a lover?'

'Oh, no!'

She had gone quite pale and serious, and her long face, which was already faded and blunted with work, looked miserable, revealing nothing except eyes like those of some good-hearted old bitch, clear, deep, and devoted.

Silence fell. Françoise, standing motionless on top of the haystack, was listening, while Jean, who was also getting his breath back, continued with his teasing, but hesitated to mention what was on the tip of his tongue. Finally, he made up his mind and let it out.

'It's a lie, then, the story that you sleep with your brother?'

The blood rushed to Palmyre's pale cheeks and made her look young again. She was taken aback and began to stammer angrily, unable to deny the rumour as strongly as she would have liked.

'Oh, how wicked of them! If you believe that . . .'

Then Françoise and Jean became cheerful and talkative again, both speaking at once, trying to wear her down and take her by surprise. Good heavens! In the ruined stable where she and her brother lived, two people could hardly move without falling over each other. Their straw mattresses touched each other on the ground, and they could easily get into the wrong one in the dark.

'Come on, it's true! Admit it's true! Anyway, everybody knows!'

Palmyre stood straight up, and in her panic and misery she flew into a rage.

'And even if it *is* true what's it got to do with you? The poor boy doesn't have much fun. I'm his sister. I might easily be his wife because none of the girls will look at him.'

As she made this confession tears ran down her cheeks, for the maternal love she felt for the crippled boy went as far as incest, and now she was heart-broken. She earned his keep for him, and at night she could surely give him what everyone else refused him, a real treat that cost them nothing. These two creatures were close to each other; they were outcasts, love was refused to them, and they could not have described how it had happened; in the depths of their dark minds lay instinctive desire and unpremeditated consent; he was like some tortured beast, while she was passive and ready for anything, and both of them succumbed to the pleasure of additional warmth, for they shivered with cold in their hovel.

'She's right! What's it got to do with us?' Jean went on in his kindly way, for he was sorry to see her so upset. 'It's their business: it doesn't do anyone any harm.'

The haystack was nearly finished now. It was almost twelve feet high, built in a solid rounded shape like a bee-hive. Palmyre, with her long thin arms, threw up the last clumps, and Françoise, standing on the top, looked taller against the pale tawny light of the setting sun. She was completely out of breath, trembling with exertion and sticky with sweat; her hair clung to her skin, her bodice hung open over her small firm breasts, and her skirt, which had lost its hooks, was slipping down over her hips.

'Oh, it's so high! I feel dizzy!'

She laughed and shivered, hesitating, for she didn't dare come down now; she put one foot forward and then withdrew it quickly.

'No, it's too high. Go and find a ladder!'

'Don't be silly,' said Jean, 'sit down! Let yourself slide down!'

'Oh no, I'm frightened! I can't!'

Then there were shouts, pleas, and coarse jokes.

'Not on your tummy, it'll make it swell! On your bottom, unless you've got chilblains!'

Jean, as he stood below, began to feel excited, as he looked up at the girl and saw her legs. His exasperation increased as he saw her so high and so far beyond his reach, while unconsciously he was overtaken with a male desire to get her down and hold her close to him.

'You won't break anything! Roll down, you'll fall right into my arms!'

'Oh no, I can't!'

He stood in front of the stack and held his arms out so that she could fall against his chest. And then, when she made up her mind, she closed her eyes and dropped down, falling so suddenly over the slippery side of the stack that her legs were wrapped round him and she knocked him over. Her skirts flew up as she fell to the ground, and she choked with laughter, saying she had not hurt herself; but as he felt her burning, sweating body against his face Jean clasped her firmly. The bitter female smell and the violent perfume of beaten hay in the open air intoxicated him and tensed all his muscles in passionate, angry desire. And there was something else, too; he was suddenly over-whelmed by an unconscious passion for this child, an emotional and physical tenderness which seemed to date from a long time ago and had grown up with their games

63

and rough laughter, culminating now in his desire to possess her then and there on the grass.

'Oh, Jean, that's enough! You're breaking me in two!'

She was still laughing, thinking he was playing. Then he met Palmyre's round-eyed stare and stood up with a start, trembling with the bewildered look of some drunkard suddenly brought to his senses by the sight of a yawning chasm. Was this the explanation? It wasn't Lise he wanted, it was this child! The thought of Lise's flesh against his own had never even made his heart beat faster, but now his whole body felt faint at the mere thought of kissing Françoise. Now he knew why he had enjoyed going to see the sisters so much and helping them. But the child was so young! He felt wretched and ashamed.

At that moment Lise was coming back from the Fouans' house. She had been thinking things over on the way. She would have preferred Buteau, because, after all, he was the father of her child. The old people were right, there was no need to hurry, and if Buteau was to say no one day Jean would still be there to say yes. She went up to him.

'I didn't get an answer,' she said. 'Uncle doesn't know anything. Let's wait.'

Jean, dazed and still trembling, looked at her but did not understand. Then he remembered—marriage, the baby, Buteau's consent, all this business which two hours ago had seemed such a good thing for both of them.

'Yes, yes, let's wait,' he said quickly. 'It's better like that.'

5

Two years had gone by in the busy monotonous life of the countryside, and as the seasons relentlessly returned Rognes had lived through the same unchanging course of events, the same work and the same rest.

Lower down in the village, on the road at the corner of the school, was a fountain, where all the women went for drinking water, for the houses had only ponds to supply water for the cattle and the land. At six o'clock in the evening the local newspaper could be read here; the least important events were recounted and there were endless comments about people who had eaten meat that day, or about some girl who had been pregnant since Candlemas. For two years the same gossip had come and gone with the seasons, continually repeated, always about children conceived too soon, men who got drunk, women who were beaten, a lot of work for a lot of wretchedness. So much had happened, and yet nothing at all.

The Fouans, whose property division had caused passionate interest, pottered along in such a dull way that they had been forgotten. Nothing had changed. Buteau was still obstinate and would not marry Mouche's elder daughter, who was bringing up his kid. And as for Jean, whom they had accused of sleeping with Lise, perhaps he didn't, after all; but then why did he keep on going to the two girls' house? It seemed strange. Things had been very calm, and then suddenly two important events, the forthcoming elections and the question of the famous road from Rognes to Châteaudun, released a great flood of gossip. When the water-jugs were filled they were left in a row and the women would not go. One Saturday evening there was almost a fight.

A fortnight later M. de Chédeville, the retiring deputy, was re-elected with a large majority. As soon as the end of August came he kept the promise he had made, a subsidy was granted to the district for opening the new road and work began at once.

On the evening after the first pick-axe blow had been struck La Bécu, her hands folded beneath her apron, was talking incessantly. For a week the chatter by the fountain had undergone a revolution due to the vital importance of the road. Some people had been paid compensation money and the others were jealous and angry. La Bécu suddenly produced a piece of news.

'Would you believe it! The Mouche girls are going to get five hundred francs!'

'It's not possible!'

And immediately all the women drew together among the pitchers which were standing about. It was quite true, the road up at Les Cornailles ran along the edge of the girls' field and took off over two hundred and fifty yards; at two francs a yard this definitely added up to five hundred francs and the ground alongside now had an increased value. What a stroke of luck!

'Well, Lise is really marriageable now, in spite of the kid. That silly Corporal chap was pretty clever to stick to her.'

'Unless Buteau comes back. His share of land's worth quite a lot more now, too.'

La Bécu turned round and elbowed the other women.

'Hush! Shut up!'

Lise was coming cheerfully along swinging her pitcher, and the women began to file past the fountain again.

Lise and Françoise had got rid of Blanchette, who was too fat and would not calve again; they decided to go to the market at Cloyes that Saturday, and buy another cow. Jean offered to take them. He had the afternoon free and his master had allowed him to take one of the farm carts, for he had heard rumours of a match between the young man and the elder Mouche girl. In fact, it was all settled; at least, Jean had promised to approach Buteau the following week and ask him about it. It had to be one man or the other, Lise's future must be decided now.

They set off about one o'clock, therefore, Jean and Lise in front and Françoise alone on the bench behind. He could feel the warmth of her knees against the small of his back and from time to time he turned round and smiled at her. It was a great pity she was fifteen years younger than he was. He was resigned now to marrying the elder sister, after much reflection and delay, but it was surely because deep down he wanted to live close to the younger girl as a relation. But then, you get carried away, you do so much without knowing why, all because you once made up your mind to it.

As they came into Cloyes, Jean put the brake on and guided the horse down the steep hill past the cemetery. As they reached the cross-roads on their way to stop at the inn he suddenly pointed to a figure going down the Rue Grouaise.

'Look! I think it's Buteau.'

'Yes, it is,' said Lise. 'He must be going to see Monsieur Baillehache. D'you think he's going to accept his share?'

Jean cracked his whip and laughed.

'Who knows! He's so cunning!'

Buteau pretended he had not seen them, although he had in fact recognized them from a distance. He stooped as he walked along, and the others watched him recede, thinking silently that it would soon be possible to sort things out. In the tavern yard Françoise, who had not said a word, got down first, climbing over one of the wheels. The yard was already full of unharnessed carts resting on their shafts, while the old buildings of the inn bustled with activity.

'Well, shall we go now?' asked Jean, as he came back from the stable.

'Yes, certainly, let's be off.'

Lise and Françoise turned down the Rue du Temple, which ran alongside the church; here the travelling salesmen set up their stalls, showing haberdashery, ironmongery, and rolls of cloth. There was a sudden exclamation from the girls.

'Oh look, Aunt Rose!'

It was, in fact, Old Fouan's wife with her daughter, Fanny, who had come in place of Delhomme to deliver some oats and had brought her mother along in the cart simply for the outing. Both women were standing waiting in front of the knife-grinder's whirring wheel. He had sharpened the old woman's scissors regularly for the last twenty years.

'Oh, it's you!'

Fanny turned round and, seeing Jean, added:

'Have you come for a walk, then?'

But when they learned that the girls were going to buy a cow to replace Blanchette, they became interested and went with them, since they had already delivered their oats. The women walked four abreast, spaced out in a line, while the young man followed them on his own. Then they reached the square.

'This way,' said Lise, turning round.

The horses were at the end, tethered to a bar, with no trappings, and only a cord fastened to their quivering necks and tails. On the left were the cows, merely held by those selling them, who moved them about to display them better.

The four women immediately fell into contemplation of a black and white cow which had been brought to market by a husband and wife. The woman, who had a very dark, stubborn face, stood in front holding the animal, while the man remained behind, motionless and poker-faced. A careful detailed inspection took place, lasting five minutes, but the women exchanged neither a word nor a look. Then they went on and stood in the same way looking at a second cow twenty paces further off. This was an enormous black beast offered for sale by a pretty young girl, almost a child, carrying a hazelwood switch. Then they stopped seven or eight times more, for the same length of time, equally silent, covering the row of animals for sale from one end to the other. Finally the four women returned to the first cow and again became absorbed.

Only this time it was more serious. They stood spaced out in a single line, examining every inch of the cow's body, gazing at it with a fixed and penetrating stare. The woman selling her said nothing either, and looked elsewhere as though she had not seen them come back and stand there.

Then Fanny leant forward and said something quietly to Lise. Old Rose and Françoise also exchanged a whispered remark. Then they all fell silent and stood still again while the examination went on.

'How much?'' asked Lise all at once.

'Forty pistoles,' replied the peasant woman.

They pretended to be completely disconcerted. They looked for Jean and were surprised to find him standing behind them with Buteau, both men chatting together like old friends. Buteau had come from La Chamade to buy a young pig and was bargaining for one now. The pigs were in a portable pen at the back of the cart which had brought them and they were biting each other and squealing, making an ear-splitting din.

'Will you take twenty francs?' Buteau asked the man selling them.

'No, thirty.'

'Oh well, go to hell then.'

And in a very gay cheerful mood he came towards the women, smiling broadly at his mother, his sister, and his two cousins, behaving as though he had seen them only the day before. The others remained calm also and seemed to have forgotten the two years of quarrels and arguments.

'Well, cousin,' he went on, 'so you've come to buy a cow? Jean told me. Well now, there's one just here. Oh, the best one in the market, a real cow, this one.'

He was pointing precisely at the black and white Cotentine.

'At forty pistoles? No thank you!' muttered Françoise.

68

'Forty pistoles for you, my pet!' he said, clapping her on the back, joking.

But she was angry and struck him back, looking furious and resentful. 'Can't you leave me alone? I don't play about with men.'

This made him more cheerful still and he turned towards Lise, who had remained serious and looked rather pale.

'What do you say, d'you want me to come into this? I bet you I'll have her for thirty pistoles. Will you bet me five francs?'

'Oh, all right. If it amuses you to try.'

Rose and Fanny nodded their approval, for they knew the young man was a fierce haggler; he was obstinate and insolent, telling lies and cheating, capable of selling things for three times their value and getting everything he wanted for nothing. They let him walk forward with Jean therefore while they lingered in the background, so that he would not appear to be connected with them in any way.

'Well, Mother,' Buteau asked the peasant woman, 'what are you selling her for?'

She had seen what was going on.

'Forty pistoles,' she repeated calmly.

At first he took this as a joke and laughed. Then he spoke to the man, who was still standing quietly on one side.

'I say, old chap, is your old girl thrown in too at that price?'

But all the time he was joking he was looking at the cow closely and found she had all the qualities of a good milker, a small head, slender horns, and big eyes, a rather full belly ridged with thick veins, her limbs somewhat slight and her tail high-set and thin. He bent down, tested the length of the udders, and the elasticity of the dugs, which were squarely-set and well-pierced; then, leaning with one hand on the animal, he began to bargain, automatically feeling the bones in her rump.

'So you want forty pistoles, do you? Don't make me laugh! Will you take thirty?'

With his hand he ascertained the strength and positioning of the bones. His fingers then moved down and went between the thighs to the place where the bare skin, of a fine saffron colour, indicated a good supply of milk.

'Thirty pistoles, is that all right?'

'No, forty,' replied the peasant woman.

He turned away but then came back to her. Then she decided to talk.

'She's a good cow, you know, really, very good. She'll be two years old on Trinity Sunday and she'll calve in a fortnight's time. You can be sure she's right for you.'

'Thirty pistoles,' he repeated.

Then, as he walked off, she glanced at her husband.

'Hey!' she shouted. 'Just so that I can get away, will you take her for thirty-five?'

'Thirty.'

'No, thirty-five.'

It seemed to be all over now. Buteau had taken Jean's arm to show quite clearly that he had given up. The women rejoined them, feeling upset, for they were sure the animal was worth thirty-five. Françoise in particular, who liked the cow, talked of settling at this figure, but Buteau became angry, saying that nobody would let themselves be robbed in this way, and for nearly an hour he stood firm in the face of his cousins' anxiety, for they trembled every time a possible buyer stopped in front of the animal. He did not take his eyes off her either. It was part of the game; you had to keep steady. It was obvious that no one was going to bring out their money quickly. They would see if anyone was silly enough to pay more than thirty pistoles, and in fact there was still no sign of a sale, although the market was nearly closing.

'Well, thirty!' repeated Buteau tirelessly, coming up to the peasant woman again.

'No, thirty-five!'

Then, since another customer was there, also haggling, he seized hold of the cow by the jaws, forced them open and looked at her teeth. Then he let go, pulling a face. Just at that moment the cow began to drop dung, which fell down softly. Buteau looked at it and pulled an even worse face. The other buyer was impressed by this reaction and went away.

'I don't want her any more,' said Buteau, 'her blood's curdled.'

This time the peasant woman made the mistake of losing her temper. This was what he wanted, and when she abused him he replied by a flood of filth. A crowd collected and everyone laughed. The woman's husband, standing behind her, still did not move. Finally he touched her elbow and suddenly she shouted:

'Will you take her for thirty-two pistoles?'

'No, thirty.'

He was just going away again when she called him back and said, choking:

'Oh well, you bastard, take her! But my God, if I had to go through that again, I'd rather give you a bloody good punch on the face first!'

She was beside herself, shaking with fury. Buteau laughed loudly and added some coarse jokes, offering to give her a lay to make up the money.

Lise had come up at once. She drew the woman aside behind a tree and paid her. Françoise had already taken hold of the cow, but Jean had to push her from behind, for she refused to budge. They had been standing about for two hours but Rose and Fanny had waited to the end, silent and tireless. Now, as they were going, they looked for Buteau, who had disappeared, and found him chatting to the man selling the pigs. He had just got his little pig for twenty francs and when he was ready to pay he first counted the money in his pocket, taking out the exact sum, and counted it again in his half-closed fist. Then came the complicated business of trying to stuff the pig into a sack, which he had brought under his smock. The old sacking gave way and the animal's hooves and snout stuck out. He threw it over his shoulder like this and carried it off, squirming and grunting, squealing horribly.

'I say, Lise!' he asked. 'What about my five francs? I've earned them!'

She gave them to him as a joke, thinking that he would not take them. But he did, and they disappeared into his pocket. Then they set off slowly towards the inn, *Le Bon Laboureur.*

'Are you off, then?' said Buteau cheerfully, as they arrived. 'Listen, Lise, why don't you and your sister stay, and we'll have a bite to eat?'

She was surprised, and as she turned to Jean he added:

'Jean can stay, too. I'd like him to.'

Rose and Fanny exchanged a glance. The boy had certainly got some idea in his head. His face never gave anything away. In any event they weren't going to get in the way.

71

'Yes,' said Fanny, 'you stay. I'm going to hurry home with mother. The others are waiting for us.'

Françoise, who had not left the cow, said drily:

'I'm going, too.'

She was quite obstinate about it, for she did not like going to the inn and wanted to take her cow home at once. She became so cross that they had to give in. As soon as the carriage was harnessed the cow was fastened behind and the three women got in.

Rose had been waiting for some admission from her son, and only now found the courage to question him.

'Haven't you got any message for your father?' she asked.

'No, nothing,' replied Buteau.

She looked him straight in the eyes.

'There's nothing new, then?'

'If there is, you'll know it when the time comes.'

Fanny flicked the horse, which set off slowly, while the cow let herself be pulled along behind, stretching out her neck. So Lise remained alone between Buteau and Jean.

At six o'clock all three of them sat down at a table in a room in the inn which opened into the café. Buteau, without indicating whether he was paying or not, went to the kitchen and ordered an omelette and rabbit. While he was out Lise urged Jean to explain himself so that the business could be settled and he need not see Buteau again. They had finished the omelette and were eating the rabbit stew, but still the embarrassed Jean had said nothing. Apparently Buteau was not thinking about the whole thing anyway. He ate heartily and laughed loudly, nudging Lise and Jean with his knees under the table in a cheerful friendly way. Then they talked more seriously about Rognes and the new road; although not a word was said about the indemnity of five hundred francs and the increased value of the land, the thought of it was at the back of their minds all the time they were talking. Buteau began to tell dirty jokes again and they clinked glasses. It was clear from his grey eyes that he was thinking of fixing up a good business deal now that the third share had become worthwhile, and his former sweetheart had a field next to his own which had almost doubled in value.

'Good God!' he shouted. 'Aren't we going to have some coffee?'

'Three coffees,' ordered Jean.

An hour went by in drinking, the brandy bottle was emptied, and still Buteau had not declared himself. He seemed to advance and then retreat, and spun things out as though he was still haggling over the cow. It seemed to be settled but he had to consider the situation from every angle all the same. Suddenly he turned to Lise.

'Why didn't you bring the child?' he asked her.

She began to laugh, realizing that this time it was settled, and she spanked him cheerfully, replying in a happy indulgent way:

'Oh, he's a real Buteau, the little devil!'

That was all. He laughed too. The marriage was fixed. Jean had been embarrassed all the time, but now he laughed with them and felt relieved. But finally he spoke and told everything.

'You know, it was a good thing you came back. I was just going to take your place.'

'Yes, I heard about that. Oh, I didn't worry. You'd probably have told me about it.'

'Oh, of course! But it's better for her to have you because of the baby. That's what we've said all along, isn't it, Lise?'

'Always, yes, that's the truth.'

All three of them became affectionate and friendly, Jean particularly, for he was not jealous and was surprised to find himself in favour of this marriage. He ordered some beer.

'My God!' shouted Buteau. 'We could certainly drink something more.'

With their elbows on the table and Lise sitting between them they now began to talk about the recent rain which had flattened the corn.

Jean paid the bill, although the invitation had come from Buteau, and this made the cheerful man completely happy. In the yard, after they had harnessed the cart, he grasped his friend by the shoulders:

'I'd like you to come, you know. The wedding will be in three weeks' time. I've been to the notary's, I've signed the deed, all the papers are ready.'

He handed Lise into the carriage.

'Come on!' he said. 'I'll take you home. I'll go through Rognes. It's not much further for me.'

Jean went home alone in his cart. It seemed quite

natural. He followed them. Cloyes was asleep and had sunk again into its utter quiet, lit by the yellow starlike street lamps, and after all the bustle of the market there was nothing more to be heard except the slow stumbling walk of some drunken peasant. Then the road stretched out in front of him, completely black. Finally he caught sight of the other cart which was taking the young couple home. It was better like that. It was as it should be, and he whistled loudly, revived by the night air, feeling free and light-hearted.

6

ROGNES was waiting impatiently for this great event, the marriage which had been delayed so long. Hourdequin, the mayor, put himself out to officiate, but had to decline the invitation for the dinner in the evening because he was forced to spend the night in Chartres owing to a lawsuit. He promised that Madame Jacqueline would come, since they were kind enough to invite her too. They had thought for a moment of inviting the Abbé Godard, in order to have some respectable guests, but as soon as they mentioned it the priest lost his temper because the marriage was fixed for Midsummer Day. He had to perform High Mass at Bazoches-le-Doyen, and since this was an endowed service how could he be at Rognes in the morning? Then the women, Lise, Rose, and Fanny, became obstinate; they issued no invitation and finally he gave in. He came at noon in such a temper that he went through their Mass in a rage, which left them feeling deeply hurt.

It had been rather cloudy in the morning but the sky had cleared, and the evening was warm, cheerful, and limpid. The table had been set in the middle of the huge kitchen facing the hearth and the stove where the meats were roasting and the sauces simmering. The fires made the room so warm that the two windows and the door were left wide open and through them came the good penetrating smell of new-mown hay.

Rose and Fanny had been helping the Mouche girls since the day before. At three o'clock there was great excitement when the pastrycook's cart appeared and all the women in the village came to their doors to look. The dessert was placed on the table at once to see how it looked, and just at that moment La Grande arrived, before time. She sat down, clasping her stick between her knees, and kept her hard eyes fixed on the food. To think that anyone had the right to spend so much money! She had eaten nothing at midday so that she would be able to get down all the more in the evening.

All the men, Buteau, Jean, who had acted as best man, Old Fouan, Delhomme, accompanied by his son Nénesse, in their black frock coats, black trousers, and silk top-hats, were playing pitch-and-toss in the yard. Monsieur Charles arrived alone, having taken Elodie back to her school in Châteaudun the day before. Without taking any part in the game he watched it with interest and made sensible comments.

But at six o'clock, when everything was ready, they still had to wait for Jacqueline. The women were letting down their skirts, which they had pinned up in order not to get them dirty near the stove. Lise was wearing blue and Françoise pink. Their dresses were made in old-fashioned styles from crude-coloured silks which Lambourdieu had sold them at twice the price they were worth, pretending they were the latest novelty from Paris. Rose Fouan had taken out the purple poplin dress she had paraded at local weddings for forty years, and Fanny, dressed in green, wore all her jewels, her watch and chain, a brooch, rings, and earrings. Every moment one of the women went out on to the road and ran to the corner of the church to see if the lady from the farm was coming. The meats were getting burnt and the rich soup, which had been served by mistake, was growing cold in the soup plates. Finally someone shouted:

'There she is! There she is!'

The carriage appeared and Jacqueline jumped lightly down. She looked charming, for she had had the good taste to show off her prettiness with a simple dress of white cretonne with red spots. She was not wearing a single jewel, apart from brilliants in her ears, a gift from Hourdequin which had caused a sensation among the neighbouring farms. But everyone was surprised when she did not send back the farm-servant who had brought her, even after the others had helped him unharness the carriage. He was called Tron, a near-giant with white skin, red hair, and a child-like expression. He came from Le Perche and had been at La Borderie for the last fortnight as yard-boy.

'Tron's staying, you know,' said Jacqueline gaily. 'He'll take me home.'

The Beauce folk did not care much for the Percherons, for they regarded them as hypocritical and sly. They looked at each other: so this great lout was one of Jacqueline's new lovers! Buteau, who had been very polite and good-humoured all day, replied:

'Of course he's staying! If he's with you that's good enough.'

Lise told them to begin and they sat down to table with plenty of bustling and shouting. They were three chairs short and ran to get two stools over which a plank of wood was placed. The spoons were already clattering on the bottom of the plates. The food was attacked and devoured in a kind of massacre; chickens, rabbits, and different kinds of meat were brought to table and disappeared in the midst of a fearful grinding of jaws. These people ate sparingly in their own homes but killed themselves with overeating in anybody else's. La Grande did not speak, so that she could eat more and she went on and on, chewing continually. It was terrifying to see what her flat, dried-up eighty-year-old body could engulf without swelling in any way.

It had been agreed that for the sake of respectability Françoise and Fanny would serve the guests so that the bride would not have to get up; but Lise could not sit still and left her chair every moment, rolling up her sleeves and carefully pouring out sauces or taking a roast off the spit. Soon, in fact, all the guests joined in; there was always somebody on their feet, either cutting a slice of bread or trying to get hold of a dish. Buteau was in charge of the wine, and it was too much for him. He had carefully arranged a cask on tap, in order to avoid spending too much time uncorking bottles, but he could not get anything to eat. Jean had to take it in turns with him to fill the glasses. Delhomme sat firmly in his chair and declared in his wise way that liquid was necessary to stop the food from strangling you. When the pastrycook's tart was brought in, the size of a cartwheel, everyone was taken aback. The force-meat balls made a great impression, too, and Monsieur

Charles was polite enough to swear on his honour that he had never seen anything finer in Chartres.

The bride and bridegroom sat opposite each other, Buteau between his mother and La Grande, Lise between Old Fouan and Monsieur Charles. The other guests sat where they wished, Jacqueline beside Tron, who gazed at her with soft stupid eyes, and Jean next to Françoise, separated from her only by little Jules, whom they had both agreed to look after. But as soon as the tart appeared he was overcome with violent indigestion and the bride had to take him away to bed. In this way Jean and Françoise finished the meal seated side by side. She was up and down all the time, her face red from the big fire in the hearth, worn out with fatigue and yet over-excited. He was anxious to help and wanted to get up instead of her, but she went on, and she was also at loggerheads with Buteau, who was a big tease when he was in a good mood and had been pursuing her since the meal began. He pinched her whenever she passed him; she struck him in a temper; then she got up on some pretext as though drawn to him, so that he could pinch her once more and she could strike him back. She complained that her thighs were black and blue.

'Then stay there!' repeated Jean.

'Oh no,' she cried, 'he mustn't think he's my man, too, because he belongs to Lise!'

When darkness fell they lit six candles. They had been eating for three hours when finally, at ten o'clock, they began work on the dessert. From then on they drank coffee, not one cup, or two, but bowlfuls of coffee all the time. The jokes became louder. Coffee gave you strength; it was a fine thing for men who were too sleepy, and every time one of the married guests swallowed a mouthful everyone split their sides.

'You certainly ought to drink some!' said Fanny to Delhomme, laughing heartily and forgetting her usual reserve.

He blushed, and calmly explained that he was working too hard, while their son Nénesse opened his mouth and roared with laughter, while shouts and thigh-slapping broke out following this conjugal confession. But the boy had eaten so much that he was bursting out of his skin; he disappeared and was not found again until everyone left, asleep between the two cows.

La Grande held out longest. At midnight she fell upon

the *petit fours* in silent despair because she knew she could not finish them. The bowls of cream had been emptied and the wedding-cake crumbs swept away. Everyone abandoned themselves to drinking, bodices were unfastened and trouser-belts undone. They all changed places and talked in little groups round the table which was covered with wine stains and grease-spots from the sauces. Singing began but was not taken up and only old Rose, her face moist with tears, went on humming a bawdy eighteenth-century song, a tune she remembered from her youth, beating time with her shaky head. There were too few guests for dancing and the men preferred to drink huge quantities of brandy and smoke their pipes, which they tapped out on the table-cloth. In a corner Fanny and Delhomme, in front of Jean and Tron, worked out to the last franc what the financial situation of the married couple would be and what their prospects were. This went on interminably; each inch of ground was estimated, for they knew the income of every person in Rognes down to the value of the household linen.

It was now one o'clock in the morning and they were talking of going home to bed. The bride and bridegroom already had a child, so there was no point in making jokes about putting them between the wedding sheets. As for the old tricks, such as scratchy hairs, or unbolting the bed, or toys which squeak when you press on them, it would have been like serving mustard when dinner is over. The best thing to do was to have another drink and then say good-night.

The Fouans and the Delhommes went home, and Monsieur Charles too. La Grande went round the table to make sure there was nothing left, and she decided to go, after telling Jean that the Buteaus would die in poverty. While the others, who were very drunk, stumbled over the pebbles on the road, her firm steady steps retreated into the distance accompanied by the regular tapping of her stick.

Tron had harnessed the carriage for Madame Jacqueline and as she mounted the step she turned round.

'Are you coming back with us, Jean? I don't think you are, are you?'

Although he had been about to climb up, he changed his mind, thankful that he could leave her to the other man. He watched her nestle against her new lover's huge body and when the carriage had disappeared couldn't help laughing. He would go back on foot, but first he went to rest for a moment on the stone bench in the yard close to Françoise, who had sat down there, overcome with heat and tiredness, waiting for everyone to go. The Buteaus were already in their room. She had promised to lock up before going to bed herself.

'Oh, how nice it is here,' she sighed, after five long minutes of silence.

Then silence fell again, in sovereign peace. The night was cool and delicious, full of stars. The scent of the hay rose so strongly from the fields by the Aigre that it perfumed the air like wild flowers.

'Yes, it's very nice,' repeated Jean finally. 'It revives you.'

She did not answer and he saw that she was asleep. She slid against his shoulder. He remained there for another hour, his mind full of confused thoughts. Evil desires overwhelmed him, then faded. She was too young. He thought that he might wait for her, that she alone would grow older and come closer to him.

'I say, Françoise, it's bedtime. We'll catch cold here.'

She woke up with a start.

'Why, yes, it's true! We'd be better in bed. Goodbye now, Jean.'

'Goodbye, Françoise.'

PART THREE

1

THE Buteau household had settled down now. The married couple had taken over the large bedroom on the ground floor and Françoise was satisfied with the room above, formerly Old Mouche's bedroom, which had been scrubbed out and furnished with a folding bed, an old chest of drawers, a table, and two chairs. She looked after the cows and led the same life as she had done before. Yet behind this tranquillity lay a hidden source of disagreement, the division of the two sisters' property, which had not been settled. The day after Lise's marriage Old Fouan, who was guardian to Françoise, had insisted that this division should be made, in order to avoid any trouble later. But Buteau had objected. What was the point of it? Françoise was too young, she didn't need her land. Nothing had changed, had it? She lived with her sister, as she had done before; she had her food and clothes, and so surely there wasn't anything to complain about, was there? As each of these reasons was put forward the old man nodded his head. But you never knew what might happen; it was best to get everything settled, and the girl herself insisted on being told what her share was, although she was ready to leave it in her brother-in-law's hands afterwards. But Buteau had won the day with his cheerful bluntness and his obstinate teasing way. The division was not mentioned any more and on all sides he extolled the pleasures of a nice family life like this.

'We've got to get on well together, that's all I want.'

For the first ten months there was no quarrel between the two sisters, nor between the married couple, but then, slowly, things began to go wrong. It began by spells of bad temper and sulkiness which led to hard words. Beneath the surface the vexed question of ownership continued its destructive work and gradually soured the love between all three of them.

It was true that Lise and Françoise no longer adored each other with the same great affection as before. Nobody ever met them now with their arms round each other's waists,

80

wrapped up together in one shawl as they walked through the twilight. They seemed to have grown apart and there was an increasing coldness between them. Since there had been a man in the house Françoise felt that her sister was being taken away from her. In the past she had shared everything with her, but she did not share this man, and in this way he had become the alien presence, the obstacle barring the way to the heart which she alone had occupied. When Buteau kissed Lise, Françoise would leave the room without doing so, for she was offended, as though someone had drunk out of her glass. As far as property was concerned she had clung to her childish ideas with extraordinary tenacity: this is mine and this is yours; and now that her sister belonged to someone else she let her go, but she wanted what was hers, half the land and half the house.

There was another reason for Françoise's anger, which she herself could not have expressed. Since Old Mouche had been left a widower the house had grown cold, there was no love in it any more, nothing to disturb her in any way, but now there was a man living there, a truly male brute who was used to seducing girls in ditches, and his games with Lise shook the inner walls and penetrated through the cracks in the woodwork. She knew everything about men and women, for she had learnt it from the animals; it disgusted and irritated her. During the day she preferred to go out and leave the couple to their dirty love-making in peace. In the evening, if they began to laugh as they left the table, she shouted that they could at least wait until she had finished washing the dishes, then she would go to her room and bang the door violently, stammering out insults, 'The swine! The swine!' between clenched teeth. In spite of everything she still imagined she could hear what was going on down below. She buried her head in her pillow and pulled the sheet up to her eyes, but she became feverish, her ears and eyes haunted by strange visions and she suffered from all the rebellious torment of her adolescence.

Worst of all, Buteau realized that all this upset her and teased her about it. Well? Why not? What would she say when she had to go through it herself? Lise laughed, too, and saw nothing wrong with it. Then he explained his views about the whole thing. Since God had been good enough to give everyone this pleasure, free of charge, then you could have a jolly good time, but you mustn't have any babies. Oh no, definitely no more babies. You always got too many of them before you were married, because you were stupid. Jules had come like this, a blasted surprise all the same, and he had to put up with it, but when you were married you had to be serious; he would rather have had himself cut like a tom-cat than start another kid. No thank you! Not another mouth to feed, for food disappeared quickly enough as it was! So he took care and watched himself when he was with his wife, for she was such an eager bitch, he said, she would take it all in at one go, and he added that he would plough deep but he wouldn't sow. Corn, yes; oh, he'd sow as much corn as the swollen womb of the earth could produce; but no brats, that was all over now!

Françoise, surrounded by these endless details, and the mating that was so close that she could feel it, became more and more restless. Her character seemed to be changing, and she was overtaken by incomprehensible moods, varying continually between cheerfulness and grumpy bouts of depression and gloom. In the morning, when Buteau unashamedly crossed the kitchen half-naked she would give him a black look. Quarrels broke out between the two sisters over trifles, such as a broken cup. Wasn't it her cup, too, at least half of it? Couldn't she break half of everything if she wanted to? Quarrels about property became bitter and left unpleasantness that lingered for several days.

About this time Buteau himself gave way to terrible bouts of temper. The earth was suffering from a fearful drought, for not a single drop of rain had fallen for six weeks. He would come home with clenched fists, depressed at seeing the harvest in danger, the poor-quality rye, the thin oats and the wheat shrivelling up before the ears had formed. It made him physically ill, like the wheat itself. He lost weight, his limbs were twisted with cramp; he was so dried up with anxiety and anger that he seemed to shrink. And one morning, for the first time, he began to argue with Françoise himself. It was a warm day. After washing himself at the well he had left his shirt open and his trousers were unbuttoned, almost slipping down over his hips; as he sat down to eat his meal Françoise, who was serving him, stood behind him for a moment.

'Can't you put your shirt in?' she broke out finally. 'It's disgusting!'

He was in a bad mood and flew into a temper.

'Good God! Can't you stop complaining about me? If it offends you, don't look. Do you want to touch something down there, you slut? You're always on about it.'

She flushed again and stammered out a reply, while Lise made the mistake of adding:

'He's right, you're getting on our nerves. If we can't do as we like in our own home, you'd better go away.'

'All right, then, I'll go!' said Françoise furiously, going out and banging the door.

But the next day Buteau was good-tempered again, conciliatory and cheerful. During the night the sky had clouded over and for twelve hours a fine, warm, penetrating rain had been falling, the kind of summer rain which revives the countryside. He had opened the window and ever since dawn he had stood there watching the rain, with his hands in his pockets.

'Now we're going to be well off,' he repeated, radiantly, 'God's on our side. My goodness, lazy days like this are better than days when you work yourself to death for nothing.'

Suddenly he heard someone open the door, and as he turned round he was surprised to see Old Fouan.

'Well, it's father! Have you come out to hunt for frogs?'

The old man battled with his big blue umbrella, left his sabots on the doorstep and came in.

'A fine drop of rain,' he said simply. 'We needed it.'

Since the property division had been finally settled, signed, and registered a year previously, he had only one occupation, which was to go and look at the land he used to own. He could always be found wandering round it, taking an interest, feeling depressed or cheerful according to the kind of harvest, complaining about his children because it was no good any longer, and if things went wrong it was their fault. This rain cheered him up again, too.

'So,' Buteau went on, 'you've come to see us? Were you just passing by?'

Françoise, who had been silent until then, now came forward.

'No,' she said drily, 'I asked uncle to come.'

Lise, who was standing by the table shelling peas, left her work and stood waiting, her arms hanging by her sides and her face suddenly hard. Buteau clenched his fists, but then put on a cheerful expression again, for he was determined not to lose his temper.

'Yes,' the old man explained slowly, 'the child talked to me yesterday. You can see now that I was right when I wanted to settle things straight away. If everyone has his share there's nothing to quarrel about. There can't be any argument. And now we've got to settle it. It's her right, isn't it? She must know what's due to her. Otherwise I'd be to blame. So let's fix a day now and we'll all go and see Monsieur Baillehache together.'

But Lise could restrain herself no longer.

'Why doesn't she put the police on us? Good God, you might think we were robbing her! Do I go about telling everyone she's so prickly we daren't come near her?'

Françoise was about to reply in the same tone when Buteau seized her from behind as though in fun.

'What a lot of nonsense!' he cried. 'We may argue but we love each other all the same, don't we? A fine thing it would be if two sisters couldn't get on together!'

The girl had shaken herself free and the quarrel might have broken out again but Buteau saw the door open once more.

'Jean!' he called out cheerfully. 'You're soaked to the skin! You look like a real drowned rat!'

In fact Jean had run from the farm, as he often did, and had only thrown a sack over his shoulders to protect himself. Now he was wet through, dripping and steaming, but laughing cheerfully. As he shook himself dry Buteau went back to the window and became more and more delighted as the rain went on and on.

'Oh, it's still falling, still falling! What a blessing! Isn't it funny the way it's raining!'

Then he turned round.

'You've come at the right moment,' he said. 'These two girls were just getting their claws out. Françoise wants the property divided so that she can leave us.'

'What? A child like her?' cried Jean, taken aback.

His desire for her had become a violent secret passion and his only pleasure was to see her in this house, where he was received as a friend. He would have asked permission to marry her twenty times already if he had not thought he was too old for such a young girl; but it was no good waiting, the fifteen years' gap between them would never close.

84

Nobody seemed to suspect that he might think of her, neither Françoise herself nor her sister, nor her brother-in-law. This was why Buteau welcomed him so cordially, for he was not afraid of any consequences.

'Child! Yes, that's the word,' he said, shrugging his shoulders in a fatherly way.

But Françoise was still tense, her eyes downcast.

'I want my share,' she insisted.

'It would be wiser,' murmured Old Fouan.

Then Jean took her gently by the wrist, drew her against his knees, and held her there, his hands trembling at the touch of her skin. He spoke to her kindly, and his voice shook as he begged her to stay. Where would she go? To strangers, or into service at Cloyes or Châteaudun? Wasn't she better off in this house where she had grown up, among people who loved her? She listened and in her turn she softened, for if she hardly thought of him as a lover she willingly obeyed him, partly from habit, largely from friendship and a little from fear, for she regarded him as a very serious person.

'I want my share,' she repeated, wavering, 'only I won't say that I'll go away.'

'Oh, you silly girl!' interrupted Buteau. 'Why are you worrying about your share if you're staying? You have everything, just like your sister, and just like me. Why do you want half of it? No, it's really idiotic. Now, listen: the day you get married you can have your share.'

Jean's eyes, which were fixed on her, wavered as if his heart had missed a beat.

'Are you listening? The day you get married.'

She did not answer, for she was depressed.

'And now, Françoise dear, go and kiss your sister. It's better that way.'

Lise was still a cheerful plump young woman and still good-hearted. She cried when Françoise put her arms round her neck. Buteau was delighted at having delayed things and shouted that, by God, they would all have a drink. He brought five glasses, uncorked one bottle and went to look for another. Old Fouan's weather-beaten face was flushed as he explained that he was in favour of what was right. They all drank, the girls as well as the men, to the health of each and everyone.

'This wine's good,' cried Buteau, putting his glass down

roughly, 'but you can say what you like, it isn't as good as the rain that's falling. Just look at that! It's still raining, all the time. Oh, it's wonderful!'

And they all crowded in front of the window, glowing with a kind of religious ecstasy, watching the warm slow rain endlessly streaming down as though they could see the tall green wheat sprouting beneath this life-giving downpour.

2

ONE day that summer old Rose, who had been feeling faint and whose legs were not very steady, sent for her great-niece, Palmyre, to clean the house. Fouan had gone out to wander round the fields in his usual way; the wretched girl got soaking wet and wore herself out scrubbing on her knees, but Rose did not leave her for a moment, while the two of them went over the same old stories again.

First of all they discussed Palmyre's unhappy life, for her brother, Hilarion, was now beating her. The half-witted cripple had become vicious, and since he did not know his own strength she was always afraid of being killed, for he got hold of her with fists strong enough to smash up stones. But she didn't want anyone to interfere; she sent everyone away who came to comfort her, because she loved her brother so much. The week before he had beaten her so violently that the whole of Rognes was still talking about the scandal, for when the neighbours had run in they had found him committing disgusting offences on her.

'Tell me, girl,' asked Rose, in the hope of receiving confidences, 'did he try to force you, the beast?'

Palmyre stopped scrubbing, kneeling there in her drenched rags, and flew into a temper without answering the question.

'What's it got to do with other people? Did they have to come and spy at our house? We don't rob anybody!'

'But, good heavens!' the old woman went on. 'If you go to bed together, as people say, it's very wicked!'

For a moment the wretched girl remained silent, her face full of suffering and her eyes gazing vaguely into the distance; then she bent down again and, punctuating each sentence with the movements of her thin arms, she stammered out a reply:

'Oh, how do we know it's bad? The priest sent for me and told me we'd go to hell. But not the poor darling boy. He's innocent, Father, I said, he doesn't know any more than a baby three weeks old; if I hadn't looked after him he'd be dead, and it's not much better for him being as he is. It's my business, isn't it? If he strangles me one day in one of those fits that come over him now I'll see if God isn't good enough to forgive me.'

Rose had known the truth for a long time and she saw that she was not going to hear anything new.

'Well, if things are that way,' she answered wisely, 'they won't ever change. But all the same, you haven't got yourself much of a life, my girl.'

And she complained that everyone had his own cross to bear. She and her husband, for instance, what misery they'd had to endure since they'd been kind enough to give up everything for their children! From that moment she never stopped. This was her endless cause of complaint.

'Good heavens! In the end you don't even look for any respect. When children are swine, they're swine. If they only paid the allowance . . .'

She explained for the twentieth time that only Delhomme brought his quarterly payments of fifty francs, oh yes, on the dot! Buteau was always late and kept trying to pay off a little from time to time. Now, although the date had gone by ten days ago she was still waiting for him; he had promised to come and pay up that very evening. As for Jésus-Christ, it was simpler still, he paid nothing, they had never seen the colour of his money.

As night fell Fouan came home to supper and she began again at table while he was eating in silence, his head lowered. Was it possible, in heaven's name, that out of the six hundred francs due to them they only had the two hundred from Delhomme, hardly a hundred from Buteau and nothing at all from Jésus-Christ, which meant they received just half of the allowance! And the wretches had signed at the notary's, it was written down and fixed by law. They didn't care a damn about the law!

Rose was finally just about to light a candle when La Grande came in with her knitting. During these long summer days there were no wakes, but to avoid wasting even a candle-end she came to pass the one hour of darkness at her brother's house before groping her way to bed. She sat down at once and Palmyre, who still had to scour the pots and pans, said not a single word more, for she was struck dumb by the sight of her grandmother.

'If you need some hot water, my girl,' Rose went on, 'get some more wood for the fire.'

She restrained herself for a moment, trying to talk of other things, for the Fouans avoided complaining in front of La Grande, knowing she would be pleased if they were to confess how much they regretted the division of their property. But Rose was carried away.

'Go on, you can put a whole bundle on, if you call that firewood! Dead twigs and scraps from the hedgerows! Fanny must really sweep out her woodshed to find us rubbish like that!'

Fouan, who had remained at table with a full glass of wine in front of him, now emerged from the silence which he had apparently wanted to preserve. He flew into a rage.

'For God's sake! Have you finished talking about the firewood? It's rotten stuff, we know it is. What d'you think I could say about this filthy vinegar that Delhomme gives me for wine?'

He raised the glass and looked at it against the candle-light.

'Look! What on earth can he have stuck in it! It isn't even the rinsings of the barrel! And yet he's honest enough. The other two would let us die of thirst, they wouldn't even fetch us a bottle of water from the river.'

Finally he drank off his wine at one gulp, but spat violently.

'Poisonous stuff! Perhaps it's meant to kill me off straight away!'

Then Fouan and Rose let themselves go without any more ado. It eased their wounded hearts; one after the other they repeated their complaints. For instance, the ten litres of milk every week; in the first place they only received six, and then, even if the milk didn't pass through the hands of the priest, it was good Christian milk, for it had been baptised with water.

La Grande, who had not opened her lips, looked at them one after the other, with her round vulture-like eyes.

'It's your own fault!' she said.

But just at that moment Buteau came in. Palmyre, having finished her work, took the opportunity to slip away, with the fifteen sous that Rose had just placed in her hand, and Buteau, standing in the middle of the room, remained motionless, preserving a careful silence, for a true peasant is never anxious to speak first. Two minutes went by. His father was forced to broach the subject.

'So you've made up your mind. Good! We've been waiting for you for ten days.'

Buteau rocked backwards and forwards.

'I come when I can. We all know on what side our bread's buttered.'

Slowly Buteau searched through his pockets. He had looked at La Grande with a frown and seemed disconcerted by her presence. She put down her knitting and was looking fixedly at him in the hope of seeing the money. His father and mother had come nearer, too, looking carefully at the boy's hand. And, as the three pairs of eyes watched him closely, he resignedly took out the first five-franc piece.

'One,' he said, placing it on the table.

The others followed with increasing slowness. He went on counting them aloud in faltering tones. After the fifth he stopped and had to dig down deeply to find another, then with a firmer voice he called out loudly:

'And that makes six!'

The Fouans went on waiting, but nothing more came.

'What d'you mean, six?' said his father in the end. 'You should be paying ten. D'you think we're fools? Last quarter you paid forty, and now you're paying thirty.'

All at once Buteau began to moan, saying that nothing was going well. The price of wheat had fallen again, the oats were doing badly. Even his horse had had a swollen belly and the vet had been twice. He would be ruined, he didn't know how to make two ends meet.

'That's none of my business,' replied the old man, furiously. 'Give me the fifty francs or I'll have the law on you!'

But he calmed down at the idea of accepting the thirty francs on account only and said he would rewrite the receipt.

'Then you'll give me the other twenty next week. I'll put that down on the paper.'

But Buteau promptly stretched out his hand and took the money from the table.

'Oh no, not that! I want it to be done with. Leave the receipt as it is or I'm off! Good heavens, it's not worth my while giving you everything I've got if I still owe you something.'

There was a fierce argument, for both father and son remained obstinate, tirelessly repeating the same words, the former angry because he hadn't put the money in his pocket straight away, and the other clutching it in his fist, resolved not to hand it over without a proper receipt. His mother had to tug at her husband's jacket a second time and again he gave way.

'All right, you blasted thief! Here's your receipt! I ought to chuck it in your face. Give me the money.'

The exchange took place fist by fist, and once the scene was played out Buteau began to smile. He went away in a good mood, quite satisfied, saying good night to everyone. Fouan sat down by the table looking worn out. Then La Grande, before she took up her knitting again, shrugged her shoulders and uttered two words, hissing violently:

'Bloody fool!'

There was a silence, then the door opened again and Jésus-Christ entered. He had been warned by Boldie that his brother was paying that evening and he had watched him on the road, waiting for him to come out before he went in. He looked kind-hearted, but he was only in a good mood because he had been drunk the day before. As soon as he crossed the threshold his eyes went straight to the six coins which Fouan had been rash enough to put back on the table.

'Oh, it's Hyacinthe!' cried Rose, who was pleased to see him.

'Yes, here I am. I hope you're all well.'

He came forward, his eyes fixed on the silver coins which shone like little moons in the candlelight. His father, who had turned his head, followed his gaze and caught sight of the money, feeling a sudden anxiety. He quickly put a plate over it to hide it, but he was too late. Bloody fool, he thought, angry at his own carelessness, La Grande is right!

'It's a good thing you've come to pay us,' he said aloud in a brutal fashion, 'for, as true as this candle gives us light, I was going to put the bailiff on you tomorrow!'

'Yes, Boldie said so,' moaned Jésus-Christ very humbly, 'and I've put myself out, because you don't want me to die, do you? What can I pay you with? Good God, I haven't even got enough bread to live on. We've sold everything. Oh, it's not a joke, come and see for yourself if you think I'm telling a story. No more sheets on the beds, no furniture, nothing. And I'm ill too.'

Rose was feeling upset now, while Fouan grew more angry.

'You've drunk everything, you lazy good for nothing! That's your funeral! Such good land, it had been in the family for years and years, and you've mortgaged it! Yes, you and your sluttish daughter, you've been having a good time for months, and if all the money's gone now, well then, you can starve!'

Jésus-Christ hesitated no longer, he began to sob.

'No father says things like that! It's against nature to refuse your own child. I'm good-hearted enough, it'll be my undoing in the end. It isn't as though you've got no money! Since you have some how can you refuse charity to your own son? I'll go and beg from somebody else. That'll be a fine thing, oh yes! A fine thing!'

He spoke through his tears and at every word he gave a sideways glance at the plate, making the old man tremble. Then he pretended he was choking and uttered only piercing cries like a man who is being murdered. Rose was terribly upset, for she was won over by the sobs, and clasped her hands, pleading with Fouan.

'Look, husband . . .'

But the latter was struggling and still refused to take any notice.

'No, no, he doesn't care a damn about us!' he interrupted. 'Will you shut up, you wretch? What's the point of yelling like that? The neighbours will come, you're driving us all mad.'

This only increased the drunken man's clamouring, and he began to scream.

'I haven't told you yet: the bailiff's coming tomorrow to seize my property! Yes, it's about an I.O.U. I signed for Lambourdieu. I'm only a swine, I'm dishonouring you, I'd better do away with myself. Just a swine, all I deserve is to jump in the river and swallow the water until I'm not thirsty any more. If only I'd got thirty francs!'

91

Fouan was overwhelmed by this scene. He jumped at the mention of thirty francs and pushed the plate aside. What was the point of keeping it there, for the scoundrel could see the coins and was counting them through the porcelain.

'You want everything! It's unreasonable, my God! Here you are, you get on my nerves! Take half of it, get out, and don't let's see you again!'

Jésus-Christ felt better at once and appeared to reflect for a moment.

'Fifteen francs,' he said. 'No, it won't be enough. Let's call it twenty, and then I'll go.'

Then, as soon as the coins were safe in his pocket he cheered them all up by telling how he had played a trick on Bécu; he had fixed up what looked like ground-lines in the private fishing area of the river Aigre, laying them in such a way that when the constable had tried to take them out he had fallen in the water.

'He's got a good heart, all the same,' said Rose, after he had closed the door.

La Grande stood up and folded her knitting, ready to go. She looked fixedly at her sister-in-law and then at her brother.

'Not a penny, you bloody fools!' she shouted at them in long-repressed anger. 'Don't ask me for a thing, ever!'

Then she left in her turn. Outside she met Buteau. He was coming back from Macqueron's, for he had been astonished to see Jésus-Christ enter looking very cheerful and his pockets rattling with coins. He had vaguely suspected what had happened.

'Oh yes, that great oaf's gone off with your money,' she told him. 'Oh, he's going to pour it straight down his throat! He doesn't care a damn about you!'

Buteau was beside himself; he banged on the Fouans' door with his clenched fist. If they had not let him in he would have broken it down. The two old people were already going to bed, his mother had taken off her bonnet and her dress and was now in her petticoat, her grey hair falling over her forehead. When they opened the door he hurled himself between them, shouting in a strangled voice:

'My money! My money!'

They were frightened and drew back, for they were still dazed and did not understand at first.

'D'you think I'm going to kill myself for my stinking

brother? He needn't do a damned stroke and I'm expected to wear myself out to keep him alive! Well, I won't have it!'

Then his father lost his temper too.

'That's enough! D'you hear? What's it got to do with you? Your money's mine now, I can do what I like with it.'

'What did you say?' Buteau went on, coming up to him, his face white and his fists clenched. 'So you want me to give up everything? Well, I think it's a filthy trick, yes, really filthy, to extort money from your children when you've got a hoard tucked away, I know you have!'

The old man was taken aback and protested wildly; his voice faltered, his strength had left him, he could no longer recapture his former authority and throw his son out.

'No, no, I haven't a thing! Will you get out!'

'Suppose I look for it! Just suppose!' repeated Buteau, who was already opening drawers and tapping the walls.

Then Rose was terrified, for she was afraid of a fight between father and son. She clutched Buteau's shoulder.

'You wretched boy!' she stammered, 'd'you want to be the death of us?'

He turned quickly towards her, seized her by the wrists, and shouted in her poor, grey, worn-out face:

'It's your fault! You gave the money to Hyacinthe! You've never loved me, you old bitch!'

And he pushed her away so violently that she collapsed on to the floor against the wall. She uttered a muffled cry, he looked at her for a moment as she lay there like some broken thing; then he went out like a madman, banging the door.

'Bloody hell!' he swore, 'bloody hell!'

The next day Rose could not leave her bed. They called Doctor Finet, who came three times without being able to ease her pain. On the third visit he found she was dying and, taking Fouan aside, he asked him as a favour if he would allow him to write the death certificate: it would save him a journey. He used this expedient for small remote villages. Yet she lingered on. When he was questioned he replied that her death was due to old age and work. When the body was worn out, nobody could go on living. But in Rognes, where the story was known, they all said that her blood had curdled. There were many people at the funeral. Buteau and the rest of the family behaved with great respect.

When the grave had been filled in at the cemetery Old Fouan went back home alone to the house where they had lived and suffered together for fifty years. He ate a slice of bread and cheese standing up. Then he wandered through the empty buildings and the garden, not knowing how to console himself. There was no longer anything to do; he went out and up on to the plateau to see if the corn was growing in his old fields.

3

THE nights were so stifling hot that year that Jean could not always sleep in his loft near the stable. He preferred to come out and lie down, fully dressed, on the paving-stones in the yard. It was not only the unbearable living warmth of the horses, or the smell of the litter, which drove him out; he could not sleep, for the image of Françoise perpetually returned, he was obsessed by the idea that she was coming to him, that he was taking her, consuming her in his embrace. Now that Jacqueline was occupied elsewhere and left him in peace his love for this girl had turned into a raging lust. Twenty times as he lay in a tormented half-sleep he had sworn to go the next day and take her. But as soon as he got up and put his head in a bucket of cold water the idea shocked him, for he was too old for her; yet the next night the torment would begin again.

When the reapers came he recognized amongst them a married woman whom he had taken to bed two years earlier when she was still a girl. One evening his desire made him so desperate that he slipped into the sheep-pen and caught hold of her feet as she lay between her husband and one of her brothers, who were both snoring with their mouths open. She did not protest and gave in to him. They devoured each other silently in the stifling darkness on the beaten soil which, in spite of being raked over, gave off such a sharp smell of ammonia from the wintering sheep that their eyes watered. And for three weeks he went back to this woman every night.

During the last days the heat was overwhelming, one day in particular when Jean was carting sheaves near Buteau's field to one of the farm fields where a large stack was to be built to a height of twenty-five feet, consisting of three thousand sheaves. The stubble had grown brittle through drought and above the wheat, which was still standing motionless, the air was burning hot. The wheat itself seemed to burn with a visible flame in the vibration of the sun's rays. There were no trees to cool the air, nothing but the short shadows cast by the men on the soil. Since morning Jean had been loading and unloading his cart beneath this blazing sky, sweating as he did so, never uttering a word, but on each trip he glanced towards the field where he could see Françoise, bent double as she worked behind Buteau, who was reaping.

Buteau had had to hire Palmyre to help him. Françoise could not do enough and he could not count on Lise at all for she was eight months pregnant. This infuriated him. How could this blasted baby have come, after all the care he had taken! He bullied his wife and blamed her for having done it on purpose, complaining for hours on end as though some beggar or stray animal had come into his house to eat up everything. After eight months he could no longer look at Lise's swollen body without insulting her.

'You and your blasted big belly! How could you be so stupid! It'll ruin us!'

In the morning she had come to work, but he had sent her home, for the sight of her heavy clumsiness made him angry. She was to come back at four o'clock and bring them some food.

'Good Lord!' said Buteau, who was determined to finish a corner of the field, 'my back's burning and my tongue's as dry as wood shavings.'

He straightened up, standing with his bare feet thrust in thick shoes, his unbuttoned shirt hanging half out of his canvas trousers, revealing the sweat-sticky hairs on his chest down to his navel.

'I must have another drink!'

He went to get a bottle of cider which he had put under his jacket to keep cool. Then when he had swallowed two mouthfuls of the tepid drink he thought of the girl.

'Aren't you thirsty?'

'Yes, I am.'

Françoise took the bottle and drank deep, showing no distaste, and as she leant back, her breasts straining against

95

the thin fabric of her dress, he looked at her. She too was streaming with sweat in her printed calico dress, which was half undone, and her white flesh showed where the bodice was unfastened at the top. The blue kerchief which covered her head and neck made her eyes look very big in her expressionless, burning face.

Without any further word Buteau went back to work, swaying from the hips as he cut down a sheaf of grass with each stroke of his scythe, and the blade made a scraping sound at each step he took. Françoise, bent double again, followed him, using her sickle to collect an armful of ears from among the thistles. At every third step she put them down in a sheaf. When he stood up, wiping his forehead with the back of his hand, and saw that she was too far behind him, her hips in the air and her head close to the ground, like a woman offering herself to a man, his tongue seemed to go even drier.

'Come on, slacker!' he shouted hoarsely. 'Don't stand about doing nothing!'

But the blue of the sky had become paler until it looked like white-hot metal, and the scorching sun seemed to be red hot. After the midday dinner came the overwhelming drowsiness of the siesta hour. Delhomme and his team, who were working close by, arranging sheaves in a stack shaped like a beehive, placing four below and one on top to form a roof, had already disappeared and were all asleep in some ditch or other. For one moment more Old Fouan could be seen, standing up. He lived with his son-in-law now, for he had sold his house a fortnight before; but he too had to lie down and he was seen no more. All that remained against the blank horizon and the scorching stubble was the distant, bony silhouette of La Grande as she gazed at a high stack which her workers had started to build among a group of half-finished smaller ones. She looked like a tree hardened by age with nothing more to fear from the sun, and she stood completely upright, without a drop of sweat on her skin, fiercely indignant that other people had gone to sleep.

'Oh, my God, my skin's cracking open!' said Buteau. He turned towards Françoise. 'What about going to sleep?'

He looked for a little shade but found none. The sun shone straight down everywhere and there was not even a bush to shelter them. Finally he noticed that at the bottom of the field the corn was still standing in a kind of little ditch and cast a narrow brown shadow.

'Palmyre!' he cried. 'Are you going to do like us?'

She was fifty paces away and replied, in a faint voice which reached them like a whisper,

'No, no, I haven't time!'

Now they no longer moved they steamed with sweat, and lay in silence, their eyes closed. All at once a leaden sleep overwhelmed them and they slept for an hour. The sweat still dripped from their limbs in the motionless, heavy, furnace-like air. When Françoise opened her eyes she saw Buteau, who had turned on one side, looking at her covetously. She closed her eyes and pretended to go to sleep again. Although he had said nothing yet she felt clearly that he wanted her, for he had seen her growing up and knew she was really a woman now. The thought horrified her. Would he dare, the swine, he whom she heard going it hard every night with her sister? He was like a stallion on heat, he had never angered her so much before. Would he dare? And she waited for him, unconsciously wanting him, resolving that if he touched her she would strangle him. Suddenly, as she closed her eyes tightly, Buteau seized hold of her.

'You swine! You swine!' she stammered, pushing him away.

'Don't be silly! Why don't you? I tell you, they're all asleep, nobody's looking.'

At this moment the deathly white face of Palmyre appeared over the corn, for she had turned at the sound of their voices, but she did not count, it was just as though a cow had stretched her head in their direction. And in fact she went on with her work, unconcerned. Every time she bent down they could hear the creaking of her back.

Buteau pulled Françoise's skirt up to her hips.

'You're a goose! Have a bit, Lise won't know!'

At the mention of her sister's name Françoise, who was weakening and felt herself overpowered, now grew tense again, and from then onwards she did not give way, striking him with her fists, lashing out with her bare legs. This man didn't belong to her, she wasn't going to take another woman's leavings.

'Go and sleep with my sister, you pig! Split her open if she wants it, give her a baby every night!'

97

As she struck him Buteau began to mutter angrily, thinking that she was only afraid of the consequences.

'You bloody fool! I promise I'll withdraw, I won't give you any babies!'

She kicked him between the legs and he had to let her go. He pushed her away so brutally that she stifled a cry of pain.

It was time for the game to end, for as he stood up Buteau saw Lise coming back with the food. He walked over to meet her and detained her so that Françoise would have time to pull her skirts down again. The idea that she might tell everything made him sorry he hadn't knocked her out with a kick, but she said nothing and merely sat down amongst the sheaves with an obstinate, insolent look. And as he began to scythe again she stayed there in an idle, lady-like way.

'What's going on?' asked Lise, lying down, too, for she was tired after her walk. 'Aren't you working?'

'No, I'm fed up,' replied Françoise, seething.

Buteau didn't dare upset her and turned on his wife instead. What the devil was she up to, sprawling there like a sow warming her belly in the sun? Oh, she'd got a fine thing there, a wonderful pumpkin that had to be ripened. She laughed at this remark, for she had kept her buxom humour. Perhaps it was true, perhaps the baby could ripen and grow like this! Under the burning sky she expanded her enormous stomach, which looked like some big sprouting plant pushing its way out of the fertile earth. But Buteau didn't laugh, he brutally made her stand up and wanted her to try to help him. She was hampered by the mass of flesh hanging over her thighs and had to kneel down, picking up the ears of corn with a sideways movement, puffing as she did so, for her misshapen belly was out of place and hung over towards her right side.

'Since you're not doing a stroke,' she told her sister, 'at least you could go home and make the supper.'

Without a word Françoise went off. The heat was still suffocating, but the plain had come to life again and the bands of men reappeared like little black dots swarming over the land as far as the eye could see. Delhomme was finishing his ricks with his two helpers, while La Grande watched her stack go up, leaning on her stick and quite ready to strike any lazy workers over the face with it. Fouan went to have a look and returned, standing absorbed in front of the work his son-in-law was directing. Then he wandered off with the heavy tread of an old man who remembers and regrets. Françoise was going along the new road, her head throbbing, for she had not recovered from the shock. Suddenly a voice called her.

'Come here! Come on!'

It was Jean, half-hidden behind the sheaves which he had been carting from the neighbouring fields since morning. He had just unloaded the wagon and the two horses were waiting, motionless in the sunshine. They were not going to build the big stack until the next day and he had simply made three heaps which were like walls flanking a kind of room, a deep, concealed hole in the straw.

'Come on! It's me!'

Mechanically Françoise obeyed the call. She was not even cautious enough to glance over her shoulder. If she had turned round she would have seen Buteau look up in surprise at seeing her leave the road. At first Jean joked with her.

"You're mighty proud, going by without saying hello to your friends!'

'Good heavens!' she answered. 'You were hiding, I couldn't see you.'

Then he complained about the way the Buteaus treated him now, but her thoughts were elsewhere. She remained silent and said only a word now and then. Of her own accord she had dropped down on the straw in the hollow as though worn out with fatigue. There was only one thought in her mind and it affected her physically in a fierce materialistic fashion—the way that man had attacked her at the edge of the field over there, the warm hands she could still feel gripping her thighs, the smell that still haunted her, the male approach she was still waiting for, as she caught her breath in an agony of repressed desire. She closed her eyes, for she felt stifled.

Jean said no more. When he saw her leaning back and relaxed like this, the blood pulsed violently through his veins. He had not planned this encounter; he held back, for he believed it was wrong to take advantage of this child. But the beating of his heart dazed him, he had wanted her so much, the idea of possessing her drove him mad, as it had done during his feverish wakeful nights! He lay down

99

close beside her; first of all he merely clasped her hand, then both hands, and almost crushed them, but he did not even dare kiss them. She did not withdraw them, she opened her eyes, raising her heavy lids, and looked at him blankly without a smile, without shame, her face drawn and nervous. This silent, almost sorrowful look made him suddenly brutal. He flung himself under her skirts and seized hold of her thighs, as the other man had done.

'No, no!' she stammered. 'Please don't, it's dirty!'

But she didn't defend herself. She uttered only a cry of pain. She felt that the earth was sinking beneath her, and in her dazed state she no longer knew whether the other man had returned or not. She found the same roughness, the same acrid male smell, the smell of sweat after heavy work in the sun. She kept her eyes tightly shut, and in the blazing darkness she was so confused that she stammered out words without thinking.

'I don't want a baby! Please stop!'

He jerked away from her and the human seed, diverted and wasted, spurted into the ripe corn, on the earth, the earth which never refuses herself, lying open and ready for every kind of seed, in her eternal fecundity.

Françoise opened her eyes again without a word, without moving, for she was dazed. Was it all over already, and didn't it give her any more pleasure than this? All she felt was the pain, and the thought of the other man came back to her, with the unconscious regret of frustrated desire. Jean, by her side, made her angry. Why had she given in to him? She didn't love this old man. He remained motionless, like her, shaken by what had happened. At last, with a gesture of annoyance he tried to say something, but no words came. Then he felt more awkward still and decided to kiss her, but she drew back, she no longer wanted him to touch her.

'I must go,' he murmured. 'Stay here a moment.'

She did not answer, looking vaguely up at the sky.

'Isn't that the best thing? Wait five minutes, then no one will see you coming out at the same time as me.'

She decided to answer.

'All right, then, go.'

And that was all. He cracked his whip, swore at his horses, and went off beside his cart, his steps heavy, his head lowered.

Buteau, however, had been surprised when Françoise disappeared behind the sheaves and as he saw Jean come out he grew suspicious. Without saying anything to Lise he set off, bending low like a crafty huntsman. Then, with a quick leap, he jumped right into the middle of the straw at the bottom of the hollow. Françoise had not moved at all and still lay in the same dazed state, her eyes gazing blankly upwards, her legs still bare. She could not deny anything and she did not try.

'You filthy trollop! You go to bed with that wretch but you kick me in the stomach! My God! We'll see about that!'

He had got hold of her already. She could see clearly from his congested face that he wanted to take advantage of the situation. Why shouldn't he have her now, since the other man had just done it? As soon as she felt his burning hands again she was repulsed as she had been before. He was there, she didn't miss him now, she didn't want him, although she was unaware of her sudden change of mood, while her whole being protested in bitterness and jealousy.

'Leave me alone, you pig! I'll bite you!'

He had to give up any second attempt, but the thought that she had had her pleasure with another man enraged him.

'Oh, I thought you were at it together,' he stammered in fury, 'I should have chucked him out a long time ago. You filthy little whore! Why did you let that stinking bastard lay you like that?'

He continued with a flood of filth. He let fly revolting words and talked about sex so crudely that she felt naked and ashamed. She was furious, too, tense and pale, but she pretended to be extremely calm.

'What's it got to go with you?' she replied to each insult drily. 'I'm free to do what I like, aren't I?'

'Well, I'm going to throw you out. Yes, as soon as we get back. I'll tell Lise how I found you, with your skirts up to your neck, and you can go and have that kind of fun somewhere else, since you like it.'

Now he pushed her in front of him and took her back to the field where his wife was waiting.

'Tell Lise, then. I'll go away if I want to.'

'If you want to! We'll see about that. You'll go away with my boot up your backside.'

He made her cut across the field at Les Cornailles, which so far had remained the joint property of herself and her sister, the field which she had wanted divided against his wishes. Suddenly he was taken aback, for an idea had occurred to him. In a flash he saw that if he threw her out the field would be cut into two, she would take half of it with her and give it to her lover, perhaps. The idea shook him and he immediately forgot his frustrated desire. No, that would be silly, you couldn't lose everything because for once a girl had turned you down. You can find that sort of fun again, but if you own land you must stick to it.

He said nothing more, going forward slowly, wondering how he could calm his violent mood before rejoining his wife. Finally he made up his mind.

'I don't like bad feeling. I get angry because you turn up your nose at me. I don't really want to upset my wife in her condition.'

Françoise thought he was afraid she would give him away to Lise.

'You can be sure of one thing: if you talk, so will I.'

'Oh, I'm not afraid,' he went on, cocksure and calm. 'I'll tell her you're lying, having your revenge because I caught you.'

As they arrived he added, rapidly, 'We'll keep this to ourselves. We'll talk about it again some time.'

4

'As long as the calf doesn't come at the same time as the baby!' Lise said every morning, and, dragging about with her enormous belly, she would linger in the cowshed looking anxiously at Coliche, whose belly had also swollen up to a great size. The end of the nine months coincided exactly with St. Fiacre's Day, for Françoise had carefully written down the date when she had taken her to the bull. Unfortunately Lise was not very certain about her date. The unwanted baby had happened in such a strange way that she had no means of knowing, but it would certainly arrive about St. Fiacre's Day, the day before or after, perhaps.

Two weeks had passed since the harvest. Françoise had

taken up her usual routine in the household again as though nothing had occurred between her and Buteau. He seemed to have forgotten and she herself avoided thinking of the things that worried her. She had warned Jean and he had not come back. He watched for her by the hedgerows, begging her to slip away and meet him in the evening by some ditch, but she was frightened and refused, concealing her coldness beneath an air of great discretion. Later on, she would say, when they had less need of her in the house. And one evening, when he had come upon her unexpectedly as she was going down to Macqueron's to buy some sugar, she obstinately refused to follow him behind the church. She talked to him all the time about Coliche, whose bones were beginning to crack and her back passage was opening. These were definite signs and he too declared that it couldn't be very far off now.

And indeed, the very day before St. Fiacre's Day, Lise was seized with bad pains in the evening after dinner, just when she was in the cowshed with her sister looking at the cow. Coliche was in pain, too, her thighs forced apart by her swollen womb and she was lowing softly.

'I told you so!' cried Lise in a fury. 'Oh, now we're in a mess!'

She bent double and held her stomach tightly with both arms, punishing it severely for causing so much trouble.

Couldn't the brat leave them in peace? she asked. He could certainly wait a bit! She felt as though insects were stinging her sides, and the pain started in the small of her back, going right down to her knees. She refused to go to bed and walked up and down repeating that she wanted to push the baby back.

About ten o'clock, when little Jules had been put to bed, Buteau, who was annoyed at seeing nothing happen, decided to go to sleep and left Lise and Françoise waiting in the cowshed by Coliche, whose pains were getting worse. Both girls began to be worried, for there was hardly any progress, although labour seemed to be over. The passage was open but why didn't the calf come? They stroked the cow and encouraged her, bringing her sugary titbits, which she refused, lowering her head as her rump was shaken by deep-set upheavals. At midnight, Lise, who had been twisted with pain all the time, suddenly felt better. In her case it was just a false alarm, with pains from time to time, but she was convinced she had pushed the baby back, and she and her sister sat up with Coliche all night, looking after her, heating cloths and laying them against her skin burning hot. The other cow, Rusty, the new one they had bought at Cloyes market, was astonished by the candle burning and followed them about with her big sleepy blue eyes.

At sunrise, Françoise, seeing that there was still nothing happening, decided to run round to their neighbour, La Frimat. She was reputed for her knowledge and had helped so many cows that people willingly went to her in cases of difficulty to save getting the vet. When she arrived she pulled a wry face.

'She doesn't look very good,' she murmured. 'How long has she been like that?'

'Twelve hours.'

The old woman kept on moving about behind the animal, examining her all over, nodding her head slightly, and looking gloomy, which frightened the two others.

'And yet,' she said, 'the water-bag's coming now. We'll have to wait and see.'

So they spent all morning watching the water-bag form, the pouch which is swollen by the waters and pushed outside. They studied it carefully, measured it, and gave their opinion. In fact, it was no different from any other waterbag, although it was rather long and too big. But at nine o'clock labour stopped again and the bag hung down miserably without moving, swinging regularly with each convulsive shudder from the cow, whose condition was clearly getting worse.

When Buteau returned from the fields to have his meal he was also alarmed and talked of sending for Patoir, although he trembled at the idea of what it would cost.

'A vet!' said La Frimat bitterly. 'D'you want him to kill her? Old Saucisse's cow burst open under his nose! No. Now watch, I'm going to break the bag and I'll find your calf for you myself.'

'But Monsieur Patoir says it mustn't be broken,' Françoise pointed out. 'He says the water in it helps.'

La Frimat shrugged her shoulders in exasperation. Patoir was a fool, and with a stroke of the scissors she cut through the bag. The water poured out like a millrace and they all stood back, but too late, for they were splashed all over. For a moment Coliche breathed more easily and the old woman was triumphant. She rubbed her right hand with butter and put it inside trying to find the position of the calf. She felt round slowly.

'I can feel the feet,' she murmured, 'but not the head. It's not a good sign when you can't find the head.'

She had to take her hand out. Coliche was shaken with a violent pain and pushed so hard that the feet appeared. That was something, at least, and the Buteaus sighed with relief. They felt they already had part of their calf and from then on they were possessed with one thought only—they must pull in order to get it all at once, for they were afraid it might go back and never come out again.

'We'd better not rush it,' said La Frimat, wisely, 'it'll come out all right in the end.'

Françoise was of the same opinion but Buteau became agitated and touched the feet every minute or so, getting angry because they protruded no further. Suddenly he took a rope and tied it in a firm knot, with the help of his wife, who was trembling as much as he was.

'Now, pull!' cried Buteau. 'All together . . . Oh the wretch, it hasn't moved an inch! It's stuck inside there . . . Come on, now! Pull! Pull again! Go on!'

The women were sweating, out of breath, but they repeated:

'Come on! Pull! Come on, you devil!'

Then there was a tragedy. The rope was old and half-rotten. It now broke and they were all flung down in the litter, shouting and swearing.

'It doesn't matter, there's no harm done,' said Lise, who had rolled over to the wall, and they hastened to help her up.

But she was no sooner on her feet than she felt faint and had to sit down. A quarter of an hour later she was holding her stomach; the pains began again as on the previous day, coming deeply and regularly. And she thought she had pushed it back! What damned bad luck, all the same, that the cow wasn't going faster, and now she'd been taken with pains again so badly that she was even going to catch her up. You couldn't escape fate! It was ordained that the calf and the baby would arrive at the same time. She sighed deeply and a quarrel broke out between her and Buteau. Why, in God's name, had she pulled on the rope? The cow's inside had nothing to do with her! She'd better get her own sorted out first! She replied by insults, for she was suffering great pain. The filthy swine! If he hadn't stuffed her in the first place her inside wouldn't be such a nuisance now!

'That's just so much talk,' said La Frimat. 'It doesn't get us anywhere.'

And La Bécu added:

'It's a relief, though, all the same.'

Fortunately little Jules had been sent to the Delhommes out of the way. It was three o'clock now and they waited until seven. Nothing happened, and the house was in an infernal state. Lise sat obstinately on an old chair, writhing and groaning; Coliche uttered only one cry as she shivered and sweated, while her condition became more and more serious. The other cow, Rusty, had begun to low in fear; then Françoise lost her head, and Buteau swore, shouting that he wanted to try pulling again. The neighbours were called in and six of them pulled, as though they were uprooting an oak tree, with a new rope, which didn't break this time. But Coliche was shaken and fell on her side, where she lay in the straw, stretched out and breathing hard, a pitiful sight.

'We'll never get that damned calf,' declared Buteau, dripping with sweat, 'and we'll lose the bloody cow too!'

Françoise clasped her hands.

'Oh, go and get Monsieur Patoir!' she begged. 'It doesn't matter what it costs! Go and get him!'

Buteau was depressed now. After a final struggle, without a word, he took out the cart.

La Frimat, who had pretended to lose interest in the cow when the vet's name was mentioned, now began to worry about Lise. She also knew a great deal about confinements and she had delivered all the neighbours' babies. She seemed anxious and did not hide her fears from La Bécu, who called Buteau back from harnessing the cart.

'Listen! Your wife's in great pain. What about bringing a doctor back, too?'

He stood there speechless and wide-eyed. Surely nobody else needed pampering? He certainly wasn't going to pay everybody!

'No, no,' cried Lise, between two spasms of pain. 'I'll manage. We haven't got money to burn.'

Buteau whipped up his horse quickly and the cart disappeared through the dusk along the road to Cloyes.

When Patoir finally arrived two hours later there had been no change: Coliche lying on her side, her breath rattling in her throat, and Lise writhing like a worm, half-sliding off her chair. This had been going on for twenty-four hours.

'Now, who've I been called for? Let's see,' asked the vet, who was a cheerful man. 'Now, old girl,' he said to Lise straight away, 'if it isn't for you, please be kind enough to get yourself into bed. That's what you need to do!'

She did not reply and did not go away. He was already examining the cow.

'My God, your cow's in a bloody mess! You always come and get me too late, and you've been pulling, I can see that. You'd split the cow in two rather than wait, wouldn't you, you damned clumsy things!'

They were all listening, their eyes downcast with an expression of respectful hopelessness. Only La Frimat pursed her lips, full of contempt. He took off his coat, rolled up his sleeves, and pushed the calf's feet back, after tying a string round them so that he could find them again. Then he put his right hand in.

'Why, yes!' he went on after a moment. 'It's just as I thought: the head's turned to the left. You could have pulled until tomorrow, it would never have come. And I'll tell you something, folks, your calf is done for. I don't want to cut my fingers on his teeth turning him round, I wouldn't get him even then, and I'd harm the mother.'

Françoise broke out into sobs.

'Monsieur Patoir, I beg you, save our cow! Poor Coliche, she loves me . . .'

And Lise, whose face had turned green in a spasm of pain, along with Buteau, who was perfectly well and unaffected by the sufferings of others, both became upset and moaned, begging him in the same way.

'Save our old cow, she's given us such good milk for years and years! Save her, Monsieur Patoir!'

'But you must understand that I'll be forced to cut up the calf.'

'Oh, to hell with the calf! Save our cow, Monsieur Patoir, save her!'

Then the vet, who had brought a large blue apron with

him, borrowed some linen trousers. He undressed completely in a corner behind Rusty, and put on only the trousers, tying the apron round his waist. When he reappeared with his cheerful bulldog face, looking fat and short in these light clothes, Coliche raised her head and stopped moaning, no doubt from astonishment. But nobody smiled, for this waiting made them desperate.

'Light some candles!'

He had four of them placed on the ground and he lay down on his stomach in the straw behind the cow, who could no longer get up. For a moment he lay there flat, peering between the animal's thighs. Finally he decided to pull on the string to bring back the feet, which he examined closely.

He had put a long narrow box on the ground beside him and, raising himself on one elbow, he took out a scalpel. Just then a hoarse groan surprised him and made him sit up.

'What, old girl, are you still there? I was just wondering—it wasn't the cow!'

It was Lise, who was now taken with true labour pains and strained downwards, her loins torn apart.

'For God's sake, go and look after yourself in your own room and let me get on with my own work here! It upsets me, on my word of honour, it gets on my nerves to hear you moaning away behind me. Come on, what's the sense in it? Take her away, you others!'

La Frimat and La Bécu decided each to take hold of Lise under one arm and get her to her room. She gave in to them, for she no longer had the strength to resist. But as they crossed the kitchen, where a solitary candle was burning, she asked for all the doors to be left open, so that she would not feel so far away. La Frimat had already prepared the bed for childbirth, country-style; a simple sheet was placed in the middle of the room on a heap of straw, along with three chairs placed upside down. Lise squatted down and stretched her legs apart, her back leaning against one of the chairs, her right foot against the second, her left foot against the third. She had not even taken her clothes off, she pressed against the chairs with both feet and she still wore slippers, while her blue stockings came up to her knees; her skirt, thrown back to her chest, revealed the huge stomach, and her plump, dead-white thighs, which were so wide open that one could see up to her heart.

Buteau and Françoise had stayed in the cowshed to pro-
vide light for Patoir; they both sat on their heels and held a
candle close, while the vet, who had lain down again, cut
out with the scalpel a section round the left ham. He
stripped off the skin, then pulled on the shoulder, which
came away and broke; Françoise went pale and collapsed,
dropping her candle and running off crying:

'Poor old Coliche, I can't bear to see it!'

Patoir was angry, particularly as he had to get up and
stamp out the fire in the straw, for the candle had set it
alight as it fell.

'That blasted child! She's as sensitive as a fine lady! She
would have had us smoked like sides of bacon.'

Françoise ran until she came to the room where her sister
lay in labour and threw herself on the chair. She was not
affected by Lise's gaping thighs and seemed to find this
natural and ordinary after what she had just witnessed in
the cowshed. She rapidly brushed away the memory of the
vet's knife cutting through the living flesh and stammered
out an account of what they were doing to the cow.

'That can't do any good! I'll have to go back,' said Lise
suddenly, who, in spite of her pains, got up to leave her
three chairs.

But La Frimat and La Bécu angrily kept her in place.
'Now, will you please sit still! What's the matter with you?'

Then La Frimat added, 'Good, now your water's
breaking, too!'

The water spurted out all at once and the straw beneath
the sheet absorbed it quickly. Now the last labour pains
began. The naked belly bore down in spite of itself and
swelled up to breaking point, while the legs, in their blue
stockings, drew up and opened again with the unconscious
movements of a diving frog.

'Now look,' went on La Bécu, 'to keep you quiet I'm
going to see for myself and I'll tell you what's happening.'

From then on she did nothing but run up and down between the bedroom and the cowshed. In the end, to save
herself the walk, she merely shouted the news from the
middle of the kitchen. The vet was continuing his dis-
memberment in the litter, which was soaked with blood and
mucilage, and he emerged filthy from head to foot from this
difficult, dirty job.

'It's all right, Lise,' shouted La Bécu, 'don't worry, go on pushing! We've got the other shoulder. Now they're taking out the head. He's got the head! Oh, what a head! It's all over now. The whole body came at once.'

Lise received the news of each stage of the operation with a heart-rending sigh. No one could tell if she was suffering on her own account or because of the calf. But suddenly Buteau brought the head to show her.

'Oh, what a beautiful calf!' they all exclaimed together.

And Lise, whose labour had not stopped, pushed harder, her muscles tense and her thighs swollen, apparently overcome with inconsolable despair.

'My God, what a terrible thing! Oh, such a wonderful calf! It's awful! Such a wonderful calf, the finest calf that ever was!'

Françoise moaned too and everyone was so full of aggressive complaints, with hostile undertones, that Patoir was offended. He ran up, but out of decency stopped at the door.

'Now listen! I did warn you! You begged me to save your cow. I know you, you devils! You won't go telling everyone I've killed your calf, will you?'

'Oh no, of course not!' murmured Buteau, going back to the cowshed with him. 'All the same, it was you who cut him up.'

As Lise lay on the floor between her three chairs, a heaving shudder ran through her flesh beneath the skin, coming down from her loins and ending at the top of the thighs in a continued swelling. Françoise, who had been in such despair that she had not noticed anything before, was all at once horrorstruck, as she stood in front of her sister, whose nakedness made her look shorter. All she could see were the angles of the raised knees to the right and left of the hump-like stomach in which a round hole had appeared. It was so unexpected, so unsightly and enormous that she was not upset. She would never have imagined such a thing, it looked like a gaping hole in some broached barrel, a wide-open window in a hayloft, surrounded with tufts of prickly black ivy. Then she noticed that another round shape, smaller in size—the baby's head in fact—was moving in and out with each spasm in a perpetual game of hide-and-seek. She was overwhelmed with such a violent desire to laugh that she had to cough lest she were thought to be lacking in sympathy.

'Be patient a bit longer,' said La Frimat. 'It'll come soon.'

She had knelt down between Lise's legs ready to receive the baby, but, as La Bécu said, it was playing tricks. It even disappeared at one moment as though it was going right back inside. Only then did Françoise withdraw her fascinated gaze from this oven door which stood open in front of her; she was immediately overcome with embarrassment and went to take her sister's hand, feeling sorry for her as soon as she looked away.

'Poor Lise, you must be in terrible pain!'

'Oh yes, I am, nobody's sorry for me! If only someone were sorry for me! Oh, it's coming back! It hurts again. It's never going to come!'

It could have gone on for a long time when there were sudden cries from the cowshed. Patoir, seeing to his surprise that Coliche was still lowing restlessly, had suspected the presence of a second calf, and in fact, when he plunged his hand in again he pulled it out, without any difficulty this time, just as though he had been taking a handkerchief out of his pocket. He was so gay and cheerful about it that he forgot decency to the point of running into Lise's room carrying the calf, followed by Buteau, who was laughing, too.

'There you are, old girl! You wanted a calf, there it is!'

And he roared with laughter, naked beneath his apron, his arms, face, and entire body covered with dung, while the calf was still wet, and its top-heavy head and surprised expression made it look drunk.

Among the general shouts of acclamation, Lise, when she saw it, was overcome with uncontrollable, endless, hysterical laughter.

'Oh, how funny he is! Oh, how silly you are to make me laugh so much! Oh, it hurts terribly, it's cutting me in two! No, no, don't make me laugh any more! I can't any more!'

The laughter roared in her plump bosom and went down into her stomach like a gusty storm. It blew her out, and once more the baby's head began to move backwards and forwards like a cannon-ball about to be fired from a gun.

But the final touch was still to come, when the vet put the calf down in front of him and tried to wipe the sweat off his forehead with the back of his hand. He marked himself with a broad streak of dung; everyone rocked with laughter and the girl in labour began to choke, uttering piercing cries like a hen laying an egg.

'It's killing me! Stop it! Your damned jokes will make me burst out of my skin! Oh heavens, it's finished me!'

The gaping hole became rounder still, large enough to engulf La Frimat, who was still kneeling down, and all at once the baby appeared, as though shot from some female cannon, red all over, its extremities weak and pale. The only sound was a gurgle as though some vast spout were being emptied. Then the baby made a mewing sound, while the mother laughed even louder, shaking like a leather bottle that was shrinking down to nothing. Cries came from one end of her body and laughter from the other. Buteau slapped his thighs, La Bécu held her sides, Patoir laughed loudly, and Françoise herself, whose hand had been crushed by her sister in her last spasm, was finally able to laugh and need not hold it back any longer. But she still thought of her sister's belly as a real cathedral which could have absorbed her husband's body completely.

'It's a girl,' said La Frimat.

'Oh no,' said Lise, 'I don't want a girl, I want a boy!'

'All right, then, my pretty one; I'll put it back and you can have a boy tomorrow.'

The laughter became louder than ever and they were practically ill with laughing. Then Lise, looking at the calf which was still in front of her, finally grew calmer.

'The other was so beautiful,' she said regretfully. 'And, all the same, we should have had two.'

Patoir went away after Coliche had been given three litres of sweetened wine. In the bedroom La Frimat undressed Lise and put her to bed, while La Bécu, with the help of Françoise, took away the straw and swept the floor. In ten minutes everything was back in place and no one would have thought that a confinement had just taken place, except for the continual wailing of the baby, who was being washed in warm water. When she had been wrapped in swaddling clothes and lain in her cradle she gradually became silent, and the mother, who was now completely exhausted, fell into a heavy sleep, her congested face looking almost black against the coarse brown linen sheets.

About eleven o'clock, when the two neighbours had gone,

Françoise told Buteau that he had better go and sleep in the hayloft. She had put a mattress on the floor and intended to spend the night there in order not to leave her sister. Buteau, silently finishing his pipe, did not answer. Everything became very quiet; there was no sound except Lise's heavy breathing as she slept. Then, as Françoise knelt down on the mattress at the very foot of the bed in a dark corner, Buteau, still saying nothing, came up suddenly behind her and knocked her down. She turned round and when she saw his tense red face she understood at once. Lust had overwhelmed him again, he had not given up the idea of having her. He must have been feeling really randy all at once to want her like this, so close to his wife, after events which had been hardly pleasant to watch. She pushed him away and knocked him over. There was a silent breathless struggle between them. He sneered at her in a strangled voice.

'Come on, now, what the hell does it matter? I can manage both of you.'

He knew well enough that she wouldn't cry out. In fact she resisted without a word, for she was too proud to call her sister and did not want to involve anyone else in her affairs, not even Lise. He was suffocating her and was on the point of possessing her.

'It would work out fine. We live together, we wouldn't have to separate.'

But he held back a cry of pain, for she had silently dug her nails into his neck. Then he became angry and mentioned Jean.

'If you think you're going to marry that bastard, you won't, not before you come of age.'

This time, as he was doing her violence under her skirt, with all the strength of his brutal hands, she gave him such a kick between the legs that he screamed. With one leap he stood up again, with a terrified glance at the bed; his wife was still sleeping and breathing evenly. He went off all the same, with a terrible threatening gesture.

When Françoise lay down on the mattress in the utter calm of the bedroom her eyes remained open. She didn't want it, and even if she did, she would never let him do it. She felt surprised too, for the idea of marrying Jean had not yet occurred to her.

For two days Jean had been working in Hourdequin's fields near Rognes, where the farmer had set up a steam threshing-machine, hired from an engineer in Châteaudun, who took it up and down between Bonneval and Cloyes. With his cart and two horses the young man brought the sheaves from the surrounding ricks and then took the grain back to the farm. The machine puffed away from morning till evening, blowing out golden dust into the sunshine and filling the whole countryside with a loud, incessant snorting sound.

Jean was sick at heart and racked his brains trying to discover a way of finding Françoise again. It was a whole month since he had held her in his arms just here among the wheat they were threshing, and since then she had always evaded him, for she was afraid. He despaired of ever coming close to her again, yet he wanted her more than ever and passion overwhelmed him. As he drove his horses along he wondered why he didn't go straight to the Buteaus and ask if he could marry Françoise. So far there had been no obvious and final breach between them. He always called out good-day to them as he passed by, and as soon as the idea of marriage occurred to him as the only means of having the girl again he convinced himself that this was his duty, that he wouldn't be an honest man if he didn't marry her.

Yet the next day, when Jean went back to his machine, he was seized with fear. He would never have risked a visit if he had not seen Buteau and Françoise set off for the fields together. He realized that Lise had always been well disposed towards him and thought he would be less afraid with her. He entrusted his horses to a friend and slipped away for a moment.

'Well, it's you, Jean!' cried Lise, who had recovered from her confinement, and was up again, quite cheerful. 'We don't see you any more. What's the matter?'

He asked to be forgiven. Then, hastily, with the typical shyness of a timid man, he came to the point. She thought at first he was making some proposition to her, for he reminded her that he had always liked her and would willingly have married her.

'So that's why I'd marry Françoise all the same,' he added immediately, 'if you'd let me.'

She looked at him in such surprise that he began to stammer.

'Oh, I know, it can't be arranged as simply as that. I just wanted to talk to you about it.'

'Good heavens!' she replied at last. 'I'm surprised, I hardly expected it because of the difference in your ages. First we must ask Françoise what she thinks about it.'

He had come with the definite plan of telling everything in the hope of making the marriage necessary, but at the last moment a scruple made him hesitate. If Françoise had not told her sister, and no one knew anything, had he the right to speak first? This discouraged him and he was ashamed of being thirty-three.

'Of course,' he murmured, 'we must talk to her about it. We mustn't force her.'

Lise, however, once she had recovered from her astonishment, looked at him cheerfully, and it was clear that the idea did not displease her. In fact she was very nice to him.

'We'll do what she wants, Jean. I don't agree with Buteau, he thinks she's too young. She's nearly eighteen; she's strong enough to have two men, not just one. And what's more, two sisters can love each other all right but now she's grown up I'd rather have a servant instead. If she says yes, marry her! You're a good sort and the older ones are often the best.'

Françoise picked up a flail with a long handle and a cornelwood flap, which were joined together with leather buckles. It was her own, polished by use and fitted with a tight string to stop it slipping. Using both hands she lifted it right up over her head and brought it down on the sheaf, so that the flap struck it firmly along its whole length. Then she worked on, lifting the flail very high again, bending it as though it had a hinge, and bringing it down again with the mechanical and rhythmic movement of a blacksmith. Buteau was working opposite her in the same way, but he brought his flail down as hers went up. They soon warmed to the work and their rhythm became faster. There was nothing to be seen except the flying tools which leapt up and spun round continuously behind their heads like birds with their feet tied together.

The blood had rushed to Françoise's cheeks, her wrists were swollen, and her skin was ablaze, vibrating with a fiery glow that was visible in the air around her. Her lips were parted and she was breathing hard. Wisps of straw adhered to her loose-flying hair. Each time she raised the flail her right knee pressed against her skirt, her hips and breasts protruded, suddenly revealing the entire lines of her figure, the very nakedness of her well-built body. A button flew off her bodice. Buteau could see the white skin below her sunburnt neck, and each violent movement of her shoulder muscles and arms made the white flesh show more. To the man this seemed even more provocative, like the movements of a strong woman who worked well; so the beating of the flails went on, the grain leapt out and rained down beneath the tick-tock action of the two panting breathless workers.

At a quarter to seven, as dusk fell, Fouan and Delhomme arrived.

'We've got to finish this,' Buteau called out to them without stopping. 'Go on, Françoise.'

She did not stop and went on beating harder, carried away by the work and the noise. This was how Jean, who had received permission to have supper out, found the two of them when he arrived. He felt suddenly jealous, as though he had taken them by surprise, working side by side at this heavy job, keeping in time, striking at the right moment, both of them sweating, so overheated and untidy that they looked as though they had been making love rather than threshing grain. Perhaps Françoise, who had been working so hard, had the same feeling, for she stopped short in embarrassment. Then Buteau turned round and remained motionless for a moment in surprise and anger.

'What have you come for?'

But Lise was just coming down with Fouan and the Delhommes. She went up to them and called out gaily:

'Why yes, of course, I didn't tell you. I saw Jean this morning and invited him to come this evening.'

Her husband's red face took on such a threatening look that she added, as though excusing herself:

'I think he's got something to ask you, Father Fouan!'

'Something to ask me?' said the old man.

Jean blushed and stammered, for he was very much put out to find things beginning this way, so suddenly in front of everyone. Then Buteau interrupted him violently, for the cheerful glance his wife bestowed on Françoise had been enough to enlighten him.

'D'you think we're a lot of damn fools? She's not for you, you old rogue!'

This harsh welcome restored Jean's courage. He turned his back and spoke to the old man.

'I'll tell you what it's all about, Father Fouan, it's quite simple. As you're Françoise's guardian I have to ask you for her, don't I? If she'll take me I'd like to have her. I'm asking if I can marry her.'

Françoise, who was still holding her flail, let it drop in astonishment. She should have expected it, all the same, but she would never have thought that Jean would dare ask for her like this, immediately. Why hadn't he mentioned it to her first? It was too sudden for her. She could not have said if she was trembling with hope or fear, and, still breathing hard from work, her bosom heaving below her loosened bodice, she stood between the two men, her hot blood racing so fast that they could feel its pulsing from where they stood.

Buteau did not leave Fouan time to answer.

'Well, you've got a cheek!' he went on with mounting fury. 'An old man of thirty-three marrying a child of eighteen! There's only fifteen years between you! Don't you think it's disgusting? D'you think you can get a chicken when you've an old tanned hide?'

Jean was angry now.

'What's it got to do with you if I want her and she wants me?'

Then he turned towards Françoise so that she could say what she felt, but she was still frightened and tense, looking as though she did not understand. She couldn't say no, but she didn't say yes. Buteau, moreover, looked as though he would kill her and thrust the 'yes' down her throat. If she married he would lose her, and he would lose her land, too. The sudden thought of this consequence finally enraged him.

'Listen, Dad! And you, Delhomme, aren't you disgusted by the thought of that child and this old chap, who doesn't even belong to the district? We don't know where he comes from, he's wandered all over the place. He failed as a carpenter, then he turned peasant, it must have been because he wanted to cover up some dirty business.'

All his hatred for town workers broke out.

'What does that matter, if I want her and she wants me?' Jean repeated, holding himself back, for he had vowed out of politeness to let her tell their little story first. 'Come on, Françoise, say something!'

'But it's true!' cried Lise, carried away by the desire to see her sister married in order to get rid of her. 'Suppose they agree? Then what would you say? She doesn't need your consent, she's decent enough not to send you packing. We're fed up with you!'

Then Buteau saw that if the girl were to speak the thing would be settled. He was particularly afraid that if her affair with Jean were known the marriage would be regarded as reasonable. Just at that moment La Grande came into the yard, followed by the Charleses, who were returning with Elodie. He motioned them to come over, not knowing what he was going to say. Then he thought of something, his face grew congested and he brandished his fist at his wife and sister-in-law.

'Blasted cows!' he yelled. 'Yes, both of them! Cows! Whores! I'll tell you something! I sleep with both of them! And if they think they can do as they like with me after that —I tell you, I sleep with both of them, the whores!'

The astonished Charles family received these words full in their faces. Madame Charles rushed forward as though to protect the listening Elodie with her body; then, pushing her towards the vegetable garden, she herself shouted loudly:

'Come and see the lettuces and the cabbages! Oh, what lovely cabbages!'

Buteau went on inventing details, describing how, as soon as one girl had had her ration, it was the other one's turn to come and be stuffed right up to her chin. He let it all out in crude terms, using filthy language, and words too revolting to be mentioned. Lise was merely astonished by this sudden attack and simply shrugged her shoulders.

'He's mad,' she said. 'My God, it's incredible, he's mad!'

'Tell him he's lying!' cried Jean to Françoise.

'Of course he's lying,' said the girl, calmly.

'Oh, I'm lying, am I?' Buteau went on. 'So it's not true you wanted some fun by the haystack at harvest time? But now I'm telling you where you can get off, you pair of trollops!'

This furious audacity paralysed Jean and left him dazed. Could he explain now that he had possessed Françoise? He thought it would be a dirty trick, especially if she did not help him. The others, moreover, the Delhommes, Fouan, and La Grande, remained silent. They did not look surprised and they obviously thought that if Buteau did sleep with both girls he was really the master and could do as he wished with them. When you have rights you must assert them.

From then on Buteau felt he was winning, for nobody had questioned his authority. He turned to Jean:

'And you, you swine! Don't come and pester me at home again! You'd better get out quick! Oh, so you won't go? Just you wait!'

He picked up his flail and made the flap whirl round. Jean had only just time to seize the other flail, which belonged to Françoise, to defend himself. The others shouted and wanted to separate them, but the two men were so angry that they drew back. The long handles could deliver blows several yards away and they swept the whole yard clear. The two men remained alone in the middle, some distance away from each other, enlarging the range of their weapons as they whirled round. They were silent now, clenching their teeth. There was nothing more to be heard except the sharp cracks as the wooden weapons struck the ground.

Buteau had dealt the first blow and Jean, who was still bending down, would have had his head broken open if he had not leapt back quickly. Tensing his muscles quickly, he suddenly raised the flail and brought it down again like a thresher beating the grain. But the other man was already beating too, the cornelwood flaps met and bent back on their straps like wounded birds in crazy flight. Three times the same encounter took place.

Delhomme and Fouan were rushing forward when the women cried out. Jean rolled down in the straw, for a treacherous whip-like stroke by Buteau, level with the ground, had caught him on the legs, but fortunately its force was broken. He stood up again and brandished his flail in rage and pain. The flap described a large circle and came down on the right, whereas the other man was expecting it on the left. A few inches more and it would have knocked his brains out. As it was, it only caught his ear and the force of the blow was deflected on to his arm, breaking it at once. The bone snapped with a sound like shattered glass.

'Murder!' screamed Buteau. 'He's killed me!'

Jean, pale-faced, with bloodshot eyes, dropped his weapon. Then for a moment he looked at them all as though dazed by the rapid turn of events and went limping off with a gesture of furious despair.

When he turned the corner of the house towards the plain he noticed Boldie, who had been watching the fight over the garden hedge. She was still chuckling about it. Jésus-Christ would shout with laughter when he heard that his brother had a broken arm after the little family gathering! She wriggled about as though she was being tickled and nearly fell flat on her back, she found it so comical.

'Oh, Corporal!' she cried. 'What a bash! The bone went crickety-crack! It wasn't half funny!'

He did not answer and walked more slowly, looking crushed. She followed him, whistling after her geese, which she had brought with her as a pretext for standing and listening behind the wall. Jean automatically went back towards the threshing machine, which was still working as dusk fell. He thought it was all over, that he would never see the Buteaus again, and that he would never be able to have Françoise. How stupid it all was! It had only taken ten minutes, a quarrel he had not sought, ending in such an unfortunate blow, just at the moment when things were going well. And now never, never again! The roaring of the threshing machine came through the dusk like a long deep lament.

PART FOUR

1

THAT day it was very windy, and warm gusty squalls brought up great clouds quickly. Whenever the sun shone through its rays were burning hot. Ever since morning Soulas the shepherd had been waiting for water that was coming from the farm, for himself, the little swineherd, and his sheep, for he was in a stubble field to the north of Rognes, far from any pool. In the pen, which consisted of movable hurdles fixed in the ground, the animals lay flat, their breath coming in rapid, painful gasps, while the two dogs lying outside were also panting with their tongues hanging out. The shepherd sat leaning against the two-wheeled hut which he moved along every time the grazing was changed. It was a narrow little shack which provided his bed, wardrobe, and food supply, and gave him some shade.

There was no sign of anything before two o'clock. The heat had increased and during the long periods of calm which suddenly began to occur, it became unbearable. The soil was reduced to dust and little whirlwinds blew up with a blinding, stifling smoke which made the men's agonizing thirst even worse.

The shepherd, who had been waiting stoically without any complaint, suddenly uttered a growl of satisfaction.

'Thank goodness, and it's not a bit too soon!'

Two carts, hardly as big as a man's fist, had just appeared on the horizon over the plain. In the first of them, driven by Jean, Soulas could clearly see the water-barrel, while the second, driven by Tron, was laden with sacks of wheat that he was taking to a windmill, a tall, wooden building five hundred yards away. The second cart stopped on the way and Tron came along in the other as far as the sheep, across the stubble, on the pretext of helping. It was a way of taking a rest and chatting for a moment.

'D'you want us to die of the pip?' cried the shepherd.

The sheep had also smelt the water-barrel and got up in a huddle, pressing against the hurdles, stretching their heads out and bleating pathetically.

'Be patient,' replied Jean. 'Now you can get drunk on this!'

They put the trough down at once and filled it with a wooden spout. Since there was a leak underneath it the dogs came along and lapped the water up, while the shepherd and the little swineherd drank greedily out of the spout itself without waiting. The entire flock lined up, there was no sound except the blissful trickling of the water, the gurgling as it went down their throats, and everyone, animals and men, delighted in splashing and soaking each other.

'And now,' said Soulas, refreshed, 'perhaps you'd be kind enough to give me a hand with moving the pens.'

Jean and Tron agreed. The pen travelled over the open stubble fields and rarely stayed longer than two or three days in the same place, just long enough for the sheep to crop the grass. This system also had the advantage of manuring a stretch of ground at a time. While the shepherd, with the help of his dogs, looked after the flock, the two men and the little swineherd pulled out the stakes and transported the hurdles fifty paces further on. Then they fixed them up again in a huge square and the sheep came to take shelter there of their own accord before the enclosure was complete.

Soulas, in spite of his great age, was already pushing his hut along, bringing it near the pen.

'What's the matter?' he asked, speaking to Jean. 'You look as though you're going to your own funeral.'

The young man had been heart-broken ever since he thought he had lost Françoise. He shook his head sadly.

'Tell me, isn't there some woman at the back of all this?' asked the old man. 'Oh, the blasted whores, they should all have their heads cut off!'

Jean looked at Old Soulas, realizing that old men can sometimes give good advice in these cases. He gave way to his need to talk and told him the whole story, how he had had Françoise and how he despaired of seeing her again after the fight with Buteau. For a moment he had even feared that the latter would take him to court over his broken arm, which prevented him from doing any work, although it was half-mended already. But Buteau had no doubt decided that it never does any good to get the law involved in family matters.

'So you had Françoise, did you?' asked the shepherd.

'Once, yes.'

He reflected for a moment seriously, and finally spoke.

'You must tell Old Fouan about it. Perhaps he'll let you marry her.'

Jean was surprised, for this simple solution had never occurred to him. The sheepfold was in place now and he left, deciding that he would go and see the old man that very evening; as he drove away in his empty cart Soulas again took up his unending watch, his thin figure standing like a grey upright streak cutting across the flat line of the plain.

In the evening Jean left his work an hour earlier than usual and went to see Old Fouan at the Delhommes' house before supper. The house stood at the other end of Rognes, on the far side of the bridge; it was a small farm which had been enlarged recently with barns and sheds, three groups of irregular buildings standing round a fairly large yard which was swept every morning and where even the manure-heaps seemed to be arranged neatly in order.

'Good evening, Father Fouan,' cried Jean from the road, his voice somewhat unsteady.

The old man was seated in the yard, a walking-stick between his legs, his eyes downcast. At the second call, however, he raised his eyes and finally recognized who was speaking.

'Oh, it's you, Corporal! You're passing this way, then?'

And he greeted him so naturally, without malice, that the young man went in. He dared not speak to him about the matter straight away, though, and his courage failed him at the thought of describing how he had taken Françoise. They spoke about the fine weather and the good effect it was having on the vines. One more week of sun, and the wine would be very good. Then the young man tried to be pleasant to him.

'You're comfortably off now, there isn't a landowner in the district as fortunate as you are.'

'Yes, that's so.'

'You've got a fine family, you couldn't easily find a better one.'

'That's true, but you know, everyone's different.'

He was gloomy again now. Since he had been living with the Delhommes, Buteau did not pay his allowance any longer, saying that he didn't want his money to feather his sister's nest. Jésus-Christ had never paid a penny and since Delhomme fed and housed his father-in-law he had made no more payments. The old man did not suffer from a lack of pocket-money, particularly since Monsieur Baillehache paid him the hundred and fifty francs per year, exactly twelve francs fifty each month, which came to him from the sale of his house. With that he could pay for pleasures such as a little tobacco every morning, his drop of wine at Lengaigne's, and his cup of coffee at Macqueron's, for Fanny was very careful and only brought the coffee and brandy out of her cupboard when someone was ill. And in spite of everything, although he had enough to enjoy himself outside and lacked nothing in his daughter's house, he was not happy there, and lived in a state of continual gloom.

'Oh yes, my goodness!' went on Jean, unaware that he was touching an open wound. 'When you're in someone else's house you haven't got a home of your own.'

'That's it, that's just it!' grumbled Fouan, and he got up as though seized with a need to revolt. 'Let's have a drink. I think I've got the right to offer a glass of wine to a friend!'

But as they reached the threshold he became timid again.

'Wipe your feet, Corporal, because, you see, they make a lot of fuss about keeping the place clean.'

Jean came in uneasily, anxious to explain everything before the master and mistress returned. He was surprised by the tidiness of the kitchen; the copper saucepans gleamed, there was not a speck of dust on the furniture, the tiles on the floor had been worn out with scrubbing. It was so clean and cold it looked uninhabited. Cabbage soup from yesterday was keeping warm by a fire damped down with ash.

'Your health!' said the old man, who had taken an opened bottle and two glasses out of the sideboard.

His hand trembled slightly as he drank, for he was afraid of what he was doing. He put his glass down with the air of a man who has taken an immense risk, and added quickly:

'Would you believe it, Fanny hasn't spoken to me since the day before yesterday, because I spat! Well, surely everyone can spit? I certainly spit when I want to. Oh no, I'd rather leave than be bothered like that!'

'You've got to make allowances,' Jean repeated after each complaint. 'If you're patient you can always get on.'

But Fouan, who had just lit a candle, became excited and angry.

'No, no, I've had enough! Oh, if I'd known what was in store for me here! I'd rather have died the day I sold my house. Only if they think they can keep me here, they're mistaken, I'd rather break stones on the road.'

He was choking and had to sit down. So finally the young man took the opportunity to speak.

'Tell me, Father Fouan, I wanted to see you about that business, you know what I mean. I've been very sorry about it but I had to defend myself, didn't I, since Buteau attacked me? Yet, all the same, Françoise and I agreed. And now you're the only man who can settle it. You could go to Buteau and explain everything to him.'

The old man had become serious. He nodded and seemed embarrassed about how to reply, when the return of the Delhommes saved him the trouble. They did not seem surprised to find Jean in their house and gave him the usual good welcome. But Fanny had immediately seen the bottle and the two glasses on the table. She removed them and went to find a cloth. Then, without looking at him, she said drily to her father, after not speaking a word to him for forty-eight hours:

'Father, you know I don't like this sort of thing.'

Fouan stood up, trembling, angered by the fact that she had made such a remark in front of others.

'What? Good heavens, can't I even offer a glass of wine to a friend? Lock it up, then, I'll drink water.'

This time it was her turn to be horribly vexed at such an accusation of avarice.

'You can drink the whole house until you burst,' she replied, going pale, 'if you enjoy it, but I don't want you to make my table dirty with glasses that leave round marks. This isn't a tavern!'

Tears had come into her father's eyes. He had the last word.

'You'd be better off with a little less cleanliness and a little more good-heartedness, my girl.'

While she was fiercely cleaning the table he stood in front of the window, looking at the darkness that was closing in, shaken with his secret despair.

Delhomme had avoided taking any part, supporting his wife's firm, sensible attitude simply by remaining silent.

He did not want Jean to go without having another drink and Fanny placed the glasses on plates. Then she made her excuse, calmly, in a low voice.

'You can't imagine how difficult it is dealing with old people! They're full of fixed ideas and bad ways. They'd die rather than improve. This one isn't bad, he's not strong enough any longer. But I'd rather look after four cows than one old man.'

As Jean emptied his glass, he saw Old Fouan leave the window and go out into the yard. He said goodbye and found the old man standing in the darkness.

'Listen, Father Fouan. Will you go to the Buteaus and get Françoise for me? You're the master, you only have to say the word.'

The old man's reply reached him through the gloom.

'I can't! I can't!' he said in a jerky voice.

Then he broke out and confessed everything. He had finished with the Delhommes, he would go away the next day and live with the Buteaus, for they had offered to take him. If his son beat him it would be less painful than pinpricks from his daughter. Jean was driven to despair by this new setback, but finally he spoke.

'I must tell you, Father Fouan, Françoise and I have made love together.'

'Oh!' said the old peasant, simply. He thought for a moment. 'Is the girl pregnant?' he asked.

Jean was certain she could not be, since they had cheated. 'It's possible,' he replied.

'Then the only thing to do is to wait. If she's pregnant, we'll see.'

At that moment Fanny appeared at the door and called her father for supper.

He turned round. 'To hell with your supper!' he shouted. 'I'm going to sleep.'

And he went upstairs to bed in a fury, without eating.

Jean took the road back to the farm, walking slowly, so depressed that he found himself on the plateau without realizing what road he was taking. The night sky was dark blue, full of stars, heavy and burning hot. As he raised his head he saw to the left hundreds of phosphorescent eyes, blazing like candles, turning towards him at the sound of his footsteps. It was the sheep in their grazing pen, which he was passing. He heard Old Soulas speaking in his low voice.

'Well, my boy?'

The dogs, who were lying on the ground, had not moved, for they could smell it was someone from the farm. The little swineherd had found the hut too hot and was sleeping in a furrow. In the midst of the bare, flat plain as it lay submerged in darkness the shepherd was the only man awake.

'Well, my boy, is it settled?'

Jean did not even stop.

'He said that if the girl's pregnant we'll see.'

He had already passed the pen when Old Soulas' reply reached him, his voice sounding low across the vast silence.

'That's fair, you must wait.'

2

THE next day Fouan went to live with the Buteaus. The move upset nobody for the old man insisted on carrying his two packets of clothes himself, making two journeys. The Delhommes tried in vain to extract an explanation from him, but he went off without a word.

Buteau was triumphant. He had been wildly jealous ever since Fouan had lived with the Delhommes, for he knew what they were saying in Rognes: it was no trouble to the Delhommes to support their father, while the Buteaus, good heavens, they hadn't got a penny. So at first he made his father eat, purely to make him put on weight and prove that nobody died of hunger in the Buteau household. Then he had the hundred and fifty franc income from the sale of the house, which his father would certainly leave to the son or daughter who had looked after him. Moreover, since Delhomme no longer kept him he would certainly begin to pay his two hundred franc share of the annual allowance again, which in fact he did. Buteau counted on those two hundred francs. He had worked everything out and told himself that he could earn a reputation as a good son without paying a penny, and with the hope of being rewarded later. This did not include the hoard which he still suspected the old man had put away, although he had never succeeded in having any proof of it.

For Fouan this period was a real honeymoon. He was

127

fêted and shown round to the neighbours. How well he looked! He certainly wasn't wasting away! The children, Laura and Jules, were always running round him keeping him busy and doing things to please him. But most of all he enjoyed returning to his old man's habits and he felt freer in the greater freedom of the house. Although Lise was a good housekeeper and clean, too, she was not as fussy or sensitive as Fanny, and he could sit anywhere, come and go as he wished, and eat whenever he wanted, keeping to the peasant habit of never passing a loaf without cutting off a slice as a safety measure against long working hours. Three months went by in this way. It was December, and terrible frosts froze the water in the jug at the foot of his bed, but he never complained, and thaws even made the room so damp that water ran down the walls like a downpour of rain. He found it natural; he had lived this rough sort of life. As long as he could have his tobacco and coffee and nobody nagged him, he used to say, he wouldn't call the King his uncle.

Things began to go wrong, however, when, one bright sunny morning, he returned to his room for his pipe, when everyone thought he had gone out. He found Buteau trying to knock Françoise down on the potatoes. The girl, who was defending herself valiantly, without a word, got up and went out, after taking the beetroot she had come to get for her cows. When the old man was left alone with his son, he lost his temper.

'You dirty swine! Trying to get hold of that child with your wife so close! And she didn't want it, I could see how she was kicking!'

But Buteau, who was still breathing hard, his face congested, refused to be criticized.

'What d'you mean by sticking your nose into things? Shut your blinkers and keep quiet or you'll be in trouble!'

Since Lise's confinement and the fight with Jean, Buteau was mad for Françoise again. He had waited for his broken arm to mend and now he would leap at her in every corner of the house, for he was certain that if he could only get her once she would do anything he wanted afterwards. Wasn't this the best way of delaying her marriage, keeping the girl and keeping the land? These two passions were inseparable —his obstinate refusal to give up anything he already had, the fierce determination to keep the field, and the frustrated male desire which her resistance turned into lust. His wife was becoming an enormous mountain of flesh and she was still feeding the baby, Laura, who was always at her breast, while the other girl, his little sister-in-law, had a good smell of young flesh and her breasts were as supple and firm as the udders of a young heifer. He did not despise either girl. In this way he would have two, one flabby and one firm, each attractive in her own way. He was cock enough for two hens, and dreamt of a pasha-like existence in which he would be cared for and pampered, gorged with pleasure. Why couldn't he marry both sisters if they agreed to it? This was the way to strengthen affection and avoid the division of property, which frightened him as much as the thought of cutting off one of his own limbs.

From then on there was violent warfare, attack and defence in the cowshed, in the kitchen, everywhere, whenever they were alone for a moment, Buteau rushing at Françoise, while she shoved him away. The same swift angry scene was repeated incessantly. He thrust his hand under her skirt and got hold of her naked flesh, seizing a lump of skin and hair as though she were some animal ready to be served. She clenched her teeth and her eyes would grow dark as she forced him to let go, striking him as hard as she could right between the legs. No word was ever spoken, all that could be heard was their hot, choking breath and the suppressed sound of the struggle. He would hold back a cry of pain, she would pull her dress down and go limping away, the lower part of her body torn and bruised, feeling that the imprint of these five fingers digging deeply into her flesh would remain there. And this would happen when Lise was in the room next door, or even in the same room, her back turned while she arranged linen in a cupboard; the presence of his wife seemed to excite Buteau and he could be sure that the girl would not break her proud, obstinate silence.

However, after Old Fouan had seen them among the potatoes quarrels began to break out. He had told Lise about it in crude terms so that she could stop her husband from doing it again. She shouted at Fouan to mind his own business, and then turned on her younger sister. It was her fault if she led men on, for men were just so many swine, you had to put up with them.

Then the slow-growing, unconscious hatred between Lise and Françoise became stronger. The wholesome affection of the past had now turned into resentment, without any obvious reason, and from morning to night they clashed with each other; the single basic cause was Buteau, who had appeared like some destructive leaven between them. Françoise, whose restlessness was increased by his behaviour, would have given in long ago if her will-power had not worked against her desire to abandon herself whenever he touched her. She took herself severely to task for it, for she clung obstinately to her simple notion of justice: she would give nothing of herself, she would take nothing from others. She hated feeling jealous and loathing her sister for having a man of her own, for she herself would rather have died of desire than share him. When he pursued her with his trousers loose and his stomach protruding, she would spit furiously on his male organs and send him back to his wife with the spit on his body. This relieved her frustrated desire, she felt she was spitting in her sister's face, showing her hurtful disdain of the pleasure in which she had no part. Lise herself was not at all jealous and was convinced that Buteau was boasting when he yelled that he slept with both of them, not that she thought him incapable of it, but she was convinced that the younger girl was too proud to give in. She was angry with Françoise solely because her refusal turned the house into hell. The fatter she grew the more she settled down in her solid flesh, feeling satisfied with life, in her cheerful, selfish way, gathering all the pleasure round her into her own person.

'I know she's my sister,' she shouted to Buteau every evening when they went to bed, 'but if she doesn't stop annoying you I'll throw her out.'

He did not see it the same way.

'That would be a fine thing! The whole district would be against us. You blasted women, I'll chuck you both into the pond together, then you'll cool down and get on with each other!'

Two more months passed, Lise was hustled about between the others, she was beside herself and nothing she did was any good. She could guess whenever her sister had refused her man again because everyone was in a bad temper, so much so that she now lived in fear of Buteau's defeats, feeling anxious when he craftily disappeared behind her sister's skirts, for she was certain he would reappear in a brutal rage, capable of smashing up the house. These were horrible days and she could not forgive the wretched obstinate girl for doing nothing to improve things.

One day in particular a terrible thing happened. Buteau went down to the cellar with Françoise to draw some cider; he came up in such a state of disarray and fury that when he found the soup too hot, he threw his plate against the wall and went out, knocking Lise down with a blow that would have felled an ox.

She got up weeping, with a swollen, bleeding cheek. She rushed at her sister.

'You're a bitch!' she cried. 'Why don't you go to bed with him then? I've had enough of it all! If you go on like this, I'll turn you out, even if I get beaten for it!'

Françoise listened, horror-stricken and pale.

'As true as God hears me,' cried Lise, 'I'd rather you did it, then perhaps he'd leave us in peace!'

She had sunk down on to a chair, sobbing, while all her plump body seemed to collapse, expressing her one desperate desire to be happy even at the price of sharing her husband. Provided she could keep her share she wouldn't be losing anything. People had silly ideas about that sort of thing, because it certainly wasn't like bread, which disappears when you eat it. Couldn't they get on better and feel closer to each other, couldn't they live a family life?

'After all, why don't you want to?'

Françoise was nauseated, she could only utter a cry of rage, her voice choking.

'You're more disgusting than he is!'

She went away on her own to sob in the cowshed, where Coliche gazed at her with big unhappy eyes. What made her indignant was not the thing itself, but the part Lise was playing as the complaisant wife, tolerating her husband's lust for the sake of peace at home; if this had been *her* man she would never have given an inch of him away. Her spite towards Lise turned into disdain; she swore she would die rather than give in now.

But from that day onwards her life became worse. Françoise became the down-trodden drudge. Lise no longer allowed her an hour's idleness, but made her get up before dawn and kept her up so late at night that sometimes the wretched girl fell asleep without finding the strength to undress. Buteau pestered her craftily, hitting her in the small of the back, pinching her thighs, giving her all kinds of brutal caresses which left her tense and bleeding, her eyes full of tears, yet still obstinately silent. He was content with little and sniggered when he saw her falter, withholding a cry as he hurt her. Her body was black and blue, streaked with scratches and bruises. In front of her sister, especially, she found the courage not even to react, to deny the very fact that these male fingers were fumbling over her body.

The whole village was astonished. Why didn't Françoise run away? The knowing ones shook their heads; she was not of age yet, she had to wait eighteen months, and as for running away and putting herself in the wrong without being able to take what she owned, good heavens, she was right to think twice about that! If only Old Fouan, her guardian, had given her some support, but he himself was hardly happy in his son's house. He was afraid of becoming involved and this made him keep quiet. Moreover, Françoise forbade him to interfere in her affairs with the courage and pride typical of a wild girl who relies only on herself.

In future every quarrel finished with the same insults.

'Well, get out, then! Get out!'

'Yes, that's what you're hoping for! I used to be too silly, I wanted to go. Now you can try killing me, but I'll stay. I'm waiting for my share. I want the land and the house, and I'll get them. Oh yes, I'll get everything!'

During the first months Buteau had been afraid that Françoise might have been pregnant by Jean. Ever since he had surprised them by the stack he had counted the days and watched her craftily, worrying about the size of her stomach, for the arrival of a child would have spoilt everything by making marriage necessary. She remained calm, for she knew very well that she could not be pregnant, but when she noticed his interest in her figure she regarded it as a joke and purposely stood with her stomach protruding to make him believe it was swelling. Now when he got hold of her she could feel him prodding her, measuring her with his coarse fingers.

'Yes, there's something there!' she told him in the end, with a defiant air. 'It's growing!'

One morning she even folded up some cloths and fastened them round her; that evening they nearly killed each other. When she saw the murderous looks he gave her she was seized with terror. Yet if she had really had a baby coming, he would certainly have struck her a blow that would have killed it. She stopped her jokes and returned to a normal posture. She even surprised him in her bedroom searching through her soiled underwear, to make sure what was going on.

'Well, have one, then!' he said, joking.

Her face went pale.

'I'm not having one,' she replied in a rage, 'because I don't want one!'

It was true. She obstinately refused to let Jean take her again. Buteau was delighted, and attacked her lover. He was a fine sort of man, wasn't he? He was so old and rotten that he couldn't give her a baby. He was treacherous enough to break a man's arm, but he wasn't even capable of stuffing a girl, he was so feeble. After that he persistently made allusions to it in front of Françoise and wore her out with jokes on the subject.

When Jean heard what Buteau was saying about him he threatened to smash his face in. He always kept a look out for Françoise and begged her to come to him, then they would see if he couldn't give her a baby, and a big one. His desire now was increased by anger, but every time she found a new excuse in the dislike she felt at the idea of starting all over again with this man. She didn't hate him; she simply didn't want him, and she must have wanted him very little to avoid abandoning herself to him as she fell into his arms behind some hedge while she was still flushed and angry after an attack by Buteau. Oh, the bastard! She spoke only of that swinish man, with passionate excitement, but as soon as Jean wanted to take advantage of her feeling and possess her she turned cold at once. No, no, she was ashamed of it. One day when she was at the end of her tether she put it off until later, until their wedding night. This was the first time she had mentioned marriage, for until then she had avoided making a definite answer when he asked her to be his wife. After that it was more or less understood he would marry her, but only when she came of age, as soon as she could have her property and demand her rights. This good sense impressed him; he advised her to be patient and stopped bothering her, except at moments when he was overcome with a desire to laugh. She was comforted and felt calmer at the thought of this vague distant arrangement and contented herself with seizing his two hands to hold him away, beseeching him with her beautiful eyes like some sensitive woman who did not want to risk having a child except with her husband.

Although Buteau knew she was not pregnant, he was afraid that it might happen if she went back to Jean. He continued to defy him and he trembled, for he heard on all sides that Jean had sworn he would stuff Françoise up to the eyes as no girl had ever been stuffed before. So he kept watch over her from morning to evening, demanding exactly how she occupied every moment, keeping her at his beck and call, threatening to whip her as though she were some domestic animal possessed of frightening strength. This was a new torture for her. She could feel her brother-in-law or her sister always at her heels and she could not even go to the manure pit to relieve herself without being spied on. At night she was locked in her room and one evening, after a quarrel, she even found a padlock fastening the shutter outside her skylight. She succeeded in escaping sometimes, all the same, and then there were terrible scenes when she returned, interrogations and sometimes inspections during which Buteau held her by the shoulders while his wife half-undressed her to have a look. This brought her closer to Jean and in the end she began to arrange meetings with him, for she enjoyed defying the others. She might even have given in to him in the end if they had been standing behind her. In any case, she finally promised he would have her and swore by all she held most sacred that Buteau was lying when he boasted of sleeping with both sisters, giving the impression that he was cock of the walk. Jean had been tortured with doubt, for at the back of his mind he realized that such a thing was possible and natural, but he seemed to believe her. When they parted they kissed like good friends, so much so that from that day she regarded him as her confidant and adviser, trying to see him at the slightest danger and risking nothing without his approval. He no longer touched her now, treating her as a comrade with the same interests as himself.

Old Fouan tried to keep out of things, but he was involved in all the quarrels. If he remained silent they forced him to take sides, and if he went out he came back to find the household in a state of chaos where his mere presence often brought out the underlying anger. Until then he had not really suffered any physical discomfort, but now privations were inflicted on him; the bread was rationed and his little pleasures were stopped. He was no longer stuffed with food, as he had been at first, and whenever he cut a slice of bread that was too thick he received harsh words. What an appetite he had! The less one worked the more one ate, then! Every three months, when he returned from Cloyes with the payment Monsieur Baillehache made him out of the three thousand francs for the house, they were waiting for him and stripped him of the money. Françoise even stole a few sous from her sister to buy him tobacco, for she, too, was left without money. Finally, the old man became very uncomfortable in the damp room where he slept; he had broken a window-pane but it had only been stuffed with straw to avoid the expense of replacing it. Oh, the children were terrible, they were all the same!

One day as Fouan was returning on foot from Cloyes after receiving his allowance at the notary's he sat down in a ditch; Jésus-Christ, who was wandering about looking at rabbit holes, caught sight of him sitting there completely absorbed, counting five-franc pieces in his handkerchief. He immediately crouched down and crawled along without a sound until he was lying just over his father. As he lay there he was surprised to see him carefully tying up a large sum of money, probably as much as eighty francs. His eyes blazed and he laughed silently, revealing his pointed teeth. The old idea of a secret hoard immediately occurred to him. The old man obviously had some hidden investments and he took advantage of his quarterly visits to Monsieur Baillehache to draw the dividends. Jésus-Christ's first thought was to start whining and get twenty francs out of him; then this amount seemed too small and another plan formed in his head. He slipped away as quietly as he had come, with the supple movement of a snake. Fouan showed no distrust therefore when he met him a hundred yards further on up the road, looking as though he too was returning idly from Rognes. They went on together, chatting, and the father inevitably spoke about the Buteaus. They were heartless, he accused them of letting him die of hunger. And his son, with tears in his eyes, kindly offered to rescue him from these brutes by taking him in at the Château. Why not? It wouldn't be dull; they had plenty of fun from morning till night in his house. Boldie cooked for two already, she could cook for three, and she cooked damned well when there was any money for food.

Fouan was astonished by this suggestion, he felt vaguely apprehensive, and refused. No, no, at his age he couldn't rush from one house to another and change his way of life every year.

'Well, father, I mean it, you can think it over. There it is; you always know that you won't be out in the street. When you've had enough of that loathsome pair you can come to the Château.'

That mild, damp November day when Old Fouan came back, Buteau wanted the thirty-seven francs fifty which he received every quarter since the sale of the house. It had been agreed that the old man would give them to him as well as the two hundred francs he had every year from the Delhommes. But this time a five-franc piece had got mixed up with those he had knotted in his handkerchief, and when he had turned out his pockets and only found thirty-two francs fifty his son flew into a rage and accused him of being a thief, alleging that he had spent the five francs, squandering them on drink and unmentionable horrors. His father was struck dumb and kept his hand on his handkerchief, feeling dimly afraid that they might look at it; he stammered out explanations and swore before God that he must have lost the coin when blowing his nose. Once more the house was in an uproar until the evening.

The reason why Buteau was in a ferocious temper was that while bringing back his harrow he had caught sight of Jean and Françoise running behind a wall. She had gone out with the excuse of getting some grass for her cows and had not appeared again, for she was aware of the scene which would greet her. Night was already falling and Buteau went out every minute into the yard in a fury, going as far as the road to see if the trollop was finally coming back from her man. He swore loudly, using filthy language, without noticing Old Fouan, who had sat on the stone bench to calm down after the quarrel, enjoying the mild warmth which made this sunny November feel like spring.

The sound of sabots was heard coming up the slope and Françoise appeared, bent double, her shoulders weighed down by a huge bundle of grass which she had tied up in an old piece of cloth. She was panting and sweating, half-hidden beneath the load.

'You blasted tart!' cried Buteau. 'If you think you can

bugger off like that, letting your lover ride you for two hours when there's work to be done here!'

He knocked her down on to the bundle of grass, which had fallen to the ground, and rushed at her just as Lise in her turn came out of the house to scold her.

'You lazy, filthy thing! Come here, let me kick you up the ass. Aren't you ashamed of yourself?'

But Buteau had already got hold of the girl under her skirt. His rage always turned into a sudden desire to possess her. He went on clutching her on the grass, his face purple and suffused with blood.

'You blasted tart!' he growled out in a strangled voice. 'This time I've got to have you, too! The sky can fall down, I'm going to get inside where the other man's been!'

Then a furious struggle began. Old Fouan could hardly see through the darkness, but he made out Lise standing beside them, watching and letting it go on; her man lay flat but the girl flung him aside every second, and he wore himself out to no purpose, taking his satisfaction all the same wherever he could. When it was over Françoise finally shook herself free.

'Swine! Swine!' she stammered breathlessly. 'You couldn't do it! That doesn't count. I don't care a damn about that, but you'll never get inside, never!'

Triumphantly she took a handful of grass and wiped her leg, trembling all over as though she herself had had some satisfaction out of this obstinate refusal. With a gesture of bravado she threw the bundle of grass at her sister's feet.

'Here you are, that's yours! It's not your fault that you're getting it back!'

Lise slapped her across the mouth and Old Fouan, who had left the stone bench, revolted by it all, intervened, brandishing his stick.

'You filthy beasts, both of you! Can't you leave her alone? That's quite enough of that.'

Lights appeared in the neighbouring houses, for the noise of this fight had alarmed everyone and Buteau hastily pushed his father and Françoise into the kitchen where Laura and Jules were huddling in a corner, terrified, in the candlelight. Lise came in, too, shattered and silent ever since the old man had emerged from the darkness. He continued to talk to her.

'It's disgusting and stupid. You were watching, I saw you!'

Buteau struck the edge of the table with his fist as hard as he could. 'Quiet! It's all over. If anyone says a word I'll hit them.'

'And if I want to say something,' asked Fouan in a trembling voice, 'will you hit me?'

'I'll hit you or anyone else. You annoy me!'

Françoise had bravely intervened between them.

'I beg you, uncle, don't get mixed up with it. You could see that I'm old enough to look after myself.'

But the old man pushed her aside.

'Don't bother, this isn't your business any longer, it's mine.'

He raised his stick.

'Oh, you'd hit me, you villain, would you? We'll see if it's not my job to punish you.'

Buteau quickly seized the stick and put it under the cupboard. He then sneered at him, looking at him wickedly and speaking straight in his face.

'Will you leave me alone? If you think I'm going to put up with your nonsense, I shan't!'

Françoise tried a second time to stand between them. Lise herself made an effort, for this new quarrel drove her to despair, but the two men pushed the women aside, coming closer to each other, breathing violence, blood fighting against blood, for the father had bequeathed this brutal violence to his son, and now the clash had come.

Fouan tried to stand up straight and recover his former authority as head of the family; for half a century everyone had trembled before him, his wife, the children, and the animals, when he held both the fortune and the power.

'Tell me you lied, you filthy swine! Tell me, or I'll make you skip, as truly as this candle gives its light!'

He raised his hand high in the air as he threatened his son, with the gesture that had kept them all in their place in the past.

When he was young Buteau used to raise his arm to protect himself when blows threatened, his teeth chattering; now he merely shrugged his shoulders with a mocking, insulting expression.

'If you think you're frightening me . . . It was all right when you were the master, going on like that.'

'I am the master, I'm your father!'

'Go on with you, you old joker, you're nothing at all. Oh, can't you leave me in peace?'

Then, as he saw the old man's shaking hand move downwards to strike, he seized it as it came and held it, crushing it in his rough fist.

'You're so damned obstinate! Must I lose my temper to make you see we don't care a damn about you now? What are you good for? You just cost money, that's all. When you've had your time and given your land to others you must just shut up and not bother them any more.'

He emphasized his words and shook his father. Then, with a final jerk, he pushed him away, until the old man, shuddering and staggering, fell over a chair by the window, and remained there, beaten, choking for a moment at the loss of his old authority, which was now dead. It was all over. He no longer counted, since he had given everything away.

Total silence fell, everyone stood with their hands hanging beside them; the children had not breathed for fear of being smacked. Then work went on as though nothing had happened.

'What about the grass?' asked Lise. 'Are we going to leave it out in the yard?'

'I'll put it in the dry,' replied Françoise.

She came back and they had supper; then the incorrigible Buteau thrust his hand into her open bodice to find a flea which she said was biting her. It didn't make her angry any longer, she even laughed about it.

'No, no, you'd get bitten somewhere else.'

Fouan had not moved, sitting stiff and silent in his dark corner. Two big tears ran down his cheeks. He remembered the evening when he had quarrelled with the Delhommes, and now the same evening had happened again, he was ashamed at being no longer master, his obstinate anger made him refuse to eat. They had called him three times; he would not have his supper. Suddenly he got up and disappeared into his bedroom. The next day at dawn he left the Buteaus and moved in with Jésus-Christ.

3

OCTOBER came, and the wine harvest was about to begin, a fine week of rejoicing when disunited families usually became reconciled again round jugs of new wine. Rognes stank of grapes for a week. Everyone ate so many that behind every hedge women lifted their skirts up and men let their trousers down. Among the vines lovers kissed each other on the mouth, with wine-stained faces. It all ended with drunken men and pregnant girls.

Jésus-Christ began to look for the secret hoard, for he decided that his father probably did not carry his money and deeds around with him. He must have hidden them somewhere. Boldie helped her father, but at first they looked everywhere in the house in vain, finding nothing in spite of their cleverness and their skill in thieving. It was only the following week that the poacher chanced to take down an old cracked pot from a shelf and there, under some lentils, he found a packet of papers, carefully wrapped up in the gummed canvas from the lining of a hat. There was not a single coin, though; the money must be hidden somewhere else, and it must be a tidy sum, for the old man had spent nothing for five years. These were deeds all right, showing three hundred francs a year in five per cent bonds. As Jésus-Christ counted and studied them he came across another sheet of paper, with a stamp on it, covered with large handwriting. When he read it he was staggered. My God! So that was where the money was going!

It was a fantastic story. Two weeks after sharing out his possessions at the notary's Fouan had become deranged, for he was heart-broken at the thought of having no more property, not even as much as a handful of corn. No, he couldn't live like that, it would have killed him, and it was then he had made this arrangement, the sort of silly thing an old man can do when he feels strongly, giving away his last few coins so that he could go back secretly to the bitch who deceives him. He, who had been so clever in his time, had allowed himself to be twisted by a friend, Old Saucisse! This furious urge to possess must have been very strong; it must have been a kind of madness in his bones, the same thing that happens to all old men when they are worn out with fertilizing the earth. It had possessed him so strongly that he had signed an agreement with Old Saucisse by which the latter, after his death, would grant him an acre and a half of land on condition that for the rest of his life he received fifteen sous every morning. Fancy doing a deal of this sort at sixty-six, and when the seller is ten years younger! The truth was that Saucisse had been crafty enough to take to his bed at this time; he was coughing and seemed to be dying, so that Fouan, stultified by his greed, believed himself the cleverer of the two and hastened to conclude what seemed a sound transaction. Nonetheless it proved that when a man is desperate, either for a woman or for a field, it's wiser to go to bed together than to sign papers, for this had gone on for five years, paying out fifteen sous every morning, and the more Fouan paid out the more desperate he was for the land, the more he wanted it. To think that he had given up all the worry of his long working life, that he had nothing more to do except die in peace while watching others surrender their bodies to the ungrateful earth, and that he had gone back to let her destroy him in the end! Men hardly ever learn wisdom, neither old nor young.

For a moment Jésus-Christ thought of taking everything, the deed and the securities, but his courage failed him, for if he did something like that he would have to run away. It wasn't like taking money; you had to wait for more of it to grow, and in a fury he put the papers back under the lentils in the cooking pot. But he became so exasperated that he could not hold his tongue. The next day the whole of Rognes knew about the Saucisse affair, the fifteen sous a day for an acre and a half of poor land, which certainly was not worth three thousand francs. In five years it had come to nearly fourteen hundred francs already and if the old rogue lived five years longer he would get both the field and the money. Everyone laughed at Old Fouan, but after ceasing to greet him in the road since he possessed nothing but his skin, they began to say good-day and take him seriously again, now that he was known to be a property-owner and have money of his own.

The family in particular were astonished. Fanny, who had been on very cool terms with her father, for she had been hurt to think he had gone to her rascally elder brother instead of coming back to her, brought him some linen, some old shirts of her husband's, but he was very harsh and referred to the phrase which still rankled with him, 'Father

will come on his knees asking us to take him back,' and he
greeted her by saying:

'So it's you who've come back on your knees to see me!'
And it stuck in her throat.

As for Buteau, he surprised them all one day by coming
to the Château, pretending he wanted to see the old man.
Jésus-Christ sneered as he brought out the bottle of brandy,
and they drank together; but his mockery turned to stupe-
faction when he saw his brother take out ten franc pieces
and put them in a row on the table.

'Father,' he said, 'we have to settle our accounts, all the
same. Here's the payment for the last quarter of your
allowance.'

The blasted cheat! After not paying a penny to his father
for years he was now trying to get the better of him by
showing him the colour of his money. But as the old man
stretched out his arm Buteau pushed him aside and picked
up the coins again.

'Oh no, that's just to show you that I've got it! I'm keeping it for you. You know where it is.'

Jésus-Christ began to see what was going on and became
angry.

'Hey! If you want to take father away . . .'

But Buteau treated the thing as a joke.

'Are you jealous, then? Suppose I have father for a week
and you have him another week, isn't that natural enough?
Suppose you cut yourself in two, dad? Here's to your health
while we wait!'

As he left he invited them to come the next day and celebrate the wine harvest in his vineyard. They could stuff
themselves with as many grapes as they could eat. In fact,
he was so nice that the two others decided he was a devil,
but amusing all the same provided you didn't let yourself
be taken in by him. They went part of the way back with
him for their own entertainment.

Months went by, the winter passed, the spring came, and
the usual life of Rognes continued. It took years before anything looked as though it had happened, for this dreary
working life went on forever. But in July, during the hot
exhausting sunshine, the forthcoming elections began to stir
up the village.

On the very Sunday morning when Monsieur Roche-
fontaine, a manufacturer from Châteaudun, was due to

arrive, a terrible scene broke ou[...]
tween Lise and Françoise. It showed [...]
nothing seems to be happening something [...]
the same. For the last link between the two sisters, [...]
always near breaking point, had now worn so thin throug[...]
the daily quarrels that it snapped, never to be mended
again, all over a stupid thing that was really quite unimportant.

As she brought the cows back that morning Françoise had
stopped for a moment to talk to Jean, whom she had just
met in front of the church. Admittedly she did this for the
sole purpose of infuriating the Buteaus, provoking them
outside the very house.

'You know,' cried Lise when she came in, 'when you want
to see your men, try not to do it in front of our windows.'

Buteau, who was sharpening a billhook, was listening.

'My men!' went on Françoise. 'I see so many of them,
don't I—and one of them would have had me, not in front
of the window, but in your own bed, if I'd wanted it.'

This reference to Buteau made Lise fly into a rage. For a
long time she had wanted only one thing, to throw her sister
out so that she could have some peace at home, even if it
meant losing half the property. The same reason made her
husband beat her, for he held the contrary view and was determined to go on scheming to the end—he had not given up
hope of taking the girl to bed as long as they both had what
was necessary. Lise was angry because she was not the mistress, and she was now tormented with a particular kind of
jealousy; she was still ready to let him lay her sister, for she
wanted the thing done with, but she was angry at seeing him
still lusting after Françoise, for she had begun to hate her
youth, her small, firm breasts, and the gleam of her white
skin as she rolled up her sleeves. If she had been boss she
would have wanted him to destroy it all, she would even
have helped him to do it; she did not mind sharing her husband, but her rivalry with her sister had become venomous,
for she was more attractive than she was and could give a
man more pleasure.

'You trollop!' she yelled. 'You lead him on! If you weren't
always hanging round him he wouldn't run after your dirty
little bottom. It's disgusting!'

Françoise went very pale for this lie shocked her deeply.
She replied quietly, cold and angry.

right, that'll do. Wait a fortnight and I shan't bother you any longer, if that's what you want. In a fortnight I'll be twenty-one and I'll go!'

'Oh, so you want to be of age, do you? You've worked it out like that to make trouble for us! Well, you little bitch, you won't go in a fortnight's time, you'll go this minute. Go on, get out!'

'All right. They need someone at Macqueron's. He'll take me. Goodbye.'

And Françoise left. There was nothing more to be said. It was all over between them. Buteau put down the billhook he was sharpening and rushed up, hoping he could box their ears and keep them quiet that way until they made it up again. But he was too late, and all he could do in his fury was to punch his wife's face until her nose bled. These blasted women! This was what he had been frightened of all along, and succeeded in putting off for so long. Now that Françoise had run away there would be nothing but trouble. He thought he would lose everything, both girl and land.

'I'll go to Macqueron's later,' he yelled. 'She's got to come back, even if I've to keep my boot up her backside all the way!'

4

THE week went by and Françoise persisted in not returning to her sister's house. There was a ghastly scene on the road. Buteau had been dragging her by the hair, but when she bit his thumb and hurt him he had to let her go. Macqueron was afraid and had to send the girl away himself, saying that he could not encourage her rebelliousness any longer.

But just at that moment La Grande was passing and took Françoise home with her. She was now eighty-eight and thought of her death only as a means of bequeathing to her heirs, along with her fortune, the worries of an interminable lawsuit. The will she had made was extraordinarily complicated and intentionally confusing, so that on the pretext of doing nobody any harm she forced them all to devour each other. This was an idea of her own; she could not take her property with her, but at least she could die with the consolation that it would destroy others. In this way her only entertainment was to see the family at each other's throats. She therefore hastened to install her niece in her house, held back for a moment by her meanness, but deciding to keep her immediately she realized that she could get a lot of work out of the girl in return for a small quantity of food. In fact, that very evening she made her wash the stairs and the kitchen. Then, when Buteau came, she received him standing, looking at him like an evil old bird of prey, and he, who had been talking of smashing up Macqueron's place, trembled and stammered, paralysed because he hoped to inherit some of her money and dared not argue with the terrifying old woman.

'I need Françoise,' she said, 'and I'll keep her, because she's not happy with you. In any case, now she's come of age you have to render accounts. We'll discuss it later!'

Buteau left in a fury, terrified by the problems he could see looming ahead.

A week later, in fact, about the middle of August, Françoise was twenty-one. Now she was her own mistress, but all she had done was to exchange one wretched existence for another, for she also trembled before her aunt; she was killed with work in this cold stingy household where everything had to shine by some natural process without the use of any soap or brushes. Cold water and strong arms had to suffice. One day, after she had forgotten herself so far as to give some grain to the hens, her head was almost broken open by a blow from La Grande's stick. Rumour said that in order to spare her horses the old woman used to harness her grandson Hilarion to the plough, and if this was an invention it was true that she treated him like any animal, striking him and killing him with work, wearing out his brute strength until he would drop from fatigue, and he was so badly fed on crusts of bread and left-overs, like the pig, that he was always faint from hunger as he grovelled in terror. When Françoise realized that she was to be the second horse between the shafts she had only one desire, which was to leave the house. It was then that she suddenly decided to get married.

She merely wanted to end the whole business. She would rather have killed herself than make up the quarrel with Lise, for her conception of justice, which had ruined her life as a child, still forced her to maintain this rigid attitude. Her

cause was the only just one, and she despised herself for
having been patient so long. She said nothing about Buteau
and only spoke harshly about her sister, without whom it
would have been possible to go on living together. Now it
was over, completely over! She lived in the one hope of
being able to get back her property, her share of the inheritance. It worried her from morning till night, and she
was angry because endless formalities were necessary. Why?
This is mine, this is yours, it didn't take more than three
minutes to settle that! Did they really think they could work
together to rob her? She suspected the entire family and
reached the stage of telling herself that only a man, a husband, could get her out of this situation. It was true that
Jean did not own an inch of land, and he was fifteen years
older than she was, but no other man had asked to marry
her, and probably no one would have taken the risk after
the stories about Buteau, for nobody wanted him as an
enemy, he was so much feared in Rognes. And then she had
been with Jean once; this had made no trouble, for there
had been no consequences, only he was very kind and very
honest. She might as well have him, since she didn't care for
any other man and was taking someone, it did not matter
whom, to protect herself and infuriate Buteau. She, too,
wanted a man of her own.

Jean was still very fond of her. His desire to possess her
had cooled greatly, now that he had wanted her for so long.
Yet he returned to her with great pleasure, regarding himself as her man, for they had exchanged vows. He had
waited patiently until she became of age, and had not tried
to oppose her decision to wait, preventing her, on the contrary, from creating too much opposition in her sister's
house. Now she could get all the support she wanted from
honest people, and so, although he criticized the violent
way in which she had left, he told her repeatedly that it was
up to her to do something. And when she was ready to
discuss the next move, he was ready too.

So the marriage was arranged one evening when he came
to meet her behind La Grande's cowshed. There was an old
rotten gate there, opening on to a yard, and they leaned
against it, he outside, she inside, with the stream of manure
from the cowshed trickling between their feet.

'You know, Corporal,' she said first, looking into his eyes,
'if you still want to get married, so do I! Now!'

He gazed at her steadily and answered her slowly.

'I hadn't mentioned it again because it looked as though I wanted your property, but you're right, all the same. We should do it now.'

Silence fell. He had placed his hand over hers, which was resting on the gate.

'You mustn't worry about Jacqueline,' he went on, 'because of the stories that went round. I haven't even touched her for three years at least.'

'It's the same in my case,' she replied. 'I don't want you to keep on thinking about Buteau. The swine tells everyone that he used to have me. Perhaps you believe him too?'

'Everyone in the district believes him,' he murmured, evading the question.

She went on looking at him. 'Oh, I believed him!' he said. 'And I could understand it, really, for I know the scoundrel; you couldn't have done anything else.'

'Oh, he tried! He bruised me all over, but I swear he never went the whole way. Do you believe me?'

'I believe you.'

To show the pleasure he felt he clasped her hand and held it, while his arm rested on the gate. He had noticed that the water running from the cowshed was soaking his shoes and he now stood with his feet apart.

'You seemed to stay in their house so willingly, it looked as though you might have enjoyed his little games.'

She felt upset and her straightforward frank expression changed.

'Especially because you didn't want it with me any more. Do you remember? It doesn't matter; I was angry I hadn't given you a baby, but it's better now that it hasn't come yet. It's more respectable like that.'

He stopped short and told her she was standing in the stream too.

'Look out! You're getting wet.'

She also moved her feet apart.

'So we agree?' she said.

'We agree. Fix the date whenever you like.'

They did not even kiss, they shook hands like good friends over the gate, then they both went their ways.

In the evening when Françoise told La Grande that she wanted to marry Jean, explaining that she needed a man to help her establish her claim to the property, the old woman at first said nothing. She had remained standing straight up, looking at her with her round eyes. She was working out the loss, the gain, and the pleasure she would find in this marriage, and it was only the next day that she gave her approval. All night, as she lay on her straw mattress, she had thought it over, for she hardly slept at all now, remaining with her eyes open until daybreak, working out what unpleasant things she could do to annoy the family. She anticipated that this marriage would entail such far-reaching consequences for everyone that she yearned for it with a real youthful fever. She could already see even the slightest drawbacks, and she imagined further complications which would cause total destruction. As a result she told her niece that she wanted to see to everything, out of affection. She emphasized this word, brandishing her cane in a terrifying way. Françoise had been abandoned, so she would act as her mother, and everyone would see what that meant.

They now had to decide which should come first—the division of the property or the marriage. La Grande pondered over it for two nights and then declared that the marriage should take place immediately. Françoise, once married to Jean, demanding her share with the help of her husband, would be more of a problem to the Buteaus. So she hurried everything along and ran round like a young girl, getting her niece's papers, asking for Jean's, and arranging everything at the village hall and the church, putting so much passion into it that she even lent them the necessary money, in return for a paper signed by the bride and bridegroom in which the sum was doubled to include the interest. She was heart-broken at being forced to offer glasses of wine to people during the preparations, but she had her sour, vinegary wine, which was so undrinkable that everyone treated it with great respect. She decided that there would be no reception because of the family troubles, only a Mass followed by a glass of the so-called wine in which to drink the health of the married couple. Fouan was feeling upset and took to his bed, saying that he was ill. The only relative present was Delhomme, who agreed to be one of the witnesses for Françoise, in order to show his high regard for Jean, who was a good chap. The bridegroom brought only his witnesses, his master, Hourdequin, and one of the farm servants. Rognes was excited about this hasty marriage, for there was so much hostility in the background, and everyone came to their doorways to watch.

It had been decided that Françoise would continue to live in La Grande's house until the division of the property was made, for she had obstinately insisted on having the house. What was the point of renting anything else for a fortnight? Jean, who was to remain a waggoner at the farm while they waited, would simply join her every evening. Their wedding night was utterly meaningless and sad, although they were not sorry to be together at last. As he took her Françoise began to weep so bitterly that the sob choked her, and yet he did not hurt her in any way, for he was very gentle. The worst thing of all was that through her sobs she told him she had nothing against him, and that she couldn't stop crying, but didn't even know she was crying. Naturally, this kind of thing was hardly likely to increase a man's desire. It was in vain that he took her again and held her in his arms. They felt no pleasure at all, less even than the first time, on the day by the haystack. He explained that these things lose their savour when they do not happen straight away. But, in spite of this uneasiness, and the shame which had made them both heart-sick, they felt in harmony and since they could not sleep they spent the night deciding how things would turn out when they had the house and the land.

The next day Françoise demanded her share of the property at once, but La Grande was not so impatient now. In the first place she wanted to make the pleasure last, drawing her family's blood by a series of pinpricks. She had made good use of the girl and her husband too, for every evening Jean paid his rent for the room by two hours of work, and she was not too anxious for them to leave and set up house on their own. However, the Buteaus had to be asked how they proposed to arrange the division. She herself, in Françoise's name, demanded the house, half of the ploughed field, and half of the pasture, giving up half the vineyard which she estimated as being worth about the same amount as the house. This was fair and reasonable, in fact, for a friendly arrangement would have avoided bringing the law into the matter, for lawyers always make too much profit. Buteau was staggered when La Grande appeared, for he was compelled to respect her because of her wealth, but he could not bear to hear what she said. He went out in a fury, afraid he might forget his own interest and strike her. Lise was left alone with her aunt, her ears burning red, and she stammered in anger.

'The house! She wants the house, does she, that worthless slut, getting married without even coming to see me! Very well, aunt, tell her that she'll have the house only over my dead body!'

La Grande remained calm.

'All right, my girl! There's no need to get excited. You want the house, too, you've a right to it. We shall see.'

For three days she went backwards and forwards between the two sisters, taking their absurd vindictive messages to each other and wearing them out to such a point that both of them nearly took to their beds. She herself was tireless, and she let it be seen how much she loved them and how grateful her nieces ought to be that she had taken on this dirty work. Finally it was agreed that the land would be divided, but that the house and the furniture, as well as the livestock, would be sold, since they could not reach an agreement. Each sister swore she would buy the house, whatever the price, and that she would sell her last stitch of clothing to get the money.

For a whole month Buteau had been angry. First of all the girl had escaped him; he was ill with repressed desire, for he could no longer grasp handfuls of flesh under her skirt, in the obstinate hope of possessing her completely one day. Ever since the marriage, the idea that the other man had her in his bed and could do as he wished with her, had finally set his blood on fire. Then there was the land, for the other man was taking it away from him too. He might as well have cut off one of his limbs. He could probably find the girl again, but the land—the land that he regarded as his own and had sworn never to give up . . . he saw red and thought of desperate means, dreaming wildly of violent crimes and murders, which only his terror of the police prevented him from committing.

Finally a meeting was arranged with Monsieur Baillehache, and for the first time Buteau and Lise found themselves face to face with Françoise and Jean. La Grande had come with them for her own entertainment on the pretext of preventing things from going wrong. All five of them entered the office in tense silence. The Buteaus sat on the right, and Jean remained standing behind Françoise on the left, as though to indicate that he had no part in this but came simply to lend authority to his wife. La Grande sat in the middle, scrawny and upright, turning her wide-open eyes and beak-like nose from one to the other in great satisfaction. The two sisters did not even seem to recognize each other, sitting without a word, without a glance, their expressions harsh. Only one glance was exchanged between the men, as rapid, eloquent, and penetrating as a knife-thrust.

Monsieur Baillehache remained calm when confronted by these fierce expressions.

'My friends,' he said, 'first of all we are going to settle the division of the land, about which you are in agreement.'

This time he demanded the signatures first. The deed was ready, only the allocation of the shares was left blank following the names. They all had to sign before the draw was made, and it was then carried out at once, in order to avoid any trouble.

Françoise had drawn number two, and Lise had to take number one, while Buteau's face went black beneath the blood which pulsed through his swelling veins. He never had any luck; now his share was cut in two. This blasted younger sister and her man now owned the section between the part on the left and the part on the right.

'Bloody hell!' he swore between his teeth. 'Blasted swine!'

The notary asked him to wait until he was in the street.

'That cuts through our land up there on the plain,' said Lise without turning towards her sister. 'Perhaps they'll agree to exchange it. It will help us and it wouldn't do any harm to anybody.'

'No,' said Françoise, drily.

La Grande nodded approvingly. It was unlucky to go against what fate had decided. This unkind stroke of destiny cheered her up, while Jean still had not moved, standing behind his wife, so determined to remain on the fringe that his face expressed nothing.

'Now,' went on the notary, 'let's try to finish. Don't let's waste any time.'

The two sisters had both agreed that he should carry out the sale of the house, the furniture, and the livestock. The sale was advertised for the second Sunday in the month, and would take place in his office. The conditions of sale stated that the buyer would have the right to enter into the enjoyment of his property on the day of purchase. Finally, after the sale, the notary would settle the various accounts between the co-legatees. All this was accepted without discussion.

But at that moment Fouan, who was to be present as the guardian of the younger sister, was brought in by a clerk, who also prevented Jésus-Christ from entering, for the rascal was so drunk. Although Françoise had been of age for a month the accounts of guardianship had not yet been rendered, which made things more complicated. It now became necessary to dispose of them in order to free the old man from responsibility. He looked at them all, his little eyes wide-open. He shook with fear, for he was more and more afraid that he would be compromised and involved with the law.

The notary read out the statement of accounts. They all listened with fluttering eyelids, anxious not to misunderstand all the time, for they were afraid that if they let one word go by it would bring them misfortune.

'Have you any objections to raise?' asked Monsieur Baillehache when he had finished.

They remained bewildered. What objections? It was quite possible that they had forgotten some things and did not understand it at all.

'I beg pardon,' said La Grande suddenly, 'but this is not the complete account for Françoise. My brother must have turned a blind eye or he would have seen that she has been robbed.'

'Oh, what's that?' stammered Fouan. 'I haven't taken a single sou of hers. I swear it before God!'

'I say that Françoise, ever since her sister's marriage, which took place nearly five years ago, remained in the household as a servant, and that they owe her wages.'

Buteau, when he heard this unexpected demand, shot up in his chair. Lise choked.

'Wages! What, pay wages to a sister? Oh, that's really too awful!'

Monsieur Baillehache had to tell them to be quiet, asserting that a minor had a perfect right to ask for wages if she wanted them.

'Yes, I do,' said Françoise, 'I want everything that's due to me.'

'And what about her food, then?' cried Buteau, beyond himself. Bread and meat didn't last long with her about. You feel her! She didn't grow fat by licking the walls, the lazy thing.'

'What about her linen and her dresses?' went on Lise furiously. 'And the washing? She made her chemises dirty in two days, she sweated so much!'

'I sweated so much,' replied Françoise, angrily, 'because I worked so hard.'

'Sweat dries up,' added La Grande, 'it doesn't make things dirty.'

Monsieur Baillehache intervened again. He explained that these accounts had to be drawn up, wages on one side, food and expenses on the other. He took a pen and tried to draw up the accounts based on what they said, but it was a formidable task. Françoise, supported by La Grande, was very demanding, saying that her work deserved high pay and described everything she did in the house, looking after the cows, the housework, the washing up, and out in the fields, where her brother-in-law made her work like a man. On their side the Buteaus, in exasperation, swelled the expense account, including meals, lied about clothing, and even asked for the money spent on birthday presents. However, in spite of their severity, in the end they owed one hundred and eighty-six francs. It left them with trembling hands and blazing eyes, wondering what they could still find to deduct. The accounts were on the point of being accepted when Buteau cried:

'Just a minute! What about the doctor, when her monthlies stopped? He came twice, that makes six francs.'

La Grande did not want agreement to follow a victory by the other side and she prodded Fouan, demanding him to remember how many days the girl had worked on the farm previously when he lived in the house. Was it five or six days, at thirty sous? Françoise cried out 'Six' and Lise 'Five', as violently as though they were throwing stones at each other. The old man was dazed, agreeing with both of them and striking his forehead with his fists. Françoise won the day and the total sum amounted to one hundred and eighty-nine francs.

'So that's everything this time, is it?' asked the notary.

Buteau, as he sat on his chair, seemed to be crushed by

this ever-growing account and he fought no longer, believing that he had reached the depths of misery.

'If you want my shirt,' he murmured miserably, 'I'll take it off.'

But La Grande had kept in reserve one last terrible blow, something very important and very simple, which everyone had forgotten.

'Listen! What about the five hundred francs indemnity for the road up there?'

Buteau leapt to his feet, his eyes bursting out of his head, his lips parted. There was nothing to be said, no possible discussion, for he had received the money and had to pay back half of it. For a moment he tried to think of something; then, finding no means of escape in the mounting frenzy which was clouding his brain, he suddenly rushed at Jean.

'You blasted swine, you've killed our friendship! Without you we'd all be living happily together as one family.'

Jean had remained very calm and silent but now he had to be on the defensive.

'Don't touch me or I'll hit you.'

Suddenly Françoise and Lise got up, each standing in front of her man, their faces convulsed with their slowly-growing hate, their claws finally bared ready to scratch each other's eyes out; neither La Grande nor Fouan seemed disposed to prevent a scrimmage, but the notary broke away from his professional apathy.

'For goodness' sake! Wait until you're out in the street! It's infuriating that we can't reach an agreement without fighting!'

When they were all silent again, although they still trembled, he added:

'You do agree, don't you? Very well, I'll draw up the accounts of guardianship. You'll sign them and then we'll proceed to the sale of the house to complete things. Now go away and behave yourselves, for stupid conduct can sometimes cost you dear.'

These words finally calmed them, but as they were going out Jésus-Christ, who had been waiting for his father, insulted the whole family, yelling that it was a crying shame, dragging a poor old man into such a filthy business, and he would surely be robbed. In his maudlin drunkenness he bore him off, as he had brought him, in a cart lined with

straw, which he had borrowed from a neighbour. The
Buteaus went one way, while La Grande pushed Jean and
Françoise into the *Bon Laboureur*, where she had herself
treated to black coffee. She was beaming.

'I had a good laugh,' she said, finally, putting the re-
mainder of the sugar in her pocket.

That day she had another idea. When they came back to
Rognes she rushed off to reach an agreement with Old
Saucisse, who was reputed to be one of her old lovers. Since
the Buteaus had sworn they would bid for the house against
Françoise until they were cleaned out, she had decided that
if the old peasant bid on his side the others perhaps would
not suspect what was going on and would let him have it.
He happened to be their neighbour and might possibly
want to enlarge his property. He accepted at once after receiving a little gift. The result was that on the second Sunday of the month the auction took place, as La Grande had
anticipated. Once more in Monsieur Baillehache's office,
the Buteaus sat on one side, Françoise and Jean on the other
with La Grande. There were other people, a few peasants
who had come with the vague idea of buying the house if it
went for nothing, but after four or five bids made sharply
by Lise and Françoise the house went up to three thousand
five hundred francs, which was its value. Françoise stopped
at three thousand eight hundred. Then Old Saucisse came
on to the scene, went beyond four thousand and added five
hundred francs more. The Buteaus looked at each other in
terror. It was no longer possible, the thought of so much
money shattered them. Lise, however, allowed herself to be
carried away, up to five thousand. She was crushed when
the old peasant all at once went up to five thousand two
hundred. It was over then and the house was knocked down
to him for five thousand two hundred francs. The Buteaus
sneered. This would make a nice sum to come to them as
soon as Françoise and her horrible man were defeated in
their turn.

But when Lise returned to Rognes and entered the old
house where she had been born and brought up she began
to sob. Buteau was so upset too that in the end he took it out
on her, swearing that *he* would have given up everything
down to the last hair of his head; but these heartless women,
they opened their purses like their legs, only when they
wanted some fun. This was a lie, for it was he who had

stopped her, and then they began to fight. He knocked her down with a blow but she got up and almost broke his leg as she lashed out against him.

The next evening there was more to come and a thunderbolt fell. In the morning Old Saucisse had gone to complete the sale and by midday Rognes knew that he had bought the house on Françoise's behalf with Jean's authorization, and not only the house but also the furniture, the donkey, and the cow as well.

The Buteaus uttered a yell of misery, as though they had been struck by lightning. Both husband and wife fell to the ground, weeping and howling, wild with despair because they had lost, and been cheated by that wretched girl. What infuriated them especially was to hear that the whole village was laughing at their stupid behaviour. Good heavens! To be taken in like this and turned out of your own house, all by a trick! But, my word, just wait!

La Grande arrived that very evening, acting for Françoise, to arrange politely with Buteau on what day they anticipated moving. He threw her out, losing all discretion, and replied in one word:

'Shit!'

She went off happily, simply shouting that the bailiff would be sent round. The very next day, in fact, Vimeux, looking pale and anxious, and more down-trodden than usual, came up the street and knocked cautiously, watched by the wives in the neighbouring houses. There was no reply. He had to knock louder and found the courage to call out, explaining that he had come to serve a notice telling them to quit. Then the attic window opened and a voice shouted out the same word, the only word:

'Shit!'

And a pot of it was emptied over Vimeux, soaking him from head to foot. He had to go back with the summons and Rognes has laughed about the joke ever since.

But La Grande had immediately taken Jean to see the lawyer at Châteaudun. He explained to them that at least five days were necessary before expulsion could be effected. A formal complaint had to be laid, a court order made, the order enforced, and then finally expulsion took place, while if necessary the bailiff would get the help of the police. La Grande discussed this in order to gain twenty-four hours and on the day she returned to Rognes, which was a Tuesday, she declared everywhere that on Saturday evening the Buteaus would be thrown into the street with sabre thrusts like thieves if they had not left the house by then of their own accord.

When Buteau was told he made fearful menacing gestures. He shouted to all and sundry that he would not leave the house alive, and that the soldiers would be forced to knock down the walls to get him out. Nobody knew if he was really mad or just pretending, for his anger had now reached such a pitch of extravagance. One morning it was seen that he had barricaded himself in, and terrible cries and howls could be heard behind the closed doors, apparently the voices of Lise and the two children. The neighbours were very upset and after a discussion one old peasant finally offered to help by placing a ladder against the window and going up to see. But the window opened, Buteau pushed the ladder down and the old man, too, who almost had his legs broken. Couldn't he do as he liked in his own home? He brandished his fists, yelling that he would flay them all alive if they bothered him any more. Worst of all, Lise appeared also with the two brats, shouting out insults and accusing the neighbours of meddling in other people's business. Nobody dared take any more notice. At each fresh outburst everyone grew more alarmed, and came to listen, shuddering, to the revolting words which could be heard in the street. Some knowing people thought that Buteau had some plan of his own, while others swore he was going off his rocker and that the whole thing would come to a bad end. The real explanation was never known.

Finally Saturday came. Buteau had become more agitated. He harnessed and unharnessed his cart from morning till night to no purpose, and as he drove it furiously about in a frightening, pointless way, people leapt aside on the road. On Saturday, at eight o'clock in the morning he harnessed it once more, but he did not go out. He planted himself on the doorstep, calling out to any passing neighbours, sneering, sobbing, and yelling about it all in crude language. Damn funny, wasn't it, to be bothered by that little tart after she'd been his bit of stuff for five years! Oh yes, she was a whore, and so was his wife! They were fine whores, those sisters, both fighting to get into bed with him first. In order to have his revenge he began to tell this lying story again, with revolting details. When Lise came out a dreadful quarrel began. He struck her in front of everyone and sent her back deflated and quietened, feeling satisfied after beating her so hard. Then he remained at the door waiting for the arm of the law, joking about him and insulting him. Had he gone whoring somewhere on the road? He expected him no longer and thought he had triumphed.

It was not until four o'clock that Vimeux appeared with two policemen. Buteau went pale and quickly shut the yard door. Perhaps he had never believed that it would come to this. A deathly, insolent silence fell over the house, which was now protected by armed force. Vimeux beat on the door with both fists. There was no answer. The policemen had to join in and batter on the door with gun-butts. A big crowd of men, women, and children had followed them and the whole of Rognes was there, waiting for the promised siege. Suddenly the door opened again and Buteau could be seen standing at the front of his cart, whipping his horse and driving right at the crowd.

'I'm going to drown myself!' he shouted in the midst of their terrified shouts. 'I'm going to drown myself!'

It was all over now, he wanted to make an end of it and throw himself in the Aigre along with his cart and horse, everything he had.

'Look out! I'm going to drown myself!'

The inquisitive crowd had dispersed in terror, fleeing before the lashing whip and the desperate speed of the cart, but as he drove it down the slope fast enough to break the wheels, men ran to stop him. This confounded blockhead was quite capable of diving in just to be a nuisance to everyone else. They caught him up and had to struggle with him, leaping to get hold of the horse's head and climbing up into the cart. When they brought him back he was silent, his teeth clenched, and his whole body tense, letting destiny do its work, protesting in silent and impotent rage.

At this moment La Grande came along with Françoise and Jean so that they could take possession of the house. Buteau merely glanced in their faces, with the black look he now wore to greet the final tragedy. But now it was Lise's turn to shout and rage like a maniac. The policemen were there, telling her repeatedly to pack her bags and go. She had to obey, since her man had been too much of a coward to protect her and fight them off. She stood with her hands on her hips, and told him what she thought of him.

'You're a fine sort of bastard, letting us be thrown out in the street! Haven't you got any guts? Can't you smash up those buggers? Go on, you poor fish, you're not a man any more!'

She shouted it in his face, exasperated by his silence. In the end he pushed her away so roughly that she shrieked, but he did not utter a word and merely glared at her.

'Come on, Mum! Hurry up!' said Vimeux triumphantly. 'We won't go until you've given the keys to the new owners.'

From that moment Lise began to move out in a sudden rage. During the last three days she and Buteau had already taken many things, such as the tools and large utensils, to the house of their neighbour, La Frimat. It was realized that they expected the eviction all the same, for they had come to an agreement with the old woman. To give them time to turn round she would rent them her house, which was too big for her, and she would keep only her paralytic husband's bedroom for herself. Since the furniture and the animals had been sold with the house Lise had only to bring her linen, her mattresses, and other small things. Everything bounced through the door and the windows into the middle of the yard, while the two children cried as though their last day had come, Laura hanging round her mother's skirts and Jules lying flat on the ground in the middle of all the things that were being unpacked. Since Buteau did not even help her the policemen kindly began to load the bundles into the cart.

But things became even worse when Lise caught sight of Françoise and Jean, who were waiting behind La Grande. She rushed forward and released the accumulated flood of her bitterness in their faces.

'You bitch! You've come to watch, along with your blasted man! All right, then, you can see what it means, it's as though you were drinking our blood. Thief! Thief! Thief!'

The word choked her and every time she brought something else into the yard she kept coming to shout it at her sister again. Françoise did not answer; she was very pale, with tight lips and burning eyes. She pretended to be conducting a painstaking inspection, watching to see that nothing was being taken away. She recognized a kitchen stool which had been included in the sale.

'That's mine!' she said harshly.

'Yours? Well, go and get it, then!' answered the other, throwing it into the pond.

The house was free now. Buteau took the horse by the bridle and Lise picked up her two children, the two last bundles; then, as she finally left the old house, she went up to Françoise and spat in her face.

'There! That's for you.'

Her sister immediately spat back.

'And that's for you!'

After the venomous hatred of this farewell Lise and Françoise wiped their faces quickly without taking their eyes off each other. Now they were separated forever, with nothing in common any longer except the hostile, rebellious family blood.

Finally Buteau opened his mouth again, yelling his last word, with a threatening gesture towards the house.

'We'll soon be back!'

La Grande followed them, so that she could watch right to the end, but she decided that now Buteau had reached rock-bottom she would turn against the others, who were leaving her too quickly, and from her point of view she already thought they were too happy. For a long time groups of people stood about talking quietly. Françoise and Jean had gone into the empty house.

Just as the Buteaus were unpacking their things in La Frimat's house they were astonished to see Old Fouan appear. Looking over his shoulder as though some evildoer was pursuing him, he asked in a timid, strangled voice:

'Is there a corner for me? I've come to sleep here.'

He had fled from the Château in terrible fright; whenever he woke during the night he saw Boldie, in her nightshirt, going round the bedroom like some thin, half-naked boy, looking for the papers which he had finally hidden outside at the bottom of a hole in the rock filled with earth. Jésus-Christ used to send the girl because she was so light and supple that she could slip everywhere barefoot, going between the chairs and under the bed like a snake. She pursued the hunt passionately; she was convinced the old man put the papers back into his clothes when he got dressed and she was furious that she could not find where he put them before going to bed. There was certainly nothing in the bed. She pushed her thin arm down into it, feeling round it skilfully while her grandfather hardly noticed her presence.

'Is there a corner for me, then?' he asked Buteau once again.

His son seemed cheered up by his father's unexpected return. It was money coming back.

'Why, of course, old man! We'll make room somehow. It'll bring us luck. My goodness, if kindness were the only thing needed I'd be rich!'

Françoise and Jean had slowly entered the empty house. Dusk was falling and the last gloomy ray of light shone through the silent rooms. It was all very old, this family home which had sheltered the work and wretchedness of three centuries, so much so that there was a lingering sadness here, as in the shadow of old village churches. The doors had been left open and it looked as though a whirlwind had blown through, while chairs lay haphazard on the floor where they had fallen in the midst of the catastrophic departure. It looked like a dead house.

As Françoise walked slowly round looking at everything, confused feelings and vague memories stirred within her. Here she had played as a child. In the kitchen, near the table, her father had died. In the bedroom, by the bed without its mattress, she remembered Lise and Buteau, and the evenings when they made love so violently that she could hear their panting breath through the ceiling. Were they going to torment her even now? She felt strongly that Buteau was still there. It was here that he had grabbed hold of her one night and she had bitten him. There, and there again! At every turn she encountered some memory which increased her uneasiness.

Then, as she turned round, she was surprised to notice Jean. What was this stranger doing in their house? He seemed embarrassed, he looked like a visitor, for he did not dare touch anything. She was overcome with a feeling of solitude, and in despair because her victory no longer gave her any pleasure. She had expected to enter the house in great delight, triumphing over her departed sister. And now the house meant nothing to her, she was stricken with unhappiness. Perhaps it was this gloomy evening light. In the end she and her man found themselves in pitch darkness, still wandering from one room to another without even having the courage to light a candle.

But a sound brought them back to the kitchen and they felt more cheerful when they recognized Gideon, the donkey, who had come in as usual and was sniffing in the side-board, which had been left open. The old cow, Coliche, was lowing in the cowshed next door.

Then Jean took Françoise in his arms and kissed her gently, as though to tell her that they would be happy in spite of everything.

PART FIVE

1

ONE afternoon Jean was driving a heavy waggon-load of manure to his field at Les Cornailles. Françoise and he had been in their house for a month and they had settled down into the active monotonous routine of the countryside. As he arrived he caught sight of Buteau in the neighbouring field, busily spreading out the manure heaps which had been placed there the previous week. The two men exchanged sidelong glances. They often encountered each other and found that they were thus forced to work side by side, since they were neighbours. Buteau was particularly unhappy about it, for Françoise's share, which had been torn out of his seven acres of land, had left him with two strips, one on the left and another on the right, which forced him to make continual detours. The two men never spoke a word to each other. If they had quarrelled they would probably have killed each other.

Jean began to unload the manure from his cart. He had climbed into it and was emptying it with his fork, standing in the manure up to his thighs, when Hourdequin passed by on the road. The farmer still had a high regard for his former servant. He stopped and chatted; he looked old, for he was consumed with anxiety over the farm and other things too.

'Jean, why haven't you tried phosphates?'

Without waiting for a reply he went on talking as though he wanted to work himself into a state of frenzy. The real answer to good crops lay in manure and fertilizers. He had tried everything and had just gone through this craze for manure, which sometimes takes hold of farmers. He had made a series of experiments, using grasses, leaves, wine-dregs, rape, and colza; then he had tried crushed bones, cooked and pounded flesh, and dried blood made into powder. He was only sorry that he could not try liquid blood since there was no slaughter house in the district.

'I've often had good results with phosphates,' he went on.

'People get cheated over them,' replied Jean.

'Yes, certainly you do, if you buy from travellers you don't know passing through the country towns. Every market should have an expert chemist responsible for analysing these chemical fertilizers, for it's so difficult to get them unadulterated. That's where the future lies, certainly; but before the future comes we'll all be ruined. We must have the courage to suffer on behalf of others.'

The stench of the manure seemed to revive him a little. He loved it, he breathed it in with real male enjoyment as though it was the very smell of the copulating earth.

But at that moment the sound of a voice made Jean turn his head. He was surprised to see Lise standing up in her cart, which had stopped at the side of the road. She was calling out to Buteau as loudly as she could.

'Listen! I'm going to Cloyes to get Monsieur Finet. Father's fallen down flat in his room. I think he's pegging out. Go home and have a look, will you!'

And without even waiting for his reply she whipped up the horse and set off again, dwindling into a small dancing figure in the distance on the straight road.

Buteau did not hurry but finished spreading out his last heaps. He was grumbling. So his father was ill! That was a nuisance. Perhaps it was only a try-on, a means of getting himself spoilt a bit. Then the notion that it might be serious after all, since his wife had embarked on the expense of a doctor on her own account, made him decide to put on his jacket.

The Buteaus were still living with La Frimat; they occupied the whole house with the exception of the ground-floor room at the back, which she had kept for herself and her paralysed husband. They found they were too crowded there and they missed their vegetable garden in particular, for, naturally, La Frimat had kept hers, since this little plot of ground allowed her to feed the invalid comfortably. This would have made them move and look for a larger house, if they had not noticed that Françoise was irritated by their proximity. Only a party wall separated the two properties. They insisted on talking very loudly so that they could be heard saying that they were just camping there and were definitely going back to their own house next door as soon as they could, so there wasn't any point in having all the bother of another move, was there? How and why they would come back they did not explain, and it was this very confidence and crazy assurance, based on unknown factors,

164

which threw Françoise into a rage and spoilt her enjoyment of the house. Lise sometimes even placed a ladder against the wall and shouted unpleasant things to her. Since the accounts had been settled in Monsieur Baillehache's office she alleged she had been robbed and never ceased to hurl revolting accusations from one yard to the other.

When Buteau reached home he found Old Fouan stretched out on his bed in the corner he occupied behind the kitchen under the hayloft. The two children were keeping an eye on him, Jules, who was already eight, and Laura, who was three, playing on the floor, pouring streams of water out of the old man's water jug.

'Well now, what's all this?' asked Buteau, standing by the bed.

Fouan had regained consciousness; his wide-open eyes turned slowly round with a fixed stare, but he did not move his head; he looked as though he had been turned to stone.

'No, father, there's too much work! We can't have any nonsense. You mustn't pass out today.'

Lise brought Monsieur Finet almost immediately. He examined the invalid at length while she and her man waited, looking anxious. The old man's death would have been a relief to them if it had happened quickly, but now it looked as though he would be ill a long time and probably cost a lot of money, while if he died before they had found his hoard, Fanny and Jésus-Christ would certainly come to bother them. In the end the doctor's silence upset them. When he sat down in the kitchen to write out a prescription they decided to ask him some questions.

'Is it serious, then?' said Buteau, frightened when he saw that the doctor had written a whole page. 'D'you think all that will make him better?'

The doctor merely shrugged his shoulders. He had gone to look at the patient again for he was interested and surprised to find that he was feverish after this slight case of cerebral congestion. He took the old man's pulse, not even trying to get any help from him as he looked up at him stupidly. He said simply when he left:

'It'll take about three weeks. I'll come again tomorrow. Don't be surprised if his mind wanders tonight.'

Three weeks! The Buteaus had heard nothing else and they were horrified. What a lot of money it would cost if there was a long list of medicines like this every day! The worst of it all was that Buteau now had to drive to the chemist's at Cloyes. It was a Saturday and La Frimat, when she came back from selling her vegetables, found Lise alone, so depressed that she was pacing up and down, doing nothing. The news had already spread through Rognes, for Boldie ran cheekily along to the house. She refused to go before touching her grandfather's hand, and went back to tell Jésus-Christ that he was certainly not dead. All at once, following the sluttish girl, La Grande appeared, apparently sent by Fanny. She stood by her brother's bed and summed him up by the brightness of his eyes as though he were an eel from the river Aigre. Then she went off, wrinkling her nose, looking disappointed that this was not the end. After that the family did not put themselves out any more. Why should they bother, since there seemed a good chance that he would survive?

Until midnight the house was in chaos. Buteau had come back in a shocking bad mood. There were mustard plasters for the old man's legs, a draught to be taken every hour, and a purge to be given next morning if he was better. La Frimat helped willingly but at ten o'clock, half-dead with sleep and not very interested, she went to bed. Buteau, who wanted to do the same, hustled Lise along. What the devil was the good of it all? It was no good looking at the old man. It certainly wouldn't make him better. His mind was wandering now and he was talking aloud in a disconnected way and seemed to imagine he was in the fields, working hard as he used to in the far-off days of his maturity. Lise was upset by these old stories muttered by her father in a low voice, as though he was already buried and returning to haunt her. She was about to follow her husband, who was getting undressed, when it occurred to her to tidy away the patient's clothes, which had been left on the chair. She shook them carefully, after searching the pockets at length, but all she found was a blunt knife and some string. Then, as she hung them up at the back of the cupboard, she noticed in the middle of a shelf, staring her in the face, a small packet of papers. Her heart missed a beat. It was the hoard! The hoard they had been looking for so hard for a month, searching in unlikely places, and there it was, right in front of her just by her hand! The old man must have been moving it to a new hiding-place when the attack had struck him down.

'Buteau! Buteau!' she called, her voice so hoarse that he

ran in wearing only his shirt, thinking that his father was dying.

He, too, was dumbfounded at first. Then they were both carried away in crazy excitement. They caught hold of each other's hands and jumped up and down like goats, forgetting the invalid, whose eyes were now closed, and as his head lay firmly on the pillow his disconnected delirious talk went on.

'Hush!' murmured Lise, turning round with a shudder.

'Oh, don't bother!' replied Buteau. 'What does he know about it? Can't you hear him talking nonsense?'

They sat down by the bed, for their legs had given way following the violent shock of triumph.

'Besides,' she replied, 'they can't accuse us of having looked for it, for, as God is my witness, I really wasn't thinking about his money. It fell into my hands. Now let's look.'

He had already unfolded the papers and was adding up figures aloud.

'Two hundred and thirty plus seventy, that's exactly three hundred. That's it, definitely; I've worked it out right. So much a quarter, it's at five per cent. Isn't it odd that these silly little scraps of paper can be money all the same, worth as much as real coins!'

Silence fell as they both looked at the papers and thought things over.

'What shall we do?' murmured Lise in the end. 'We ought to put them back, I suppose.'

'No!' said Buteau with a violent gesture.

'Oh, but we ought to! We must put them back! He'll look for them. He'll make a fuss. That would lead to a lot of trouble from the rest of the family.'

She stopped short for a third time, overcome when she heard the old man sob. He sobbed out of wretchedness, in terrible despair, with sobs that seemed to come mysteriously from the whole of his past life, for he repeated only one phrase in a voice that grew more and more hollow:

'It's all over! It's all over!'

'D'you think,' Buteau went on violently, 'that I'm going to let this crazy old man keep his papers? He might tear them up or burn them! Oh, no, I certainly won't!'

'Yes, that's true,' she murmured.

'Well, that's enough now. Let's go to bed. If he asks for

them I'll tell him I'm looking after them. And the others had better not bother me!'

They went to bed after hiding the papers under the marble top of an old washstand which seemed safer than putting them at the bottom of a locked drawer. The old man was left alone without a candle in case it should cause a fire. He went on chattering and sobbing deliriously all night.

The next day Monsieur Finet found him calmer and better than he had hoped. Oh, those old plough-horses, their souls were riveted to their bodies! The fever that he had feared seemed to have abated. He prescribed iron and quinine, rich men's drugs, so expensive that Buteau and Lise were again horrified.

A week later Monsieur Finet was astonished to find Fouan getting up, not very strong, but insisting on walking, for as he said, if you don't *want* to die, then you *don't* die. Buteau, standing behind the doctor, sneered, for he had stopped giving the prescriptions after the second one, saying that the best thing was to let the illness work itself out. On market day, however, Lise had been weak enough to bring back a draught which had been prescribed the day before, and since the doctor came on Monday for the last time Buteau told him that the old man had almost had a relapse.

'I don't know what they stuck in your bottle but it made him damned ill.'

That evening Fouan decided to speak. Since he had got up he had walked round the house anxiously, his mind a blank, no longer remembering where he might have hidden his papers. He searched everywhere and desperately tried to remember. Then a vague memory came back to him. Perhaps he had not hidden them, perhaps they had stayed there on the shelf. But then, if he was mistaken, and nobody had got them, was he going to arouse suspicion himself by admitting the existence of the money which had been painfully hoarded in the past and then hidden so carefully? He struggled with himself for two days more, torn between fury at this sudden disappearance and the self-enforced need to keep his mouth shut. Yet the facts became clearer; he remembered that on the morning when he had had the attack he had put the packet in this place, intending to slide it into the crack of a beam in the ceiling which he had just discovered as he looked round from his bed. He was so tormented by his loss that he let the whole secret out.

'Where are the papers?' he asked in a hoarse strangled voice.

Buteau blinked, looking extremely surprised, as though he did not understand.

'What? What do you mean? What papers?'

'My money!' shouted the old man, drawing himself up to a great height with a menacing expression.

'Your money! You've still got some money, have you? You swore so hard that we'd cost too much and you hadn't a penny left! Oh, you damned cunning old chap, you've got some money, have you?'

He swayed in his chair, sneering and laughing, feeling triumphant that he had had the suspicion in the past, for he had been the first to suspect the hoard. Fouan trembled in every limb.

'Give it back to me!'

'Give it back to you? Why should I have it? I don't even know where your money is!'

'You've robbed me! Give it back to me, damn you, or I'll make you give it up by force.'

And in spite of his age he grasped him by the shoulders and shook him. But his son then got up and seized him in his turn, unhurriedly, simply shouting violently in his face:

'Yes, I've got it and I'm keeping it! I'm keeping it for you, do you understand, you old fool? You're going off your head! Yes, it was high time to take those papers away from you, you were just going to tear them up. It's true, isn't it, Lise? He was tearing them up!'

'As true as I'm here. It happens when you don't know what you're doing.'

Fouan was terrified when he heard this. Was he really mad, for he couldn't remember anything! If he had really wanted to destroy the papers like a child playing with pictures, then this wasn't worthy of him and he was only fit to be killed. His breath failed him. He had neither courage nor strength.

'Give them back to me, will you?' he stammered, in tears.

'No!'

'Give them back to me, I'm better now.'

'No, no, you'll only wipe your bottom with them or use them to light your pipe. No, thank you!'

And from then on the Buteaus obstinately refused to give up the deeds. They spoke about them openly, moreover, and told a dramatic story, saying how they had arrived in the nick of time to take them out of the invalid's hands just as he was starting to tear them up. People appeared to believe them superficially, but secretly they suspected they were lying. Jésus-Christ was particularly angry; to think that this hoard, which could not be found in his house, had been wormed out by the others immediately, that he had held it in his hands one day and had been stupid enough to leave it intact! There was no point in being regarded as a scoundrel if you didn't behave like one. He swore he would settle accounts with his brother when his father died.

Fouan, on his side, trailed about from house to house and told the story everywhere. Whenever he could stop a passerby he complained about his miserable lot. In this way one morning he went into the next door yard, to his niece's house.

Françoise was helping Jean load a cart of manure. He was standing in the pit, emptying it with his fork, while she stood in the cart taking the forkfuls and spreading it out, pressing it down with her heels so that the load could be heavier.

The old man stood in front of them leaning on his stick and began to complain.

'Isn't it infuriating to think they've taken my money away from me and won't give it back! What would you do in my place?'

Françoise let him repeat the question three times. She was very upset that he had come to talk like this and she received him coldly, for she wanted to avoid any possible argument with the Buteaus.

'You know, uncle,' she replied finally, 'it's nothing to do with us! We're only too glad to be out of that hell-hole,' and turning her back on him she went on trampling down the load in the cart with dung up to her thighs, and as her husband sent up forkfuls one after the other, she was almost submerged. She disappeared then in the midst of the warm steam, and although the manure gave off asphyxiating fumes when it was moved she felt at ease and quite confident.

'I'm not mad, am I, that's quite clear,' Fouan went on, without appearing to have heard her. 'They ought to give me my money back. D'you think I'd be capable of tearing up the deeds?'

Neither Françoise nor Jean breathed a word.

'You'd have to be mad, wouldn't you, and I'm not mad. You can see that I'm not!'

Françoise suddenly stood up on top of the loaded cart. She looked very tall, healthy, and strong, as though she had grown there and this fecund smell emanated from her. She had a full bosom now and as she stood there with her hands on her hips she looked a true woman.

'Oh no, uncle! Oh, no, we've had enough! I've told you not to get us mixed up in all that dirty business, and now we've got away from it perhaps it would be better if you don't come to see us any more.'

'So you're sending me away?' asked the old man, trembling.

Jean thought he should intervene.

'No, it's just that we don't want any quarrelling. We'd have to spend three days fighting if you were seen here. Everyone wants peace and quiet, don't they?'

Fouan remained motionless, looking from one to the other with his pale, short-sighted eyes, then he went away.

'Very well, if I need help I must go somewhere else; I mustn't come to you!'

They let him go, feeling uneasy, for they were by no means evil yet. But what could they do? They could not have helped him in any way and they would certainly have lost their appetite and their sleep over it. While her husband went to look for his whip Françoise carefully picked up the lumps of manure which had fallen down and threw them back on to the cart with a shovel.

The next day a violent scene broke out between Fouan and Buteau. In fact, every day they began to argue about the deeds again.

'Give them back to me!' repeated the father obstinately, while the son refused, telling him every time to shut up.

But gradually things became worse, especially since the old man was looking round to find where his son could possibly have hidden the hoard. Now it was his turn to go over the whole house, knocking on the cupboards, tapping the walls to see if they sounded hollow, and whenever he was alone he got rid of the children and went on with his search in the same passionate way as a boy runs after a servant girl the moment his parents have gone out. One day Buteau returned unexpectedly and saw Fouan stretched out full length on his stomach looking under the chest trying to see if there was a hiding place there. This made him furious, for his father was getting close. What he was looking for down below was in fact above, hidden and pressed down by the heavy weight of the marble.

'My God, you old fool! Now you're pretending to be a snake! Will you please get up!'

He pulled on his legs and stood him up with a jerk.

'Can't you stop poking about in every corner? I'm tired of feeling that every nook and cranny of the house is being searched.'

Fouan was annoyed at being taken by surprise, and looked at him, repeating in a sudden fury:

'Give them back to me!'

'Shut up!' Buteau shouted in his face.

'Oh, I'm too miserable here! I'm going away!'

'All right then! Get out! Good riddance, and if you come back then, my God, you've got no guts.'

He seized him by the arm and flung him out.

2

FOUAN went down the hill. His anger had abated quickly and he stopped on the road further along, dazed at finding himself outside, not knowing where to go. Three o'clock struck from the church, a damp cold wind was blowing on this grey autumn afternoon and he shivered, for everything had happened so quickly that he had not even picked up his hat.

When he came to the river he leant against the parapet of the bridge for a moment. Darkness would soon be upon him, and he was worried. Where would he sleep? He had not even a roof over his head. The sight of Bécu's dog made him envious, for the animal had at least a hole in the straw where it always spent the night. Automatically he crossed the bridge and found himself in front of the Delhommes' little farm. When he realized where he was he turned suddenly to one side and went behind the house so that he would not be seen. There he paused again, leaning against the stable wall. He could hear his daughter Fanny talking inside. Had he been thinking of coming back to her house? He did not even know, his feet had brought him there of their own accord. He could not make out what she was saying. She must have been arguing with a servant, and her voice rose; he heard her, in dry, hard tones, using no coarse words, say things to the wretched girl which hurt her so much that she sobbed. He was hurt, too; his feeling had evaporated, and he grew tense, knowing that if he had pushed open the door he too would have been greeted by his daughter in the same unpleasant tone.

'Dad will come on his knees asking us to take him back again.' He imagined her repeating the remark that had broken all links between them for ever, like the stroke of an axe. No, no, he would rather die of hunger or sleep behind a hedge than see her triumph, with the pride of a woman who knows she is beyond reproach. He detached himself from the wall and with difficulty walked away.

Fouan thought that everyone was watching him, and in order to avoid the road he went up the right bank of the river beyond the bridge and soon found himself among the vineyards. He intended to go up on the plain, avoiding the village, but he had to go past the Château to which his legs also seemed to have brought him back, like some old beast of burden who instinctively returns to the stables where he used to feed. From the corner where he stood he could tell that some feast was going on, some drunken party which would last until morning. His stomach was hollow and he felt himself drawn closer; he recognized voices and smelt the stewed beans that Boldie cooked so well whenever her father wanted to celebrate the arrival of some friend. Why shouldn't he go in and have some fun with the two scoundrels? He could hear them shouting at each other in the smoky room. They were comfortably warm and so drunk that he felt jealous. His hand reached out for the door but a shrill laugh from Boldie suddenly froze him. It was she who frightened him now for he could still see her in her shift coming up close to him like a thin naked serpent, searching him, devouring him. And then even if her father helped him get the papers back, the girl would take them away again. All at once the door opened, the slut came to look outside, for she had become aware of some presence. He only had time to hide quickly behind the bushes. Then he made off and through the dusk he could see her green eyes shining.

When he reached the plateau he felt relieved, as though

173

he had been saved from the others and would cheerfully die of his solitude. He wandered aimlessly about for a long time. Night had fallen and the icy wind lashed against him. Six o'clock struck; everyone in Rognes was having supper. His limbs felt weak and he could only walk slowly. Between two squalls a shower of rain fell, cutting sharply against his skin. He was soaked through but went on walking and was caught in two more showers. Without knowing how he came there he found himself in front of the church outside the ancient family house where the Buteaus lived.

No, he could not find shelter there, they had driven him away. It began to rain so hard that his courage failed him completely. He went up to the Buteaus' side door and looked into the kitchen, from where there came a smell of cabbage soup. His wretched body had come back in total submission. His physical need for food and warmth drove him on, but as the Buteaus went on eating they talked, and their words stopped him.

'Suppose Father doesn't come back?'

'Oh, don't worry, he's too fond of his stomach, he'll come back when he's hungry!'

Fouan went away, for he was afraid that he might be seen standing by the door like a dog coming back for something to eat after a whipping. He was choking with shame and a wild resolution formed in his mind that he would just lie down and die. They would see whether he was too fond of his stomach! He went down the hill again and sank down on the end of a log in front of Clou's forge. He came to himself when he recognized La Grande on her way home from the Delhommes' house, where she had gone in order to save lighting a candle. He got up, and his limbs creaked with the effort. He followed her at a distance but not quickly enough to reach the house at the same time as she did. He hesitated in front of the closed door and his heart sank. Finally he knocked three times, so timidly that La Grande did not hear him. Eventually she came.

'Who is it?' she asked.

'It's me.'

'Who are you?'

'It's I, your brother.'

She had certainly recognized the voice at once and did not hurry, for she enjoyed forcing him to speak. There was a silence.

'What d'you want?' she asked.

He was trembling and dared not reply. She opened the door again roughly, but as he was coming in she barred the way with her thin arms, leaving him in the street, while the driving rain still streamed down through the gloomy darkness.

'I know what you want! They came to tell me at the wake. Yes, you've been stupid enough to let yourself be robbed again! You haven't even been able to keep the money you hoarded up, and you want me to take you in, don't you?'

Then, when he began to make excuses and stammer out explanations, she flew into a rage.

'As though I hadn't warned you! Haven't I told you often enough that it's a silly coward's trick to give up your land? All right, then, now it's just as I said it would be, you're hounded out by your wretched children, running about in the dark like a beggar, without even a stone to rest your head on.'

He stretched out his hands, weeping, and tried to thrust her aside, but she stood her ground and finished what she wanted to say.

'No, no! Go and ask the people who've stolen your money to give you a bed. I don't owe you anything! The family would accuse me of meddling in their affairs again. It isn't that at all though: you gave away your property. I'll never forgive you!'

As she drew herself up, with her withered neck and her round eyes, she looked like some bird of prey. She banged the door violently in his face.

'It's your own fault! You can die in the street!'

Fouan remained there, tense and motionless, outside the door, while behind him the rain continued its steady downpour. In the end he turned round and went off again into the pitch-black night, and the torrential, slow-falling icy rain.

Where did he go? He was never very clear about it afterwards. He came across a fence and followed it as far as a little door, which opened. The ground gave way beneath him and he rolled into a hollow. It was cosy there, warm and dry. But he heard a grunting sound; he was in a pig-sty, and the pig had got up, thinking that food was coming. He pushed his snout against Fouan's ribs, but the old man was so weak that the fear of being eaten alive drove him out. He could not walk any further and lay down outside, huddling against the door, curling up tightly so that the edge of the roof would protect him from the rain. But it still soaked his legs and icy gusts of wind froze his wet clothes on his body.

The next day only one thing concerned him: how long would it take to die? He suffered less from the cold. It was hunger that tortured him most. He was certainly going to die of hunger. Another night, another day perhaps. During daylight he did not weaken, he preferred to meet his end like this rather than go back to the Buteaus. But a terrible anguish took hold of him as dusk fell again. He was terrified of spending another night in this incessant rain. The cold seemed to penetrate into his bones and an intolerable hunger gnawed at his chest. When the sky grew black he felt he was drowning, borne away on this streaming tide of damp darkness; his brain was no longer in control, his legs walked of their own accord, and his animal instincts carried him along. It was then, without intending to do so, that he pushed open the door to the Buteaus' house and found himself in the kitchen again.

Buteau and Lise were just finishing yesterday's cabbage soup. When he heard the door he turned round and looked at Fouan, who said nothing, his clothes dripping wet and steaming. There was a long silence.

'I knew you wouldn't have the guts!' sneered Buteau, finally.

The old man stood there, inscrutable and motionless. He did not say a word.

'Come on, wife, you can give him his feed, he's come back because he's hungry.'

Lise had already got up and brought a plate of soup, but Fouan took it and sat at the side on a stool as though refusing to join his children at table. He drank it up greedily in big spoonfuls, and his hunger was so desperate that his whole body trembled. Buteau finished his meal unhurriedly, rocking on his chair, picking up pieces of cheese from a distance and eating them off the tip of his knife. He was watching the old man, as he ate greedily, and he followed the movements of the spoon, mocking him.

'My word! Your walk in the fresh air seems to have given you an appetite! You mustn't do that every day, it would cost too much to feed you!'

His father went on noisily swallowing the food but he did not say a word. The son went on talking.

'So the old devil sleeps out at night! Perhaps he went to see the girls! Perhaps that's how you got such an appetite, was it?'

There was still no reply, still the same obstinate silence, only the violent gulping sound as he swallowed great spoonfuls of soup.

'Hey, I'm talking to you,' shouted Buteau irritably, 'at least you could be polite enough to answer me!'

Fouan did not even raise his staring, anxious eyes from the soup-plate. He seemed blind and deaf, as though he were alone, miles away, and wanted to show that he had come back only for food, pretending that his stomach was there but his heart was not. Then he scraped the bottom of the soup-plate with his spoon in order to get the last drop. Lise was moved when she saw how hungry he was and allowed herself to intervene.

'Leave him alone, if he wants to keep quiet.'

'He's not going to start treating me like dirt again,' Buteau went on angrily. 'I'll let it pass this time. Are you listening, you obstinate old devil? Let it be a lesson to you. If you bother me any longer I'll let you die of hunger out on the road.'

When Fouan had finished he rose from his chair with difficulty, still preserving a deathly silence, which seemed to grow even deeper; he turned his back and dragged himself under the stairs to his bed, where he flung himself down fully clothed. Sleep overwhelmed him at once, and he did not seem to be breathing, as though crushed by exhaustion. Lise went to look at him and told her husband that he was probably dead. Buteau went too but shrugged his shoulders. Oh, no, old men didn't die like that, but he must have walked a long way to be in such a state. Next morning, when they went in to have a look the old man had not moved and he was still asleep in the evening. He did not wake up until the second morning, after thirty-six hours of unconsciousness.

'Oh, so there you are again!' said Buteau with a sneer. 'I thought you'd go on sleeping and wouldn't be eating any more bread.'

The old man neither looked at him nor replied, but went out to sit down at the side of the road and take the air.

Then Fouan became obstinate. He seemed to have forgotten the deeds which they had refused to give back to him. At least he said no more about them and did not look for them. Perhaps he was indifferent, in any case resigned. But his break with the Buteaus was complete; he remained silent as though he were isolated and buried. Never, in any circumstances, for any reason, did he speak a word to them. Communal life continued; he slept and ate there, he saw them, was close to them from morning till night, but there was no glance, no word. He seemed to be blind and dumb. He dragged himself about like a ghost among the living. When they were tired of paying attention to him and getting no response they left him to it. Buteau and even Lise herself also stopped speaking to him; they tolerated him like a piece of furniture which had been moved, and finally they ceased to be aware of his presence. The horse and the two cows were more important.

Buteau acted on his father's behalf, receiving money and signing for it on the pretext that the old man was weak in the head. The allowance of a hundred and fifty francs coming from the sale of the house was paid directly to him by Monsieur Baillehache. He had difficulty only with Delhomme, who had refused to pay the two hundred francs' allowance to anyone except to his father-in-law. Delhomme demanded that he should be present, but as soon as his back was turned Buteau seized the money. That made three hundred and fifty francs, but he complained that he could add as much and more without having enough to feed the old man. They never mentioned the deeds again. They slumbered there; they would see about them later. As for the interest payments, he alleged that they still served to pay off the money due to Old Saucisse under the agreement, fifteen sous every morning for the purchase of an acre and a quarter of land. He insisted that this contract could not be dropped for there was too much money involved. However, there was a rumour that Old Saucisse had been threatened and in terror he had agreed to break the contract and give him back half the money he had received, a thousand francs out of two thousand, and if the old twister kept quiet it was only because he was a vain old rogue who did not want to be caught in his turn. Buteau sensed that Old Fouan would die first, for he felt that if the old man were given a push he would certainly not be able to get up again.

Fouan, whose obstinate pride had stopped him from returning to the Delhommes, for he had been cut to the quick by his daughter's remark, succeeded in enduring everything in the Buteau household, from unpleasant remarks to blows. He no longer thought of his other children. He accepted things in such total resignation that the idea of leaving never occurred to him at all. Things would be no better anywhere else, so why go? Whenever Fanny met him she passed by unmoved, having sworn that she would never be the first to speak to him again. Jésus-Christ, who was more good-natured, had been angry with him over the unpleasant way in which he had left the Château, but he had amused himself one evening by making him horribly drunk at Lengaigne's tavern, then taking him back to the Buteau house, causing a fearful scene and throwing the house into an uproar.

Fouan lost his last interest in life when he could no longer walk. It soon became so painful for him that he could barely go further than the village. On fine days he had three or four favourite resting-places: the logs in front of Clou's forge, the bridge over the Aigre, and a stone bench near the school. He went slowly from one to the other, taking an hour to go two hundred yards, dragging his sabots as though they were heavy carts, and his whole body was misshapen as he lurched unevenly along. Often he would forget himself for a whole afternoon, sitting hunched up at the end of a beam, drinking in the sunshine. He sat there dazed and still, with his eyes open. People passing by no longer greeted him, for he had become an object. His pipe was too tiring for him and he stopped smoking for it weighed too heavily on his gums, while the effort of filling and lighting it exhausted him. He wanted only to sit quite still, for he became cold and shivery as soon as he moved, even in the hot midday sun. After the loss of his will-power and authority he had reached the final degeneration, like an old, ailing abandoned animal, aware of the wretchedness of having once lived like a man.

'Well, Fouan,' a neighbour asked him on one occasion, 'you're still going strong?'

'Oh,' he grunted, 'it takes a devil of a long time to die, but it isn't because I don't want to.'

And he meant what he said, for with peasant stoicism he accepted death and had longed for it ever since he had given up his property and the earth claimed him again.

3

THE winter ploughing was almost finished and one dark, cold February afternoon Jean had just taken his plough to his big field at Les Cornailles where he still had to do two good hours' work. He wanted to sow one end of the field with a Scottish variety of wheat, an experiment which had been advised by his former master, Hourdequin, who had even put a few bushels of seed at his disposal. He took care to plough a perfectly straight furrow, so straight that it looked as though it had been marked out with string. His horse, its head lowered, its feet sinking into the soil, drew the plough at an even continuous pace. Whenever the ploughshare got stuck Jean freed it of mud and weeds by shaking both wrists until it slid forward again, leaving behind it soil which moved as though it was alive, rich-looking and banked up, bared to its entrails.

When he reached the end of the furrow he turned and began another; soon he was almost intoxicated by the amount of earth he had turned over, for it gave off a strong smell, the smell of dark secret places where seeds germinate. His heavy tread and fixed gaze left him finally in a be-wildered state. He would never become a real peasant. He was not born to the soil; he remained a former town worker, a trooper who had been through the Italian campaign. He could see and feel what peasants do not see or feel, the vast, sad tranquillity of the plain, the deep breathing of the earth in sunshine and rain. He had always dreamt of retiring to the countryside, but how silly he had been to imagine that on the day when he put down his gun and his plane the plough would satisfy his desire for peace and quiet! The earth was calm and good to those who loved it but the villages that clung to it like nests of vermin, the human insects living off its flesh, were enough to dishonour it and poison the atmosphere. He could not remember ever having suffered as much as he had done since the distant day when he had arrived at La Borderie.

Yes, indeed, what unhappiness these ten years had brought! First of all his long wait for Françoise, and then the hostility with the Buteaus. Not one day had passed without some unpleasant incident, and now that he had Françoise and they had been married for two years, could he

say that he was really happy? He still loved her but he had
seen clearly that she did not love him, that she would never
love him as he would like to have been loved, with open
arms and open heart. They lived together happily, their
household prospered, they worked and saved. But it was
not satisfactory, somehow, he felt that she was distant and
cold, preoccupied with something else, even when he held
her close to him in bed. She was now five months pregnant,
and the child had been conceived without pleasure, which
can only mean unhappiness for the mother. The thought of
the child had not even brought them closer together.
Jean suffered in particular from an impression which became increasingly clear to him and he had even been aware
of it the night when they went into their house, a feeling
that he would remain a stranger to his wife, a man from
another district, reared elsewhere, no one knew where; a
man who did not think like the men of Rognes, who seemed
built in a different way, without any possible link with her,
although he had given her this baby. One Saturday just
after their marriage, when she had been furious with the
Buteaus, she had brought back from Cloyes a sheet of
stamped paper so that she could make a will and leave all
her property to her husband, for it had been explained to
her how the house and the land would revert to her sister
if she were to die without heirs, while only money and
furniture were joint property of husband and wife. Then
without any explanation, she seemed to have changed her
mind. The sheet of paper was still in the cupboard and it
was blank. Jean had felt a deep and secret sorrow over this,
although he was an interested party, but he saw in it a lack
of affection. As he stopped and let his horse rest he was
surprised to notice Old Fouan coming along the new road
from Rognes.

Jean was just finishing his ploughing when Delhomme,
who was returning on foot from a neighbouring farm,
stopped at the edge of the field.

'I say, Corporal, have you heard the news? It looks as
though there's going to be a war.'

'War? Who with?'

'The Prussians, so they tell me. It's in the papers.'

Jean stared in front of him. Memories of Italy returned,
he saw again the murderous battles, from which he had
been lucky enough to escape without being hurt. At that

time he had looked forward so ardently to living a quiet life somewhere, and to think that this mention of war by a passer-by on the road set all his blood alight!

'But, good God, we can't let the Prussians play hell with us!'

Delhomme did not agree with him. He shook his head and said it would be the end of the countryside if the Cossacks came again, as they had done after Napoleon. Fighting didn't do anyone any good, it was more sensible to get on well together.

'I think other people can do the fighting. I've deposited money with Monsieur Baillehache. The young men are drawing lots tomorrow, but whatever happens, Nénesse won't go to the front.'

'Yes, of course,' said Jean, who felt calmer now. 'I'm the same, I don't owe the country anything more, and now that I'm married I don't care a damn if there's any fighting. So it's the Prussians! Well, they'll get a thrashing, that's all!'

'Goodbye, Corporal.'

'Goodbye!'

Jean had finished ploughing and decided to go to La Borderie straight away to get the seed he had been promised. He left the plough at the end of the field and leapt on his horse. As he rode away he thought of Old Fouan again but when he looked round he could not see him anywhere. The old man must have gone to shelter from the cold behind a stack of straw in the Buteaus' field.

When he reached La Borderie Jean called out but could get no answer; everyone must have been working outside. He went into the empty kitchen and when he rapped on the table, he heard Jacqueline's voice coming up from the dairy in the cellar. It was reached through a trap-door which opened right at the foot of the stairs, so badly placed that everyone was always afraid of accidents.

'Hello, who is it?'

He knelt down on the top step of the steep little staircase and she recognized him from below.

'Well, it's you, Corporal!'

He could see her too, in the dim light which came through a grating in the dairy wall. She was working there among the bowls and pans. Her sleeves were rolled up to her arm-pits and her naked arms were white all over with cream.

'Come down then . . . You're not frightened of me, are you?'

She spoke in the same familiar tone as she had done in the past and laughed in her usual attractive way. But he felt embarrassed and did not move.

'I've come for the seed that the master promised me.'

'Oh, yes, I know . . . Wait, I'll come up.'

And when she emerged into the full daylight he could see how fresh she looked, with her bare white arms and the wholesome smell of milk about her. She looked at him with her pretty perverse eyes.

'Well, aren't you going to kiss me?' she asked him in the end, jokingly. 'You don't have to be impolite just because you're a married man now!'

He kissed her, pretending to peck her on both cheeks, to show that they were just good friends. But she disturbed him, physical memories excited him and a slight shudder ran through his whole body. Although he loved his wife so much, he had never felt like this when he was close to her.

'Well, come on,' said Jacqueline, 'I'll show you the seed. Just imagine, even the kitchen-maid's gone to the market.'

She went across the yard and into the barn, going behind a heap of sacks. It was there, lying in a heap against the wall, kept in place by planks of wood. He had followed her, and felt slightly disturbed at being alone with her in this deserted spot. He at once pretended to be interested in the wheat, which was a fine Scotch variety.

'Oh, how big the seeds are!'

But she laughed her cooing laugh and brought him quickly back to the subject which interested her.

'Your wife's expecting, I hear, you've been going strong, haven't you? Tell me, is it good with her, is it as nice as with me?'

He flushed deeply, and she was delighted to see the effect she had on him.

'Are you still going with Tron?'

She didn't seem upset and spoke freely, treating him like an old friend.

'Oh, he's all right, the big silly, but you know he's not very sensible. He isn't half jealous! Oh yes, he makes scenes, he won't let me have anyone except the master, and even then he doesn't like it. I think he comes at night to listen and make sure we're sleeping.'

Jean laughed, but she did not, for she was secretly terrified of the giant, saying he was crafty and not to be trusted, like all the Percherons. He had threatened to strangle her if she was unfaithful to him. She was afraid whenever she went with him, in spite of her liking for his big limbs. She was so slim that he could have crushed her between the fingers of one hand. But she shrugged her shoulders prettily, as though to say she had coped with worse.

'You know, Corporal,' she went on with a smile, 'it was better with you, we got on so well.'

She went on looking at him with her fascinating eyes, and plunged her arms into the wheat. He was caught again, he forgot he had left the farm, that he was married, that his wife was expecting a child. He seized her wrists right down in the seed, his hands moved up her arms, which were white over with flour, right up to her girlish breasts which seemed to have grown hard with too much lovemaking. This was what she had wanted ever since she had caught sight of him above the trap-door; she wanted him again, and she wanted the vicious pleasure of taking him away from another woman, his legitimate wife. He took hold of her and pushed her down on the heap of corn, she was enraptured and cooed with delight. Suddenly a tall thin figure appeared behind the sacks. It was Soulas the shepherd, coughing violently and spitting. Jacqueline leapt to her feet, and Jean muttered breathlessly,

'Very well, then, I'll come back and take some . . . The seeds are so big!'

She was furious. The shepherd did not go away.

'It's really too much this time,' she muttered through clenched teeth, looking at his back. 'Even when I think I'm alone he comes to bother me. I'll have him thrown out all right.'

Jean had cooled down; he left the barn quickly and untied his horse in the yard, ignoring the signs from Jacqueline, who would have concealed him in the farmer's bedroom rather than give up her pleasure. But he wanted to escape and repeated that he would come back the next day. He set off on foot, holding his horse by the bridle, but as he reached the gate he saw that Soulas was waiting for him.

'So there's no honesty in the world,' said the old shepherd, 'if you come back to her too? Kindly tell her to keep her mouth shut, if she wants me to do the same. Oh, there'll be ructions, just you wait!'

Jean replied only with a rough gesture, refusing to be involved any further. He was ashamed of himself and angry at what he had almost done. He thought he loved Françoise, but her presence no longer roused him to these moments of wild desire. Did it mean he loved Jacqueline more? Had that bitch really got some hold over him? All the past came back to him and he felt angrier still when he realized he would come back to her yet again, in spite of his revulsion. He shuddered as he leapt on his horse and set off at a gallop, in order to get back to Rognes more quickly.

That afternoon, as it happened, Françoise had decided to go and cut some lucerne for her cows. She usually did this work herself and as she set off she thought she would see her husband ploughing the field nearby; she did not care to risk going there on her own, for she was afraid of meeting the Buteaus, who were so angry at no longer owning the entire field that they were always trying to pick some unpleasant quarrel or other. As she reached Les Cornailles she was surprised to see Jean nowhere about, although she had not told him she was coming. The plough was there, so where on earth could he be? She was terribly upset then at the sight of the Buteaus, who were standing by the field waving their arms in fury. For a moment she was on the point of turning back, but then she was indignant at being afraid, for she had every right to go to her own land. So she went on, carrying her scythe over her shoulder.

The truth of the matter was that whenever Françoise met Buteau like this, especially when he was alone, she felt very upset. She had not spoken to him for two years, but whenever she saw him a tremor ran through her entire body. Perhaps it was anger, perhaps it was something else too. On several previous occasions on her way to the lucerne patch she had caught sight of him like this. He turned his head once, twice, three times, and looked at her with his yellow-grey eyes. She shuddered slightly and quickened her pace in spite of herself, while he began to walk more slowly. The last time they had met she had been so frightened and so hampered by her big belly that when she tried to step from the road into the lucerne patch she had fallen down flat; and he had burst out laughing.

That evening, when Buteau maliciously told Lise how her sister had fallen down they looked at each other with a glance that revealed the same thought: if the little bitch had killed herself and her child too, her husband would be left with nothing, the land and the house would revert to them. La Grande had told them about the will which had been postponed since the coming child had made it superfluous. Just think—suppose Françoise were to die without an heir, how satisfactory that would be, what a stroke of divine justice! Lise's hatred had become so venomous that in the end she disowned her sister and swore she would hold her head down on the executioner's block if it would get them back their home, after the blasted girl had thrown them out in such a disgusting way. Buteau was not so demanding, and declared only that it would be a good thing if the kid pegged out before it was born.

Then, when the two of them went to bed and she blew out the candle, Lise laughed in a strange way, saying that until a brat had actually come there were ways of stopping it. Silence fell, then he asked why she spoke like that. Lying close against him, whispering in his ear, she made a confession; last month she'd been upset to find she'd been caught again and so, without telling him, she had gone to see La Sapin, an old woman in Magnolles who was a witch. He'd have been delighted, wouldn't he, if she'd told him she was expecting again! La Sapin had simply got rid of it with a needle. He listened, indicating neither approval nor disapproval, showing his satisfaction only by saying as a joke that she should have got hold of the needle to use it on Françoise. She laughed too, and threw her arms round him, whispering that La Sapin had told her another way it could be done, such a funny way! Oh, how? Well, a man could undo what another man had done—he only had to lay the woman, make the sign of the cross on her stomach three times and recite an *Ave* backwards. Then any baby that was there would disappear into thin air. Buteau stopped laughing, they pretended they didn't believe it, but the ancient superstitions which lay in their very bones made them shudder, for everyone knew that the old woman in Magnolles had turned a cow into a weasel and brought a dead man back to life. If she said that this method would work, then it must be true. Lise asked him very coyly, if he would try the *Ave* in reverse and the three signs of the cross, so that she could see whether she felt anything. No, nothing! So the needle must have done the trick. It would have done real harm to Françoise. He laughed, wondering if he could do it. Oh, well, why not, since he had had her already? Never! Now he protested, while his wife dug her nails into his flesh in a fit of jealousy. They fell asleep in each other's arms.

From that night the thought of the coming child who would take their house and land from them forever haunted them, and whenever they met the girl they immediately looked at her stomach. When they saw her coming along the path they summed her up and were alarmed to find that the pregnancy was well advanced and that it would soon be too late to do anything.

'By God,' yelled Buteau, as he returned from the ploughed field that he was examining, 'that thief has taken off at least a foot of our land! He can't deny it, there's the boundary.'

Françoise had continued to approach, walking calmly along in the same way, concealing her fear. Then she understood the reason for their angry gestures, for Jean's plough must have made inroads on their land. Boundary disputes of this kind were continually arising and never a month passed without some violent argument between the four of them. It was bound to end in blows and law-suits one day.

'Do you hear?' Buteau went on, raising his voice, 'you've come on to our ground, I'll make you pay for this!'

Françoise did not even turn her head and went into her lucerne patch.

'We're talking to you!' shouted Lise, beside herself. 'Come and look at the boundary, if you think we're lying. You've got to see the damage.'

Her sister's silence and apparent contempt made her lose all sense of proportion. She walked towards her, clenching her fists.

'Listen, what the hell do you think you're doing? I'm your elder sister, you ought to respect me. I'll make you go down on your knees and ask forgiveness for all the dirty tricks you've played on me.'

She stood in front of her, blind with rage and spite.

'Down on your knees, you bitch!'

Françoise said nothing, but she spat in her sister's face, just as she had done when the other couple had been turned out of the house. Lise shrieked, then Buteau intervened, pushing her roughly out of the way.

'Leave her alone, this is my business!'

Oh, yes, he could deal with her! He could twist her neck and break her back like any rotten tree! He could grind her up into food for the dogs or use her like a tart. She wouldn't stop him, she'd be glad to help. And from that moment she drew herself up and kept a look out to make sure that nobody disturbed him.

'Get on with it then, there's no one about!'

Buteau walked towards Françoise, and when she saw him, with the hard look on his face and his arms tense, she thought he was going to strike her. She had not put down her scythe, but she was trembling. He caught hold of the handle, snatched it from her and threw it into the lucerne. Her only chance of escape now was to go back, and she went into the neighbouring field, moving towards the stack that stood there, as though she hoped it might protect her. He did not hurry in any way and seemed also to be driving her in that direction, gradually opening his arms wider, his face now relaxed in silent laughter which bared his gums. Suddenly she realized that he didn't want to beat her. No, he wanted something else, he wanted what she had refused him for so long. Then she trembled more violently, as she felt her strength ebbing away, she who had been so firm in the past and fought back so hard, swearing he would never get her. Yet she wasn't a child any more, she had been twenty-three on St. Martin's Day, she was a woman now, with lips that were still red and eyes as big as silver coins. She was aware of a melting sensation, her limbs became so warm and soft that she could hardly walk.

But Buteau still forced her backwards.

'You know it's not all over between us yet,' he said at last, in a low passionate voice. 'I want you and I'll have you.'

He had succeeded in getting her with her back against the rick. He seized her by the shoulders and threw her down on the ground. Then she began to struggle desperately, as she had always done during the years she had resisted him. He held her firmly and avoided her kicks.

188

'You're expecting already, you bloody fool, there's no risk: I won't give you another one, you can be sure of that.'

She burst into tears, a kind of hysteria seized her, she defended herself no longer, her arms and legs twitched nervously; he couldn't take her, for at each attempt she threw him to one side. Anger made him brutal and he turned towards his wife.

'Don't be so blasted lazy! What's the good of standing there watching? Give me a hand, get hold of her legs, if you want me to do it!'

Lise had remained standing motionless ten yards away, alternately scanning the distant horizon and watching the others, her face completely expressionless. When her husband called her she did not hesitate; she came forward, seized her sister's left leg, pulled it away from the other and then sat on it, crushing it with her weight. As she lay pinned to the ground, Françoise went limp, her nerves shattered, her eyes closed. Yet she was still conscious, and as Buteau took her she was carried away by such a thrill of pleasure that she clasped him violently with both arms, uttering a long cry. Rooks that were flying overhead were frightened by the sound. Above the rick appeared the pale face of Old Fouan, who had been sheltering there from the cold. He had seen everything and he must have been afraid, for he concealed himself in the straw again.

Buteau got up, and Lise stared at him. She had been concerned only with one thing, to make sure that he did all that was necessary; he had been so absorbed that he had forgotten the whole point of it, the sign of the cross and the *Ave* repeated backwards. She was shattered. So he had done it for his own pleasure!

But Françoise left him no time to explain himself. For a moment she had remained on the ground, yielding as it were to the violent pleasure of love which she had never experienced before. Suddenly she knew the truth: she loved Buteau, she had never loved anyone else, she never would. This discovery filled her with shame and fury, for all her notions of justice were aroused. A man who was not hers, the man who belonged to the sister she hated, the only man she could never have without being a bitch! And she had just let him go the whole way, she had held him so tightly that he must have known she loved him.

189

She leapt up, distraught and untidy, spitting out her suffering in broken phrases.

'You filthy swine! Yes, both of you! You've destroyed me!'

'People get guillotined for less! I'll tell Jean, you bastards! He'll deal with you!'

Buteau cheerfully shrugged his shoulders, pleased that he'd got his way in the end.

'Don't make such a fuss. You were dying for it, I could feel you going it all right. We'll try it again one day.'

This joke brought Lise's rising anger to a head, and all the accumulated fury caused by her husband's behaviour now broke over her younger sister.

'It's true, you whore, I saw you! You got hold of him, you forced him to do it! I always said you were at the back of all my troubles! Just you dare tell me now that you didn't seduce my husband, yes you did, the very day after we were married, when I was still wiping your nose for you!'

Her jealousy broke out, coming strangely after the way she had let Buteau go ahead, but it was caused not so much by what had just happened but by the fact that her sister had taken away half of everything that was hers. If this sister had never been born she wouldn't have had to share everything with her. She detested her for being younger, fresher, and more desirable.

'You're lying,' cried Françoise. 'You know very well you're lying!'

'Oh, it's a lie, is it? So you weren't after him, you never even chased him down into the cellar?'

'Me? And just now, did I do it? You cow, you held me down, yes, you nearly broke my leg. I don't understand, you must be some revolting creature or else you want to kill me, you bitch!'

Lise replied with a swinging blow. This brutality drove Françoise mad and she rushed at her. Buteau didn't interfere now, he stood sniggering with his hands in his pockets, like some vain cockerel watching two hens fighting over him. The struggle went on, becoming furious and vicious, bonnets were torn off, the women buried their nails in each others' flesh at every vulnerable spot. They had pushed each other back into the lucerne field. Lise screamed, Françoise dug her nails into her neck; then she saw red, she conceived the clear-cut, desperate wish to kill her sister. To the left of Françoise she caught sight of the scythe, the handle lying across a tuft of thistles, the blade pointing upwards. In a flash she knocked Françoise over with all the strength she possessed. The wretched girl stumbled, turned, and fell to the left, uttering a terrible cry.

The scythe had pierced her side.

'My God, my God!' stammered Buteau.

It was all over. It had taken only one second, the irreparable deed was done. Lise, aghast to see her wish fulfilled so quickly, saw the torn clothes drenched with blood. The blade must have pierced through to the child in the womb, for why should there be so much blood? Old Fouan's pale face appeared over the rick once again. He had seen what had happened, and he blinked anxiously.

Françoise no longer moved, Buteau came up to her but dared not touch her. A gust of wind blew and froze him to the marrow, while his hair stood on end as he shuddered with terror. He grasped Lise by the hand and some unknown force drove them along the deserted road. The low sombre sky seemed to come down on top of their heads. The rush of their footsteps sounded like a crowd of people sent to pursue them; they ran over the bare lonely plain, Buteau's smock billowing out, Lise carrying her bonnet in her hand, her hair flying loose, both of them panting out the same words.

'She's dead!' they cried, like hunted beasts. 'My God, let's run!'

They ran faster, and they said nothing more, unconsciously uttering vague sounds in tune with their flying feet.

'Dead, my God!' The words came through their snivelling. 'Dead, my God! my God!'

They disappeared.

A few minutes later, when Jean came trotting back on his horse he was horrified.

'What on earth's happened?'

Françoise had opened her eyes again but she still did not move. She looked at him sadly for a long time. She made no answer, as though she were already far away, thinking of other things.

'You're hurt, you're bleeding, answer me, I beg you!'

Old Fouan came up and Jean turned to him.

'You were there, what happened?'

Then Françoise replied, speaking slowly.

'I came for some grass. I fell on my scythe . . . Oh, it's all over!'

She looked at Fouan, her eyes told him something else, something that only he and the family should know about. In spite of his dazed look the old man seemed to understand.

'Yes, it's true,' he repeated, 'she fell, she hurt herself. I was there, I saw her.'

Jean had to run to Rognes to find a stretcher. On the way back she fainted again. They were afraid they would not get her back alive.

4

THE very next day, a Sunday, the young men of Rognes were going to Cloyes to draw lots for military service, and just as La Grande and La Frimat rushed along to undress Françoise and put her to bed with the greatest possible care, the drum was beating down on the road, sounding a real knell for the wretched world from the depths of the gloomy dusk.

Jean had lost his head; he had set off to find Doctor Finet, when near the church he met Patoir, the vet, who had come to attend to Old Saucisse's horse. He forced him to come and look at the injured woman, although the other tried to say no. When he saw the appalling wound he refused point-blank to do anything. It was useless, there was nothing to be done. When Jean brought back Monsieur Finet two hours later the doctor reacted in the same way. There was no hope, he could only give sedatives to ease the agony. The five months' pregnancy complicated the case, the baby was moving, dying from its mother's death, for the flank of her fecund body had been torn open. The doctor tried to bandage the patient but before he left, promising to come back the next day, he declared that the poor woman would not live through the night. But she did, all the same, and was still alive the next morning when, at about nine o'clock, the drum began to beat again, summoning the conscripts to assemble before the school.

It had rained all night, Jean had heard a real deluge

falling as he sat at the back of the bedroom, in a dazed state, huge tears gathering in his eyes. Now he could hear the drum, as though muffled in crêpe, through the damp, mild, morning air. The rain had stopped, but the sky had remained a leaden grey.

Doctor Finet did not reappear until about ten o'clock, and seemed very surprised to find Françoise still alive, for he thought he would have nothing to do beyond writing the death certificate. He examined the wound and nodded, preoccupied by the story that he had heard, although he suspected nothing. They had to tell him about it again; how the devil had this wretched girl managed to fall on to the blade of a scythe? He left again, outraged by this clumsiness and annoyed because he would have to come back again to sign the death certificate. But Jean had remained gloomy, watching Françoise, who closed her eyes in silence whenever she felt her husband's questioning look upon her. He guessed that someone had lied, and that she was hiding something from him. At dawn he had slipped out for a moment and run to the lucerne patch, for he wanted to look at it; he could see nothing definite, footsteps obliterated by the pouring rain during the night, a patch of ground which had been trampled over, no doubt where Françoise had fallen. After the doctor had gone he sat down again by the dying girl's bedside, alone with her, for La Frimat had gone to have her dinner and La Grande had had to go to look at her own house.

'Are you in pain? Tell me!'

She closed her eyes tightly and did not reply.

'Tell me, you're not hiding something from me, are you?'

She might have been dead already, if it had not been for her painful rapid breathing. Since the day before she had been lying on her back, and seemed stricken with stillness and silence. She was consumed with high fever but her will-power, in the depths of her being, seemed to stiffen and resist any delirium, for she was so afraid of uttering a word. Her character had always been strange, she was damned obstinate, people used to say, as obstinate as all the Fouans, never doing what other people did, and she had notions which staggered outsiders. Perhaps she was following some deep family feeling, something stronger than hatred and the need for revenge. What was the use, since she was going to die? These things were buried with the family, in the district where they had all grown up, things which must never, at any price, be mentioned before a stranger; and Jean was the stranger, this young man whom she had never been able to love, whose child she was carrying, the child who would never be born, who was lost now, as though she was being punished for having started it.

But ever since he had brought her back dying, Jean had thought of the will. All night the idea had kept on recurring to him that if she died like this he would only have half of the furniture and the money, a hundred and twenty-seven francs, which was in the cupboard. He loved her well enough, he would have given his eyes to keep her, but what deepened his sorrow was the thought that in losing her he might lose the land and the house. Yet until now he had not dared to speak to her about it; it was so hard, and then there had always been people there. In the end, when he realized that he would never know any more about how the accident had happened, he mentioned the other problem.

'Perhaps you have some matters to settle?'

Françoise lay there tensely and did not seem to have heard. There was no change in her closed eyes and inscrutable face.

'You know, because of your sister, in case you come to any harm. We've got the paper there, in the cupboard.'

He brought her the stamped paper and as he went on, his voice became embarrassed.

'Would you like me to help you? I don't know if you've still got the strength to write. It's not for me, it's just the idea that you wouldn't want to leave anything to the people who've done you so much harm.'

Her eyelids flickered slightly, proving that she had heard. But she refused, and he was left astonished, unable to understand. Probably she herself could not have said why she was pretending to be dead like this, before she was nailed into her coffin. The land and the house did not belong to this man who had come into her life by chance, like some passer-by. She owed him nothing, the child would go with her. On what authority would the property pass out of the family? Her childish, obstinate conception of justice protested: this is mine, this is yours, let's part and say goodbye. Yes, it was like that, and there were other vaguer things too, her sister Lise had faded and vanished into the past, only

Buteau was present, and in spite of his cruelty she loved him, desired him, and forgave him.

But Jean became angry, for the same passion for the earth had possessed him and poisoned his soul. He raised her, tried to sit her up and place a pen between her fingers.

'Now come, it's impossible! Surely you don't love them more than me, those villains will have everything!'

Then at last Françoise opened her eyes and he was shattered by the look she gave him. She knew she was going to die, her eyes seemed to grow larger and they revealed a look of utter despair. Why did he torment her? She couldn't, she wouldn't. She uttered only a low cry of pain. Then she fell back, her eyes closed again, and in the centre of the pillow her head no longer moved.

Jean was ashamed of his brutality and felt so uneasy that he was still holding the paper in his hand when La Grande came back. She understood and took him aside, asking whether there was a will. He stammered out a lie, saying that precisely he was hiding the paper for fear that Françoise was upset. La Grande appeared to approve, still remaining on the side of the Buteaus, for she foresaw that terrible things would happen if they were the heirs. She sat down by the table and began to knit again.

'I'll certainly cause no trouble to anyone . . . My will's been in order for a long time. Everyone's got his share, it wouldn't be honest if I gave preference to anyone . . . You're in it, children. It'll come one day!'

Jean was not listening; he was looking vacantly out of the window. Ever since the morning he had noticed that Old Fouan had come to the house several times, dragging himself round on his two sticks. Suddenly he saw him again, his face glued to a window pane, trying to make out things in the bedroom; Jean opened the window and the old man was quite taken aback, muttering that he had come to ask how things were going. Very badly, the end had come. Then he craned his neck and gazed at Françoise from a distance for so long that he looked as though he could not tear himself away. When Fanny and La Grande caught sight of him they said again that Lise should be sent for. Everyone in the family must come, things couldn't end like this. But when they wanted to send him for her the old man was frightened and went off, shivering. He muttered brokenly between his gums:

'No, no, impossible, impossible.'

Jean was struck by his fear, while the women gave up trying. After all, it was the sisters' own affair, nobody would force them to become reconciled. At that moment a sound was heard, faint at first, like the buzzing of a big fly, then it grew stronger and stronger, like a gust of wind blowing through the trees.

'It's the drum,' said Fanny, with a start. 'There it is! Goodbye.'

She vanished, without even kissing her cousin for the last time.

La Grande and La Frimat had gone to the door to see. Françoise and Jean were left alone; perhaps, in her stubborn, motionless silence she heard everything, and wanted to die like some animal run to earth in the depths of its hole; he stood in front of the open window, torn by uncertainty and drowned in sorrow which seemed to come from people and things, from the whole immense plain. Oh, how the sound of the drum swelled and throbbed through his whole being, the unending sound that brought back distant memories to mingle with his present sorrow, memories of barracks, battles, and the miserable life of the poor wretches who had neither wife nor children to love them!

Then he heard the women moving about and whispering. He shuddered at the sound. Françoise was dead. She had not opened her eyes or spoken again. She seemed to be sleeping, her face was very white, thin, and stubborn.

A shadowy form moved away from the window and rushed off into the darkness. Jean thought it must be some dog on the prowl. It was Buteau, who was running to tell Lise that her sister was dead.

5

THE next morning Françoise's body was laid out and the coffin was placed across two chairs in the middle of the bedroom. Jean was surprised and indignant when he suddenly saw Lise and Buteau enter one after the other. His first instinct was to throw them out at once, for these heartless relations had not even come to kiss the dying girl for the last time, but they now arrived the moment the coffin lid was nailed down, as though relieved they would never see her again. But the members of the family who were present, Fanny and La Grande, stopped him. Quarrels round a corpse brought bad luck, and in any case nobody could stop Lise making amends for her bitterness by deciding to keep vigil over her sister's body.

And the Buteaus, who had relied on the respect due to the dead, moved in. They did not say they were taking possession of the house again, they merely did so quite naturally, as if it went without saying now that Françoise was no longer alive. Lise sat down for a moment and then so far forgot herself as to open the cupboards and make sure that the things had not been moved during her absence. Buteau was already wandering round the stable and the cowshed as though he owned them. By evening both of them seemed to have settled in again. The one thing that embarrassed them was the coffin, which occupied the centre of the bedroom, but they only had to be patient for one more night. Next day there would be room enough from early in the morning.

Jean paced up and down among the family, looking lost and not knowing what to do with himself. At first the house, the furniture, and Françoise's body seemed to be his, but as the hours passed everything appeared to detach itself from him and pass into the hands of the others. By nightfall nobody spoke to him any more; he was no more than an outsider whom they tolerated. He had never felt so painfully aware of being a stranger and having no relative of his own among these people who were all linked by family ties and all thought the same way when it came to excluding him. Even his poor dead wife no longer belonged to him, so much so that Fanny, when he spoke of keeping vigil by the corpse, tried to send him away, saying there were too many people there; but he persisted and had even thought of taking the hundred and twenty-seven francs out of the cupboard, to make certain it would not fly away. Lise must have seen the money when she opened the drawer, along with the sheet of stamped paper, for she had begun to whisper rapidly to La Grande. It was after that, when she was certain that there was no will, that she settled down again in the house so comfortably. But she wouldn't have the money. Jean was afraid of what might happen the next day and told himself that at least he would keep that. Then he sat up all night on a chair.

The funeral took place early next day at nine o'clock. The Charleses came, as well as Delhomme and Nénesse. It was a respectable funeral and nothing was overdone. Jean wept, Buteau wiped his eyes. At the last moment Lise had said that her legs were giving way and she'd never find the strength to follow her poor sister's body. So she remained alone in the house while La Grande, Fanny, La Frimat, La Bécu and other neighbours went to the cemetery, on the way back they all lingered purposely in front of the church and finally witnessed the scene which they had anticipated since the previous day.

Until then the two men, Jean and Buteau, had avoided each other's eyes, for they were afraid a fight would break out before Françoise's body had grown cold. Now they both walked towards the house with the same resolute air and glanced at each other sideways; they would see. Jean immediately realized why Lise had not attended the funeral; she had wanted to stay on her own so that she could at least bring in most of her things. An hour had been enough, she had thrown the bundle over La Frimat's wall, and moved the more breakable things in a wheelbarrow. She had brought Laura and Jules back into the yard, boxing their ears while she was about it, and they were already having a fight there, while Old Fouan, whom she had also pushed round, was having a rest on the bench to get his breath back. The house had been reconquered.

'Where are you going?' Buteau asked sharply, stopping Jean in front of the door.

'I'm going home.'

'Home? D'you call this home? This isn't your home, it's ours.'

Lise had run up and yelled out insults even more violent.

'Well, what does that rotter want? He'd been poisoning my poor sister long enough, that's quite obvious, otherwise she wouldn't have died from the accident. She showed how she felt because she's left him nothing. Hit him, Buteau! Don't let him come in, he'll pass the disease on to us!'

Jean was shattered by this harsh attack and tried to discuss things again.

'I know that the house and land revert to you, but I have half of the furniture and the livestock.'

'Half? You've got a cheek!' went on Lise, interrupting him. 'You filthy pimp, you dare take half of anything! You didn't even bring a comb here with you and all you had was the shirt on your back. You wait for women to bring you property, that's a dirty way to live!'

Buteau supported her and made a sweeping gesture across the threshold.

'She's right, you'd better leave. You had your jacket and your trousers, take them with you. We won't keep them from you.'

The family, especially the women, Fanny and La Grande, stood about thirty yards away and appeared to approve by remaining silent. Jean went white at this insult and was stricken to the heart at being accused of such a vile, calculating attitude. He lost his temper and shouted as loud as the others.

'Oh well, if you want to have a row about it, all right, we'll have one! In the first place, I'm going home; it's my house until the property has been divided. Then I'll go and find Monsieur Baillehache, he'll seal up the house and appoint me as guardian. This is my home, so you can damn well get out!'

He came forward with such a threatening air that Lise stood away from the door, but Buteau leapt at him and a fight began. The two men rushed into the centre of the kitchen and the quarrel went on inside.

'Show me the paper which authorizes you to have the house!'

'To hell with papers! We're in the right, and that's good enough!'

'Then come with the bailiff and the policemen, like we did.'

'I don't care a damn for the bailiff and the policemen! Only criminals need them. An honest man can settle his own affairs.'

Jean had retreated behind the table, desperately anxious to win, for he didn't want to leave the house where his wife had just died, and it seemed to contain all the happiness he had ever known. Buteau was also furiously determined not to give up the place he had reconquered and he realized the business had to be settled.

'And then,' he went on, 'that's not the whole story, we're bloody well fed up with you!'

He jumped on to the table and came down on top of the other man, but Jean seized a chair, hit him across the legs with it and knocked him down. Next he retreated into the bedroom next door and barricaded himself in. Then Lise suddenly remembered the money, the hundred and twenty-seven francs she had seen in the cupboard drawer. She thought that he was running to take it, got there first, opened the drawer and yelled with fury.

'The money! The bastard stole the money last night!'

From that moment Jean was lost, for he had to protect his pocket. He shouted that the money was his, that he was quite ready to settle accounts and that they would certainly owe him more. But Lise and Buteau did not listen. She rushed at him and struck him more fiercely than her husband; with a violent push Jean was thrust out of the bedroom and into the kitchen again, where all three of them circled round in confusion, bumping against the furniture. Jean kicked himself free of Lise; she came back and dug her nails into the back of his neck, while Buteau took a flying leap and rushed at him, using his head as a battering ram; Jean fell sprawling in the road outside.

They stayed there and barred the door with their bodies.

'You're a thief! You've stolen our money!' they shouted. 'Thief, thief, thief!'

Jean picked himself up.

'Very well,' he replied, stammering with pain and anger, 'I'll go to the judge at Châteaudun and he'll let me come back into my home. I'll have the law on you and sue you for damages. I'll be back.'

With a last threatening gesture he disappeared, going up towards the plain.

Then the Buteaus uttered a savage cry of victory. At last they had chucked him out into the street, Jean the stranger, the usurper, and they had come back into the house; they had always said they would come back. The house! The house! The idea that they were back again in the old family house filled them with crazy delight and they rushed through the rooms, screaming at the tops of their voices just for the pleasure of screaming in their own house. The children, Laura and Jules, ran up and started banging on an old saucepan like a drum. Old Fouan, who had remained on the stone bench, watched them with a disturbed look, without a smile.

Jean walked on, his eyes gazing into nothingness, not knowing where his feet were taking him. At first he had though of rushing to Cloyes to see Monsieur Baillehache and establish his right to live in the house. Then his anger abated. If he went back one day he would have to leave the next, so why not accept this terrible grief immediately, for it was all over now. And those bastards were right, poor he had come, poor he was going away. But above all, what broke his heart and forced him to accept the situation was the thought that Françoise must have wanted things to be this way, since she had not left him her property; so he gave up his plan for immediate action, and when his anger blazed up again, as he walked along, he merely swore he would bring the Buteaus to justice and get his share back, half of everything that fell into the common domain. He'd show them if they could strip him like this!

Jean looked up and was astonished to find himself in front of La Borderie. Instinctively, without realizing it, he had come back to the farm to find shelter, and in fact if he did not want to leave the district this was surely the way of staying, he could live and work there. Hourdequin had always had a high regard for him, he would certainly welcome him now.

But he was alarmed to see Jacqueline running across the yard in a state of frenzy. Eleven o'clock was striking and he found he had arrived in the midst of a terrible catastrophe. In the morning when she came downstairs Jacqueline had found the trap-door to the cellar open, the trap which was placed at the foot of the staircase in such a dangerous position. At the bottom lay Hourdequin, dead, his back broken on the steps. She cried out, the men came running up, the whole farm was horror-struck. Now the farmer's body was lying on a mattress in the dining-room, while Jacqueline sat in the kitchen, her features distorted, her eyes dry.

As soon as Jean came in she spoke to him and consoled herself by talking in a strangled voice.

'I told him so often! I wanted this trap-door moved. But who can have left it open? I know it was closed yesterday evening when I came up. Ever since this morning I've been racking my brains to think what can have happened.'

'Did the master go downstairs before you?' asked Jean, who was horrified to learn of this accident.

'Yes, it was only just daylight. I was asleep. I thought I heard a voice calling him from downstairs. I must have been dreaming. He often got up like this and always went down without a light, he liked to keep an eye on the men just as they were getting up. He can't have seen the trap was open, he must have fallen. But who, who on earth can have left it open? Oh, it'll kill me!'

A suspicion occurred to Jean, but he immediately thrust it aside. This death brought her no profit, her despair was genuine.

'It's a tragedy,' he murmured.

'Oh yes, a tragedy! It's a great tragedy for me!'

She collapsed on a chair, overwhelmed, as though the walls were falling down on top of her. The master whom she had hoped at last to marry! The master who had sworn he would leave her everything in his will! And now he was dead, before there'd been time for him to sign anything. She would not even have any wages, his son would come back and kick her out as he'd sworn to do. Nothing! A few jewels and some linen, just what she stood up in. It was a disaster, a crushing blow.

What Jacqueline did not mention, for she had forgotten about it, was that the day before she had arranged for Soulas the shepherd to be dismissed. She alleged he was too old and unfit for his work, for she was furious at finding him always lurking behind her and spying on her. Hourdequin, although he did not agree with her, had given in, for now he was at her beck and call, he was completely dominated and reduced to buying nights of pleasure by submitting to her like a slave. Soulas had been dismissed with kind words and promises, but he had looked at the master fixedly with his pale eyes. Then slowly he had begun to tell the truth about the slut who had caused his dismissal: the succession of men, and now Tron, after so many others; the story of this last man and the insolent, impudent randiness which everyone knew about, it was so well-known in the district that people said the master must have a liking for farm servants' leavings. Hourdequin was completely distraught and tried in vain to stop him, for he wanted to remain in the dark. He didn't want to know anything, for he was terrified he would be forced to send Jacqueline away. The old man went on methodically to the very end without omitting one solitary occasion when he had surprised her with a man, and gradually consoled himself, pouring out all the long-accumulated bitterness in his heart. Jacqueline was unaware of this exposure, for Hourdequin had rushed out into the fields, afraid he might strangle her if he set eyes on her. Then when he came back he had simply dismissed Tron on the excuse that he left the yard in a filthy state. Then she had had a suspicion but she had not dared to defend the cowman, and only arranged that he would sleep there that night, for she hoped to settle the matter in the morning, so that she could keep him. And now this incident had faded from her mind after the fatal blow which had destroyed her ten years of laborious scheming.

Jean was alone with her in the kitchen when Tron appeared. She had not seen him since the day before and the other servants were wandering round the farm anxiously, doing nothing. When she saw the man from Le Perche, the tall stupid creature with his white skin, she cried out. The strange way in which he entered was enough to enlighten her.

'It was you, you opened the trap-door!'

Suddenly everything became clear to her, while he went pale, his eyes staring and his lips quivering.

'You opened the trap-door and you called him so that he'd fall down!'

Jean was horrified by this scene and drew back. But neither of them seemed aware of his presence, they were in the grip of such violent passions. Tron, lowering his head, admitted it in muffled tones.

'Yes, I did it. He sacked me. I'd never have seen you again, and I couldn't stand it. And then, earlier on, I thought that if he were dead we'd be free to live together.'

She listened to him, tense and nervous.

'Once it was done I thought you'd be pleased. I didn't tell you anything about it because I didn't want to worry you. And now he's gone I've come to take you, so that we can go away and get married.'

'You!' burst out Jacqueline cruelly. 'But I don't love you, I don't want you! So you've killed him to have me! You must be even more stupid than I thought! Fancy doing such a silly thing before he'd married me and made his will! You've ruined me, you've taken the bread out of my mouth! Don't you see, it's my back you've broken, you beast! Can't you understand? And you think I'm going to go away with you! Just look at me! D'you think you can treat me like that?'

He listened to her in his turn, open-mouthed, staggered by this unexpected reaction.

'Because I've been nice to you and we've had a good time together d'you imagine you're going to bother me all my life? Get married? Oh no, oh no! If I wanted a man, I'd find one who wasn't so stupid. Oh, go away, you make me sick! I don't love you, I don't want you. Go away!'

He was shaking with anger. Had he committed murder for nothing? She was his. He would take her by the scuff of her neck and carry her off.

'You're a proud thing,' he muttered. 'All the same you'll come. If you don't I'll settle things with you as I did with him.'

Jacqueline walked towards him clenching her fists.

'Just try, then!'

He was very tall, well-built and strong, and she was very fragile and small, with her pretty, slender figure, but it was he who drew back. She terrified him, for her teeth were sharp and her eyes shone steely-bright, like knives.

'It's all over! Go away! Rather than go with you I'd never see a man again! Get out! Get out!'

And Tron went, moving backwards, retreating like a cowardly beast of prey, giving way to his fear and craftily putting off his revenge until later. He looked at her and said once again:

'Dead or alive, I'll get you!'

Jean escaped from the kitchen and found himself on the open plain beneath a rainy March sky, but he saw nothing, for he was overwhelmed by this episode coming on top of his own misfortune. He had had his fill of bad luck and anxiety on his own account made him walk more quickly in spite of his grief over Hourdequin's fate. He did not breathe again until he reached the first houses in Rognes; he told himself that the farmer's sin had killed him, and began to think about the great truth that men would be much happier without women. The memory of Françoise returned to him and he was stricken with grief.

Then he walked more slowly, for he didn't know where to look for work. Out of the hundred and twenty-seven francs he had already paid for his wife's funeral, the cross, and the grave in the cemetery. He had barely half the sum left; he could easily make it last three weeks and then he would see. He was not afraid of hardship; his one thought was the idea that he should not leave Rognes because of the lawsuit. Three o'clock struck, then four, then five. Everywhere it was the same story: money and women, they brought death and they brought life. It was not surprising if they were the cause of all his trouble, too. His legs felt weak. He realized that he had not eaten anything yet and went back towards the village, deciding to take a room at Lengaigne's tavern, but as he crossed the square in front of the church the sight of the house from which he had been thrown out that morning brought him to life again. Why should he leave his two pairs of trousers and his overcoat with those bastards? They were his, he wanted them, even if it meant another fight.

Night was falling and Jean could barely distinguish Old Fouan, who was sitting on the stone bench. A candle was burning in the kitchen, and as he came up to the door Buteau recognized him and rushed to bar the way.

'Good God, you again! What d'you want?'

'I want my two pairs of trousers and my overcoat.'

A fearful quarrel broke out. Jean obstinately demanded the right to search through the wardrobe while Buteau, who had got hold of a sickle, swore he would slit his throat if he crossed the threshold. Finally Lise's voice could be heard shouting inside.

'Oh, go on, give him back his rags! You wouldn't wear them, they'd infect you!'

The two men fell silent. Jean waited. But behind him on the stone bench, Old Fouan was dreaming, his thoughts elsewhere.

'You'd better get out!' he muttered in his hoarse voice. 'They'll kill you just as they killed the girl.'

Suddenly Jean understood everything, both Françoise's death and her obstinate silence. He had already suspected something and now he no longer had any doubt that she had saved her family from the guillotine. Fear made his hair stand on end, he could neither speak nor move, when suddenly Lise hurled his trousers and overcoat through the open door right into his face.

'There they are, your filthy things! They stink so badly they'd have given us the plague!'

He picked them up and went off. Only when he was on the road outside the yard he brandished his fist towards the house and shouted out one single word which pierced the silence:

'Murderers!'

Then he disappeared into the blackness.

Buteau was shattered, for he had heard what Old Fouan had murmured in his dream and the word shouted by Jean struck him physically like a shot in the stomach. Was the law going to come into this business now, when he thought it was all over and buried along with Françoise? As soon as he had seen the soil scattered on the grave that morning he had breathed again, but now he realized that the old man knew everything. Had he just pretended to be stupid so that he could watch them? Buteau was so upset that he felt quite ill when he came in and left half his supper. When Lise heard what had happened she shivered and could not eat anything either.

They had both looked forward to their first night in the house they had won back, but it was a ghastly, miserable night. They had put Laura and Jules to bed on a mattress in front of the wardrobe and the children were still awake, while their parents could not close their eyes, and they tossed and turned as though they were lying on burning hot coals until finally they began to talk in subdued voices. What a burden the old man was now that he had reached second childhood! He was a real worry and cost so much that they were left without a penny; it was incredible how much bread he ate and how greedy he was, helping himself to meat, letting wine trickle down into his beard, and he was so dirty it made you sick just to look at him. And now, on top of that he was always going about with his trousers undone and had been surprised exposing himself in front of little girls. The old beast was completely finished, it was a disgusting end for a man who had been no worse than any other in his time. Really, the only thing to do was to finish him off with a pick-axe, since he couldn't make up his mind to die of his own accord.

'When you think you've only to breathe on him and he'd fall down!' murmured Buteau. 'And he still goes on! He doesn't mind getting in our way. These damned old men, the less they do the less they earn and the more they cling to you. He'll never die.'

Lise, lying on her back, then spoke, too.

'It was a bad thing he came back here. He'll be too comfortable; he'll get a new lease of life. If I'd a prayer to make I'd have asked God not to let him sleep a single night in the house.'

Neither of them mentioned their real anxiety, the idea that the old man knew everything and could give them away, even innocently. This was really the limit. He cost them money, he was a nuisance to them, he stopped them from enjoying the benefits of the stolen deeds, and they had put up with all this for a long time; but to think that one word from him would send them to the guillotine, oh no, that was going too far! Something had to be done.

'I'm going to see if he's asleep,' said Lise suddenly.

She lit the candle again, made sure that Laura and Jules were asleep and then went into the room where the beetroot was stored, where the old man's iron bedstead had been set up again. When she came back she was shivering, the tiled floor had chilled her feet, and she snuggled down under the blanket, coming close to her husband, who took her in his arms to warm her again.

'Well?'

'Well, he's sleeping. His mouth's wide open like a fish, he can't breathe.'

There was silence as they lay in each other's arms, but they could hear their thoughts working beneath their skins. An old man who could hardly breathe would be so easy to finish off—just something pushed into his throat, a handkerchief or even your fingers, and that would be the end of him. In fact they would be doing him a great service. Wasn't it better to sleep quietly in the cemetery rather than be a burden to others and to oneself?

Buteau continued to hold Lise tightly in his arms. Now they were both very warm, as though some desire had set their blood alight. All at once he let go of her and jumped out on to the floor.

'I'll go and have a look too.'

Carrying the candle he disappeared, walking barefoot, while she held her breath and listened, her eyes wide open in the dark. But minutes went by and no sound reached her from the next-door room. In the end she heard him come back without the light. She heard the sound of his feet moving softly over the floor and he was so agitated that he could barely restrain his heavy breathing. He came up to the bed and felt over it to find her, then whispered in her ear:

'You must come. I daren't do it alone.'

Lise followed him, her arms extended for she was afraid of knocking into things. They no longer felt the cold but their nightshirts hampered them. The candle stood on the floor in a corner of the old man's room. In the dim light they could see him lying on his back, and his head had slipped off the pillow. He was so stiff and dried up by old age that apart from the painful rattle of his breath through his wide-open mouth he might have been taken for dead. He had lost his teeth and there was a black hole between his lips; the two of them leant down to see if any life remained at the bottom of it. For a long time they stood there watching side by side, their hips touching. But their arms grew weak; it was so easy and yet so difficult to pick up anything that came to hand and stop up the hole. They went away, then they came back; their tongues were dry, they could not have said a word, only their eyes spoke. With a look she indicated the pillow. Come on then, what was he waiting for? His eyelids flickered as he pushed her forward in his place. Suddenly Lise, in a moment of exasperation, seized the pillow and brought it down hard on the old man's face.

'You blasted coward! Must women always do the job for you?'

Then Buteau rushed forward and pressed with his whole body, while she climbed on the bed and sat down, pushing with all the weight of her naked buttocks. They were both in a frenzy. They pushed with their fists, their shoulders, and their thighs. The old man had shuddered violently, his legs had stretched out with a sound like broken springs. He jumped like a fish thrown on to the grass, but it did not last long. They were holding him down too roughly; they felt him growing flatter as existence left him. There was a long shudder, a last twitch, and then nothing at all. He was as flabby as a piece of cloth.

'I think that's done it,' muttered Buteau breathlessly.

Lise was still sitting there huddled on the bed; she stopped jumping up and down, but waited to see if the body still showed any sign of life.

'That's it, it's all over.'

She slid off the bed, her nightshirt rolled up to her hips. She lifted the pillow. But then they groaned in terror.

'My God, he's completely black! We're finished!'

It would have been impossible to say he had got himself into such a state on his own. They had crushed him in such a frenzy that they had pushed his nose down to the back of his mouth and his face was purple, he was as black as a nigger. For a moment they felt the earth tremble beneath them. They heard the police running up, the clanking of prison chains, the blade of the guillotine. They were overcome with terror and remorse at doing the job so badly. How could they improve it now? It was no good washing him with soap, he'd never be white again.

The sooty colour of his face filled them with anguish, but then they had an idea.

'We could set fire to him,' murmured Lise.

Buteau was relieved and took a deep breath.

'That's it! We'll say he did it himself.'

Then as the thought of the deed came back to him he clapped his hands and his entire face lit up with triumphant laughter.

'My God, yes! We'll say he burnt the papers along with himself! Then there'll be nothing to explain!'

He immediately went to find the candle, but she was afraid of setting the house on fire and did not want him to bring it near the bed at first. There were some bundles of straw in the corner behind the beetroots and she took one, set it alight and began burning the old man's hair and beard, which were very long and white. There was a smell of spilt grease and a crackling sound, with little yellow flames. Suddenly they jumped back aghast as though some icy hand had seized them by the hair. In the appalling pain caused by the burning their father, who had not been completely suffocated, had just opened his eyes and from the atrocious black mask with its great broken nose and its burning beard he looked at them. His expression of pain and hatred was horrible, then his entire face fell to pieces and he was dead.

Buteau was wild with terror and uttered a roar of fury when he suddenly heard the sound of sobbing at the door. It was the two children, Laura and Jules, in their nightshirts, who had been awakened by the noise and drawn by the bright light into the bedroom through the open door. They had seen, and they were howling with fright.

'You blasted vermin!' cried Buteau, rushing at them. 'If you say a word I'll strangle you! Take that to remind you!'

He struck them and knocked them down. They got up, they did not cry but ran back to their mattresses where they snuggled down and did not move again.

Buteau wanted to finish things off now and in spite of what his wife said he set fire to the mattress. Fortunately the room was so damp that the straw burnt slowly. Thick smoke rose from it and they opened the skylight, for they were half suffocated, then the flames shot up to the ceiling. Their father's body crackled and the unbearable smell of burning flesh grew stronger. The old house would have burnt up like a hayrick if the straw had not begun to smoke again as the boiling flesh melted. Nothing remained across the iron bedstead except the half-blackened body in its disfigured, unrecognizable state. One corner of the mattress had been left untouched and the end of one sheet was still hanging down.

'Let's be off!' said Lise, who, in spite of the great heat, was shivering again.

'Wait!' replied Buteau. 'We have to tidy things up.'

He placed a chair beside the bed, and put the old man's candle there, lying on its side to give the impression that it had fallen on the mattress. He was even cunning enough to burn some paper on the floor. Then there would be ash, and he would describe how the old man had discovered his deeds the day before and kept them.

'It's done now. Let's get back to bed.'

Buteau and Lise rushed back, and jumped into bed, but the sheets were icy and they had to clasp each other in a violent embrace to get warm again. Day broke before they went to sleep. They said nothing. They shuddered and heard their own hearts beating loudly. The door to the other bedroom had been left open and this worried them, but the idea of shutting it worried them more. Finally they dozed off, without letting go of each other.

In the morning all the neighbours ran up when they heard Buteau's desperate calls for help. La Frimat and the other women found the candle that had fallen over, the half-burnt mattress and the papers reduced to ashes. They all cried that it was bound to happen one day, they had said so a hundred times, for the old man had reached his dotage and they were lucky their house had not burnt down with him.

6

Two days afterwards, on the morning when Old Fouan was to be buried, Jean woke very late after a sleepless night in his little bedroom at Lengaigne's tavern. He had not yet gone to Châteaudun for the lawsuit, the only thing which prevented him from leaving Rognes. Every evening he put it off until the next day, and as his anger subsided he hesitated all the more. A last struggle with himself had kept him awake in a feverish state, for he did not know what decision to take.

The Buteaus were murderous brutes and an honest man should have got their heads cut off. When he first heard of the old man's death he understood the dark deed clearly enough. The villainous pair must have burnt him alive to stop him from talking. After killing Françoise they had been forced to kill Fouan. Whose turn was it now? He realized it would be his turn: they guessed that he knew the secret. They would certainly shoot him in some quiet spot if he persisted in staying in the district, so why not denounce them immediately? He decided to do so; he would go and tell the story to the police as soon as he got up. Then he hesitated again for he was nervous of being a witness in this big case. He would probably suffer as much as the guilty parties. What was the point of making even more trouble for himself? It probably wasn't very courageous but his excuse was that by saying nothing he was obeying his wife's last wishes. Twenty times during the night he decided to go ahead, then he decided not to, and the thought that he could not face his duty upset him.

Then about nine o'clock Jean got up and dipped his head into a basin of cold water. Suddenly he took a decision: he would say nothing. He would not even start a lawsuit to get back half of the furniture. It wasn't worth it. His pride restored his confidence and he was glad he did not belong

to this wicked family. He was glad he was an outsider.
They could devour each other and if they were all destroyed
then the world would be well rid of them. What was the
point of pursuing one couple, when the whole tribe should
have been exterminated? He preferred to go away.

At that moment Jean caught sight of a newspaper which
he had brought up the day before from the tavern. He had
been interested in an article about the forthcoming war, for
terrifying rumours had been circulating for the last few
days. He did not realize that the news had awoken an
unconscious desire which had lain dormant in the depths of
his mind but now came to the surface and caught fire all at
once. His last hesitation about leaving, the thought that he
did not know where to go, was now swept away as though
by a great blast of wind. Yes, he would go to the war, he
would join the army again. People were too horrible, and
the thought of killing some Prussians comforted him. Since
he had found no peace in this district, where families sucked
each other's blood, he might as well return to the slaughter.

When he went downstairs he ate two eggs and a piece of
bacon. Then he called Lengaigne and settled his bill.

'Are you leaving, Corporal?'

'Yes.'

'Won't you be coming back?'

'No.'

The tavern-keeper was astonished and looked at him,
keeping his thoughts to himself. So the man was fool
enough to give up his rights?

'What are you going to do now? Are you going to take up
carpentry again?'

'No, I'm joining the army.'

The tavern-keeper was so surprised that he was unable to
repress a contemptuous laugh. What a half-wit he was!

Jean had already taken the road to Cloyes when a last
feeling of tenderness stopped him and made him climb up
the hill again. He did not want to leave Rognes without saying goodbye at Françoise's tomb. And there was something else, too, he wanted to take a last look at the vast
rolling expanse of the sombre plain which he had finally
come to love during his long hours of solitary work.

He stood by Françoise's tomb, which was in the middle
of a row, and the grave prepared for Old Fouan was open
beside hers. The cemetery was overgrown with weeds, for

the local council had never got round to allocating fifty
francs towards its upkeep. Crosses and railings had rotted
where they stood, only a few rusty stones had withstood
the opposition, but the charm of this solitary place lay in its
very abandonment and its profound calm, disturbed only
by the cawing of the aged rooks as they circled round the
steeple. Jean was aware of the peace of death as he looked
at the great plain where seeds were springing up and bringing it back to life. Then the church bell began to toll slowly,
three strokes, then two more, then a full peal. Fouan's body
was on the way to the cemetery.

The gravedigger, who was bandy-legged, came limping
along and looked at the grave.

'It's too small,' said Jean, who felt moved, and wanted
to see the funeral.

'Oh, well,' replied the lame man, 'when he burnt himself
up he shrunk.'

It was a respectable Mass, although it was taken too
quickly. When it was over the sprinkler passed from hand
to hand and then the procession formed again: the cross,
the choir-boys, Clou with his trombone, the priest, panting
in his haste, the coffin carried by four peasants, the family,
and then the rest of the people who had followed. Bécu had
begun to ring the bells again so hard that the rooks flew
away from the steeple, croaking in fear. The procession
entered the cemetery immediately and had only to go
round the corner from the church. The music and singing
broke out more loudly through the deep silence in the misty
sunshine, and in the open air the coffin suddenly appeared
so small that everyone was struck by it. Jean, who had
remained there, was shattered. Oh, poor old man, so
shrunken with age, so ravaged by the wretchedness of life,
that he fitted comfortably into this little toy box; he would
not take up much room, he would not be a burden to this
earth, the vast earth which had been his one passion,
consuming him until his muscles had dried up. The body
had reached the edge of the open grave; Jean's glance
followed it and went beyond, over the wall, going right
across the Beauce, and in the fields which unfolded one
after the other he saw the sowers, far away in the distance,
repeatedly making the same movement as the living wave of
seed rained down into the open furrows.

When the Buteaus caught sight of Jean they exchanged

an anxious look. Had the bastard come to wait for them here and make a terrible scene? As long as they felt he was in Rognes they would not be able to sleep in peace. The choir-boy carrying the cross had just set it in the ground at the foot of the grave, while the Abbé Godard, standing before the coffin, which had been placed on the grass, quickly recited the last prayers; but everyone's attention was distracted when they saw Macqueron and Lengaigne, who had arrived late, looking persistently towards the plain. They all turned in the same direction and saw a large column of smoke rolling across the sky. It must have been coming from La Borderie. It looked as though the haystacks behind the farm were on fire.

'*Ego sum* . . .' began the priest in a fury.

The faces turned back towards him and all eyes were again fixed on the body.

'Amen!' said the choir-boy carrying the holy water, loudly.

The Abbé Godard immediately went on in his angry voice:

'*De profundis clamavi ad te, Domine* . . .'

As he proceeded, Jésus-Christ, who had taken Fanny aside, began to attack the Buteaus again violently.

'If only I hadn't been so drunk the other day! But it's damn silly to let ourselves be robbed like this.'

'We've been robbed all right,' murmured Fanny.

'Those bastards have got the deeds,' he went on, 'they've been getting money from them for a long time; they came to an agreement with Old Saucisse, I know. My God, aren't we going to take them to court about it?'

She drew back and refused firmly.

'Oh no, I won't. I've got enough business of my own. You can if you like.'

Then Jésus-Christ made a gesture of fear and resignation too. He could not push his sister forward, and he wasn't very happy about the way he stood with the law.

'Oh well, everyone imagines the worst about me. Never mind, an honest man has his reward, he can keep his head high.'

La Grande, who was listening, saw him straighten up in a dignified, courageous way. She had always said he was very simple in spite of being a scoundrel. She felt sorry for him; to think that a big chap like that didn't go and fight it out with his brother to get his share! And to show what she thought of both him and Fanny she repeated her usual promise without any introduction, as though it had fallen from the sky.

'Oh, you can be certain I won't do any harm to anybody. The will's in order, it has been for a long time. Everyone will have his share; I wouldn't die happy if I was giving any preference to anyone. Hyacinthe is in it and you, too, Fanny. I'm ninety now. I'll be leaving you one of these days.'

But she didn't believe a word of it, for she was convinced she would never die; her obstinate love of property was too strong. She would bury them all. Now her brother had gone, that was another one. Everything here, the coffin, the open grave, and this last ceremony seemed to be for the neighbours, not for her. Tall and thin, with her stick under her arm, she stood among the tombs without any emotion, feeling merely curious about why other people were so sorry to die.

The priest stammered out the last verse of the psalm.

'Et ipse redimet Israel ex omnibus iniquitatibus ejus.'

He took the sprinkler from the holy water vessel and shook it over the coffin, raising his voice.

'Requiescat in pace.'

'Amen!' replied the two choir-boys.

And the coffin was let down. The gravedigger had fastened the ropes, two men were enough, for it weighed no more than the body of a child. Then the procession filed past again. The sprinkler passed once more from hand to hand and everyone shook it, making the sign of the cross over the grave.

Jean had come closer and as he took it from the hand of Monsieur Charles his eyes plunged down into the grave. He was feeling dazed after looking for so long at the vast plain where the sowers were sowing the wheat for the bread of the future. He could see the coffin in the ground, and it looked smaller still, with its narrow pinewood lid, pale yellow like the corn; as the thick clods of earth rained down, covering it half over, he could see no more than a light-coloured blotch looking like a handful of this same corn that his comrades on the distant plain were scattering along the furrows. He shook the sprinkler and passed it to Jésus-Christ.

'La Borderie's on fire!'

There was no longer any doubt about it, for flames were rising from the roofs, wavering faintly in the bright sunlight. A thick cloud of smoke was moving slowly towards the north. Just then they noticed Boldie, who was running along from the farm. When she went to find her geese she had noticed the first sparks and had enjoyed the spectacle up to the moment when she had decided to run along and tell the others. She jumped astride the little wall and cried out in her shrill girlish voice:

'Oh, it isn't half burning! It's that devil Tron. He came back and set it on fire. In three places, too, in the barn, the stable, and the kitchen. They found him just as he was lighting the straw; the waggoners have beaten him up, and the horses, the cows, and the sheep were all getting roasted. My goodness, you should have heard them yelling! I've never heard such a row!'

Her green eyes shone and she burst out laughing.

'And Jacqueline, too! You know she's been ill since the master died. Well, they'd forgotten her in bed. She was on fire already. She just had time to escape in her nightshirt. Oh, it was funny to see her running through the fields with nothing on! She jumped up and down with both her front and back showing and everyone shouted "Hey! Hey!" to keep her going, for they don't like her very much. One old man said, "She's leaving just as she came, with only her chemise on her back!" '

She rocked with laughter again.

'You ought to look, it's too funny. I'm going back.'

She jumped down and ran off quickly again towards La Borderie, which was still burning.

Monsieur Charles, Delhomme, Macqueron and almost all the peasants followed her, while the women, led by La Grande, left the cemetery and went along the road in order to have a better view. Buteau and Lise had remained behind and she stopped Lengaigne, for she wanted to question him about Jean without appearing to do so. Had he found work then, since he had taken lodgings in the district? When the inn-keeper replied that he was leaving to join the army again, Lise and Buteau were intensely relieved and they both made the same remark.

'How stupid he is!'

Now it was all over they were going to start living a

happy life. They glanced at Fouan's grave, which the gravedigger was just filling in, and as the two children lingered on to watch, their mother called them.

'Come on, Jules and Laura! Be good, do as you're told or the man will take you away and bury you in the ground like that.'

The Buteaus left, pushing their children in front of them, the children who knew everything, and looked very sensible, with their big, black, deep, expressionless eyes.

POSTSCRIPT

EMILE ZOLA's novel *Earth—La Terre*—is acknowledged to be one of the most powerful novels of the nineteenth century. The story first appeared as a serial in the magazine *Gil Blas*, in 1886; the final version, published in book form the following year, amounts to nearly a quarter of a million words.

When he began to work on *Earth*, Zola was about forty-five and had already published fourteen of the twenty novels known as the *Rougon-Macquart* Series, the 'natural and social history' of two related families over five generations. By describing the conditions under which different branches of the family lived, Zola intended to present a realistic portrait of all sectors of French society. He wanted to show how industrial development was affecting life in Paris, in provincial towns of various types, and in the remote countryside. His interpretation of political and economic trends led him to believe that the future could bring only disaster for France. At the same time he wished to prove that human conduct can be analysed 'scientifically', and that heredity in particular plays a vital part in the destiny of every individual. He believed that the individual, as a microcosm of society, could be no more certain of happiness than the community to which he belonged.

Earth is set in an imaginary village, Rognes, one of many scattered over the vast plain of Beauce, a farming district which includes most of the two 'departments' in the northern part of central France named Eure-et-Loir and Loir-et-Cher. The centre of Beauce has always been the famous cathedral town of Chartres, frequently mentioned in this novel. The time is the late 1860's, and the close of the story coincides with the outbreak of the Franco-Prussian war in 1870.

Zola collected a great amount of material for his novel, visiting farms, villages, and towns in the Beauce district, attempting to make contact with uncommunicative peasants, taking notes of case-histories, as he always did, studying relevant documents and books. The result of this work was a vivid, detailed background to the story, descriptions of all seasonal activities of village life, ploughing, sowing, reaping, the wine-harvest, sheep-shearing, sheep-grazing, and the wakes during the long winter evenings; village intrigues of various kinds supply a number of sub-plots, involving the parish priest, the rivalry between the two tavern-keepers in Rognes, flirtations among young people, and a school-master with revolutionary ideas. There are countless incidents which have their own grotesque, earthy humour ('Mother Caca' who collects human manure for her vegetable garden, or Gideon, the donkey who gets drunk), but entertaining and precise as these descriptions are, they have little more than historical interest for the contemporary reader, and many of them have been shortened or omitted in this translation. It is the central theme, the remarkably 'modern' story of the Fouan family, that holds our attention today. It would have been impossible to omit any scene from this brutal, violent drama which is as relentlessly true today as it was at the end of the last century.

The presentation of the Fouan family is an outstanding example of Zola's realism, and of his interest in heredity. Buteau, Fouan's younger son, has inherited his father's passion for the land and his mother's avarice, to such an extent that he kills both his parents and is ready to destroy his sister-in-law and her unborn child. Fouan's sister, La Grande, is mean to the extent of inhumanity; she forces her own grandchildren, Palmyre and Hilarion, to live in such degrading poverty that they develop an incestuous relationship. The 'bourgeois' branch of the family, Charles Badeuil and his wife, formerly Laure Fouan, respectable and serious-minded though they appear, made their fortune by running a brothel in Chartres, and although their daughter and their grand-daughter were educated in convents, both girls successively feel neither surprise nor disapproval on discovering their parents' source of income but carry on the establishment with great efficiency.

In this version of *Earth*, the 'Charleses' do not appear as often as in the original story, for Zola intended them as symbols of the hypocritical middle-class rather than as essential characters in his plot; the same is true of the farmer Hourdequin, whose role in the original text was to express Zola's pessimistic views about the approaching crisis in French agriculture, due to ignorance, lack of scientific method, and the narrow-minded obstinacy of the peasant land-owners.

Only one member of the Fouan family loses something of his importance in this version, Old Fouan's kindly, weak-minded, drunken elder son known as 'Jésus-Christ', who plays no vital part in the story, remaining isolated in his poacher-like existence and supplying comic relief in chapters of Rabelaisian humour. The extraordinary scenes that take place in his 'Château' suggest that he might have formed the central character in a separate and very different book. Compared with our standards today, the great novelists of the nineteenth century wrote three books in one, for their public, particularly the readers of serials, demanded complexity and variety where we now prefer simplicity, unity, and a swift pace.

Zola's story and treatment are astonishing even today, when few forms of sordid or unnatural behaviour are left unexplored by fiction-writers. When *Earth* first appeared in France, public opinion was outraged by its savagery and by the portrayal of peasants as money-grubbing, bestial creatures. Soon after the novel was published five younger writers, apparently at the suggestion of Zola's literary enemies, issued a manifesto condemning *Earth* as obscene and suggesting that a book containing so much sexual violence could only have been written by a man who was impotent. But the novel sold well, serious literary critics soon realized that it was a masterpiece, and Zola was awarded the Legion of Honour.

The first English translation, *Soil*, made in 1888, led to a private prosecution. The publisher was fined, and only a fiercely censored version was made available to the public. Eight years later the poet Ernest Dowson retranslated the book for a literary society which published several of Zola's novels for private subscribers only. The British novelist and critic Angus Wilson regards *Earth* as one of Zola's three greatest novels, the others being *Germinal*, about miners whose starvation wages drive them to rebellion, and *L'Assommoir*, about alcoholism in the slums of Paris. In France *Earth* still gains thousands of new readers every year, and since its appearance in a cheap edition French booksellers have found that it occupies a high place on the best-seller lists. It is a key book in the whole output of Zola, whose influence on twentieth century writing is still a living force, not yet fully appreciated.

MARGARET CROSLAND